> ## "You know more ... e than most men I've dated!"

Cori couldn't help but moan as she lay on the examination table.

Ben stood up and pulled off the latex gloves. The expression on his face was wry. "Why don't you get dressed and we'll talk in my office."

"What's wrong?" She tried to grab his sleeve and almost fell off the table when she missed.

"In my office."

"In my office," she mocked. "Doctors are the same everywhere. They have to do everything their way." By the time she was dressed and entered his office, she was convinced she was dying of a rare disease.

"All right, just give it to me straight," she ordered. "It's some exotic parasite tunneling its way through my body. Or something equally gruesome. I'm not going to give birth to one of those creatures they had in *Alien*, am I?"

Ben started to smile, then sobered. "Not exactly."

"Then what?

"All right, I'll give it to you straight. I'd say you're about ten weeks pregnant."

Dear Reader,

His idea of a "long night" is a sexy woman and a warm bed—not a squalling infant! To him, a "bottle" means champagne—not formula! Yeah, Ben Cooper is about to get a rude awakening. He's about to become an "Accidental Dad"!

Linda Randall Wisdom takes you on a rollicking ride into parenthood—as small-town doc Ben Cooper gets snagged by heiress-on-the-run Cori Peyton *and* her little bundle of joy!

And who better than Linda Randall Wisdom to capture your fantasies? This veteran author has been nominated for every major award, and her next book celebrates her fiftieth published novel!

Don't miss the companion novel to this— Cathy Gillen Thacker's *Daddy Christmas*, available right now!

Happy reading!

Debra Matteucci
Senior Editor & Editorial Coordinator
Harlequin Books
300 E. 42nd St.
New York, NY 10017

Linda Randall Wisdom

MOMMY HEIRESS

Harlequin Books

TORONTO • NEW YORK • LONDON
AMSTERDAM • PARIS • SYDNEY • HAMBURG
STOCKHOLM • ATHENS • TOKYO • MILAN
MADRID • WARSAW • BUDAPEST • AUCKLAND

ISBN 0-373-16608-7

MOMMY HEIRESS

Prologue

Peyton Estate
Bel Air, California

"Courtney, you may be my daughter and I love you, but there is no way in hell I will give you five million dollars for a broken-down piece of property."

"I'm talking about a wonderful investment, Daddy, not a broken-down piece of property," Cori argued. "And it's practically an historical monument in England. With your British roots, that should please you."

Sean Peyton glowered at his daughter under heavy brows. That same glower had intimidated many a business mogul over the years. Unfortunately, it had no effect on his only daughter.

"I was never British," he groused, glaring at her across the polished surface of his walnut desk. "I was born in Cornwall."

"Close enough." Cori walked around his desk and perched herself on the edge, crossing her legs at the knee. She leaned over, circling his ear with her fingernail. The smile on her face was that of a daughter who knew how to wrap her father around her little finger. "Think about the advantage this business would offer me, Daddy," she crooned. "You've been begging me to do something with my life. Opening a bed and breakfast in the house would be perfect for me. Everyone has always said what a wonderful hostess I am."

He jerked his head away from her teasing touch. But as he gazed at his child, warmth overtook the frost of his glare. "What do you know about running a hotel?"

"I've certainly stayed in enough of them over my lifetime to know what goes on in one. I would hire qualified staff to handle everything else. I'll just be there to greet the guests and plan special activities for them," she explained.

Sean shook his head in wonder. What had happened in the past fifteen years to the little girl he loved more than life itself? Trouble was, he already knew the answer. Her mother had died so suddenly, leaving them both grief stricken, and because Cori looked so much like Elizabeth, he spoiled her shamelessly. It was Cori's nature to be warm and loving—she was actually one of the most unselfish people he knew—but it hadn't stopped her from believing she could have anything she wanted just by asking Daddy for a check. And, God help him, he had done that too many times.

"Cori, my love, a successful business owner knows everything that goes on with his trade," he told her. "You can't even make a bed."

"So I'll learn if it's that important to you!" She fidgeted. "I would really like to get away!"

Now he knew exactly what was going on.

"It's because of that bastard!" he said in his rumbling voice that still held a hint of his Cornish ancestors.

She wrinkled her nose in distaste. "All right, I'll be the first to admit Rufus was a big mistake. I'll even admit he only wanted me for my money. Does that make you happy?''

Sean looked down and noticed he held his pen so tightly his fingers were white. "The man didn't have one ounce of common sense in his body. Not to mention—what mother names her child Rufus? Sounds more like an Irish setter than a man. If you could even use that term when referring to him. It's a good thing you didn't marry him, girl, because I would have had to disinherit you."

"I already admitted he was a mistake!" She rolled her eyes. "But that's why I want to get away. Buying the house and turning it into an inn would be a perfect catharsis for me. So if you would just deposit the amount in my account, I would be very happy. Don't worry, Daddy, I'll pay you back out of my profits." She leaned down and started to slide open his top desk drawer. He quickly shut it.

"Courtney, I love you dearly, but I will not loan you the money." Even as he spoke, he noticed the storm already brewing in her navy-blue eyes. "To be honest, you are talking about a business proposition and you have no concept of what is involved in running any kind of business."

"I took business classes in college," she argued, stung by his refusal.

"And you never bothered sticking any of them out, either. What do you have to show for it? Not a degree, that's for sure." He took a deep breath, needing to make her understand. "What if something happened to me tomorrow?"

She suddenly looked stricken. She reached forward and grabbed his hands between hers, rubbing them gently as if infusing her own life force into him. "Oh, Daddy, you're not sick, are you?"

He hated himself for worrying her. "No, I'm just asking you what you would do if I wasn't here and you discovered you had nothing."

Cori shook her head. "Daddy, I'll always have you. And you made sure I always carry my credit cards with me," she teased.

Sean took a deep breath. He knew his daughter wasn't the least bit dumb. Too many intelligence tests proved that. So why didn't she stop to think? He hated what he was going to do, but he had no choice. She was going to have to learn what the real world was all about, no matter how painful the lesson.

"No money," he stated flatly. "In fact, if you are so keen on buying an English country house to turn into an inn, you'll just have to find the money yourself. I will not loan you the money and I will not see you go to England. If you have to pine for that idiot Rufus, you can do it here."

Cori hopped off his desk. "But, Daddy, I need to get away," she insisted.

He shook his head again. Perhaps it would have been easier if he had refused her more often years ago.

To her credit, Cori didn't throw a tantrum. Instead, distress crossed her delicate features and darkened her blue eyes.

"Then I suppose you won't mind if I go for a long drive to clear my head?" she said with a haughty toss of her golden blond hair that reminded Sean of his own dear Elizabeth.

"Darlin', you feel free to take a drive and, afterward, we will sit down and talk about your future in the working world," he said with an expansive sweep of his arms. "I'm sure we can find something here for you that will keep you occupied."

Cori walked to his office door with only a slight sniffle to betray her sorrow.

"You wait and see, Daddy. One day I'll show you I'm not the child you think I am," she declared before marching out.

Sean heaved a sigh as the door closed after her.

"I can only hope. But I'm afraid I won't be holding my breath."

Chapter One

Cal's Gas and Oil
Farrington, Kansas

"I've got good news for ya and bad news for ya." The lanky mechanic wiped his hands on a rag that looked as if a clean spot couldn't have been found on it. The name Jess was stitched over his left chest pocket.

"Do us both a favor and give me the good news first."

"I can fix your car."

Cori brightened up. "That's great! Why are you saying you have bad news?"

He looked apologetic. "I just can't fix it right now."

Cori looked as if someone had punched her in the solar plexus.

"What do you mean you can't fix it right now?" She surveyed her surroundings, seeing the dark interior of the garage, inhaling air redolent with the pungent aroma of gas and oil, not to mention the less than attractive aroma belonging to Jess who stood a short distance from her. Her French perfume bravely fought the other scents and lost.

Dressed in grease-stained cotton coveralls, his face and hair streaked with the same slippery substance, he looked like a creature out of a horror movie. But his grin, white teeth gleaming against his smeared face, was pure mid-western.

"Gotta fix up the doc's truck first," he explained, pointing his thumb over his shoulder. "It's real important he has his truck for emergencies."

Cori had seen enough of the small town to hazard a guess "the doc" was probably their only hope for medical care.

"How long will it take after you finish his truck?"

"Depends if I can get the parts. The guy I need to talk to is out to lunch. Look, why don't you go on down the street to Myrna's. Relax, have something to eat and I'll call you down there," he suggested.

Cori looked around. Since the day had turned blistering hot, the idea of a cold drink was appealing.

"There would be no problem calling me there?" she asked.

He shook his head. "Look around town if you want to," he offered. "Like I said, I just gotta get Doc's truck up and runnin'. It shouldn't take too long. It's just a brake job." He glanced at her Jensen Healey with undisguised envy. "Sure is a sweet little car. How much they go for?" His eyes bugged out when she told him. "No kiddin'?" He shook his head. "Tell ya what, miss, I'll even put clean coveralls on before I work on it."

Cori's smile was like blinding sunlight. "Thank you." She pulled her bag out of the car and started to leave the garage. She turned back around. "Where is this Myrna's?"

"Can't miss it. It's six doors down." He clutched the grease-covered rag to his chest as he watched her walk outside. Gil, his brother and partner in the garage, walked up behind him.

"She shore is pretty," Gil commented.

Jess nodded. "Like someone out of the movies."

The two young men remained frozen to the floor as they watched the young woman, dressed casually in an above-the-knee denim skirt and pink tank top, walk down the dusty road. Her golden blond hair was partially covered by a denim billed cap. While billed caps were nothing new in town, this one was; for one, it didn't carry the name of a local feed store, and second, the denim bill was covered with delicate white lace.

"If I had any brains I'd take a *long* time working on her car," Jess commented.

"If you had any brains, you'd realize she's pure class," Gil told him, walking back outside when he noticed Mrs. Hammond had driven up in her ancient Studebaker.

THE FIRST THING Cori noticed when she walked down the sidewalk was the curious looks people directed her way. She decided they weren't used to having a lot of visitors and put it out of her mind.

She took her time walking down the tree-lined street, pausing to look in store windows. She could see the sleepy little town was like so many she had driven through the past two days. Many of the buildings hadn't been painted in a while and were now faded from the merciless sun. At the dress shop, she stopped, noting the yellow shorts and top featured in the window.

"Needs more pizzazz," she murmured, and continued on two more doors down to Myrna's Coffee Shop.

The white building was brightened up with bright green gingham curtains in the windows and a small sign in the window that proclaimed If You Eat At Myrna's And Leave Hungry, It's Your Own Fault.

The moment she stepped into the air-conditioned interior, the low rumble of conversation stopped abruptly.

Men, seated around various tables and in booths, openly watched her walk toward the counter. The women tried to hide their glances.

Cori perched on one of the vinyl stools. A waitress wearing a blue gingham uniform and white apron walked over. The woman's hair was so red it was almost orange, and it was teased high into a bouffant straight from the sixties.

"Coffee?" She held up a glass pot.

Cori shook her head. "Do you have Diet Coke?"

"Sure." She handed her a plastic-coated menu. "Ralph's special today is meat loaf." She walked away.

Cori studied the menu, amazed by the offerings that ranged from country-fried steak to fried chicken to steak and eggs served all day long. Her nerves had been running on high since she realized driving alone across half the country might not be a good idea. Yet, she still wasn't ready to go back home and see her father again. She took a deep breath. Her stomach had been upset lately and sleep hadn't been offering her the usual peace she was used to. She only hoped she wasn't getting sick.

"Haven't they heard the words cholesterol and fat here?" she murmured, feeling her stomach roil a bit when she noticed the waitress serve a large bowl of chili to one of the customers. She turned to give the waitress a smile when the woman deposited a large ice-filled glass of cola. "Could I have a salad, please? With low-cal ranch dressing on the side. Oh, and Jess at the garage is looking at my car and he said he'd call me here. He said it wouldn't be a problem."

The woman smiled and shook her head. "Honey, it's no problem at all. But I wouldn't expect your car to get fixed right away. I bet he won't be able to look at it until he finishes that brake job on the doc's truck. Are you sure you only want a salad? Darlin', you're so tiny you could blow away in a strong wind."

"Just a salad is fine, thank you. It's really too warm for anything else." Cori peeled the paper off her straw and stuck it in her drink. She discovered just how thirsty she was when she drank almost half the glass. Before she could blink, the waitress had swept up her glass and refilled it.

"It's hot out there, all right." The woman leaned on the counter. "Where ya from?"

"California."

She brightened up. "Really? You from Hollywood?"

Cori hid her smile at everyone's assumption a person from California came from the fabled tinsel town.

"No, I'm from Bel Air. It's near Beverly Hills."

Her eyes widened. "Honest? I've heard of that place. I read about it in a magazine. They say it's real ritzy there. So what do you do there? Model?" Her gaze swept over Cori, taking in the silk tank top and denim skirt that might have looked casual, but probably cost more than she made in six months.

"No, my father has his own business." Cori wasn't used to such open curiosity and wasn't entirely sure how to handle it.

"Movies?"

She shook her head. "Finance." How did one explain your father dealt with billions of dollars a year?

"Oh." She nodded. "A banker."

"Sophie, we gonna get any more coffee today?"

She looked up. "You'll get it when I'm ready and not until then." She smiled at Cori. "Men. Can't keep 'em. Can't shoot 'em. You think about orderin' the meat loaf. You need some meat on your bones, girl."

Cori glanced around. "What I need is my car working," she murmured, picking up her glass and sipping her drink. She reached inside her purse and pulled out a paperback book. She had barely opened it when she felt a presence on her right.

"Hear you have car trouble."

She kept her forefinger in her book to hold her place as she turned her head. The man seated on the stool could have been sixty or eighty. Dressed in ancient denim overalls and a faded blue flannel shirt with the sleeves neatly buttoned at the wrists, displaying gnarled hands that showed a lifetime of hard work. He looked the picture of the farmer. Especially with the navy billed cap advertising John Deere set on top of his mostly bald head.

"Yes, I do." She smiled at him. "News must travel fast in this town."

"With not much else going on, newcomers are our best source of entertainment. Where ya from?"

"Los Angeles."

His lips pursed in a low whistle. "What the hell, pardon my language, you doin' all the way out here, darlin'?"

"Hell, pardon my language, if I know."

The man's laughter erupted from his chest. He slapped his knee with a gnarled hand.

"You stay around, cutie, and we'll get along fine." He patted her hand and moved off the stool, shuffling his way back to a table filled with his cronies.

"Here's your salad." A plate landed near Cori's elbow.

Cori turned back to the counter and stared at a creamy mound on top of the largest heap of greens she had ever seen.

"I asked for the dressing on the side," she said in a barely audible voice.

"Honey, around here, Ralph puts the dressing on top and you're lucky he does that," the waitress brusquely informed her before bustling off.

Cori picked up her fork and carefully scraped most of the dressing to the side of the plate. She picked up the paperback and quickly found herself engrossed in the fast-paced mystery as she ate.

"You own that fancy car out at Cal's?"

Cori's lips had just closed over her fork. She managed a polite smile as she chewed and swallowed.

"Yes, I do."

This man looked like her other visitor's twin, except his cap advertised Martin's Feed and Seed and his shirt was red and blue stripes.

"Pretty car."

"Thank you." She wondered what else he was going to ask. She easily guessed there were no secrets kept in this town.

The man's head bobbed up and down in a nod. "Expensive?"

"It's British made." She didn't think he'd like to hear the car probably cost more than he made in a lifetime. Cori was considered flighty at times, but she would never dream of hurting someone's feelings.

"British! Dammit, woman, doncha know you're supposed to buy American-made cars!" He shook his head. "Honey, they're only out to get our money, you know that, don't you? Look how they tried to rule us all those years ago. Them selling us cars is just their way of gettin' even for losing the Revolutionary War."

Cori's eyes widened under his tirade. "I—"

"Zeke, leave the girl alone. She's trying to eat her meal," the waitress scolded.

Cori looked at her rescuer with gratitude.

"Her car ain't even American made," he told the woman.

"That's her business, not yours. Now shoo!"

He grumbled a few times as he slid off the stool and ambled off toward his friends who had been watching the proceedings with great interest.

"Nosey old goat," Sophie grumbled, then speared Cori with a sharp look. "I guess you're not used to that in the big city where a person don't even care about their neighbor. Here, we look out for each other."

"It's not always that way where I come from," Cori felt obligated to protest even as a tiny voice in her mind reminded her that she didn't know the name of the people who lived in the neighboring mansion. For that matter, she never really cared to find out. "Do you think it's going to take them long to fix my car?" she asked with a shred of desperation. After her day, she knew it was time to head home.

The waitress shrugged. "Depends how long it will take to fix Doc's."

She felt her shoulders wilt. "His is more important, yes, I understand."

"It is when he's the only medical help we've got for a hundred miles around." She walked off when one of the men called her name.

As Cori read her book and ate her salad, she felt everyone's eyes on her. And heard assorted murmurs around the restaurant. This wasn't the first time she had been the center of attention, but it was the first time she felt a bit uncomfortable about it. She didn't linger over her meal and impatiently waited for her check. Maybe she could persuade the mechanic to work on her car. And if persuasion didn't work, she figured bribery would.

She paid the check and left Sophie a tip. She had barely taken three steps away from the coffee shop before she realized she had an entourage. The four men who had been sitting at the rear table, including her two interrogators, were behind her.

She ignored them—and the heat beating down on her head—and made her way back up the street. She couldn't help but hear their whispered conversation.

"Wow, she's really pretty. You think she's Meg Ryan? She sure looks like her."

"Now why the hell would Meg Ryan be all the way out here?"

"You don't know everything. Maybe she's out here making a movie."

"No, I don't think she's Meg Ryan, you nincompoop. 'Sides, she wouldn't be out here without Dennis Quaid."

"She doesn't look like Meg Ryan to me, either. She looks more like Michelle Pfeiffer, but with shorter hair."

"You idiot, she's not Michelle Pfeiffer, either. You take a look at those legs. Nobody but Sharon Stone has legs like those."

Cori thought of turning around and correcting their misconceptions, except she guessed they were having too much fun with their argument. Besides, by then she was smiling as she reached the garage.

She had just stepped onto the property when she noticed a tall, lean man, dressed in jeans and a black T-shirt, talking to Jess, then shaking his hand and climbing into the dark blue truck she remembered seeing in the garage hoisted up on a rack.

"Obviously, Doc got someone to pick up his precious truck that he needs so desperately," she murmured, intrigued by the brief sight of brown hair, tanned skin and what looked like a very nice body.

Cori walked into the garage and Jess greeted her with a sheepish grin.

"I called about the parts for your car, ma'am," he told her. "I can get them in about a week."

"A week! No, you don't understand. I need my car today!" She dug through her purse and pulled out her wallet. "Look, call them back. Tell them I'll pay extra for immediate delivery." She handed him one of her credit cards.

Jess gaped at the gold card she held out. He took it gingerly between grease-stained fingers and walked back to the office. He picked up the phone and rapidly punched in numbers. In a moment, he was speaking quietly into the receiver. A moment later, he gave her the thumbs-up.

"I'll just need to get authorization from the credit company for the repairs," he explained, picking up the phone again. "My boss insists on it."

Cori looked around, noticed the cluster of admirers, flashed them a smile and turned back to the office where Jess listened with a frown wrinkling his brow. He said something, then hung up. He walked back slowly.

"I'm real sorry, Miss Peyton, but they said your credit card was no good."

"What? Well, there must be a mistake. I used it this morning to pay my hotel bill." She shook her head as she gave him another card from her wallet, then extended her hand for the first card. "I'll have to check into it tonight."

He held up the card in one hand and a pair of scissors in the other. "They said I have to cut it up and send it back to them. They pay me for doing it."

"What?" She reached out to grab it back, but he was faster. Before Cori's eyes, her credit card was cut into four pieces. "This is ridiculous! What did they say?"

Jess hung his head, unhappy to be the bearer of bad news. "The lady said your account was canceled."

"Canceled?" she parroted, ignoring the murmurings from behind. Didn't these men have anything better to do than stand there and eavesdrop on what should be a private conversation? "Why would anyone want to cancel my credit card?" The moment the words left her mouth, the realization lit up inside her brain. "May I use your phone?"

He shifted uneasily. "You'll have to use the pay phone around back."

"Thank you," she snapped, marching around back. She looked over her shoulder. Oh, yes, she still had her shadows. "Don't you have something to do?" she asked frostily.

It didn't deter them.

"Not a thing," one of the men assured her with a broad smile.

"The phone's right over there," one of the other ones offered, pointing past her.

"Thank you." Cori dialed the number, then her calling-card number. All she got was a computer voice telling her that her card was no longer valid. She dug through her wallet, pulled out change and dropped it in the slots. "Collect call to Sean Peyton from Cori," she said in a clipped voice, turning her back on the men.

She wasn't surprised when the company operator accepted the charges and immediately routed the call to her father's office.

"Where the hell are you?" Sean's voice boomed in her ear.

"Somewhere in the Midwest." By now she could feel her nerves starting to unravel. First her car, then her credit card. What next? "One of the 'I' states, I think. Illinois, Iowa, one of those. I never could keep them straight."

"Toto don't realize she's in Kansas," one of the men snickered.

Cori's shoulders stiffened. "Do you mind?" She glared at the group. "This is a personal call."

"Don't worry, darlin', we'll give you all the privacy you need," one of the men assured her as they stepped one pace back. "We just wanted you to understand that you're in the great state of Kansas. Farrington, to be exact."

Cori took a deep breath.

"What is going on there?" Sean demanded.

"You canceled my Visa," she accused him.

"That's right, and all your other cards, too."

"What!" She was stunned. "All of them? Why?"

"Because I want you to come to your senses and come home. You've had enough time to pout. Now it's time for you to get back where you belong. We can talk more calmly about your idea for that inn."

Cori held her breath. Her father never gave in without a reason. "And?"

"And if you want to work so badly, you can come into the office and work for me. There's no reason why you can't start in Phyllis's department. It's a good entry-level job for you and you can work your way up there. Learn the meaning of a dollar. Once you show me you have a logical head on your shoulders for business, we'll talk about the inn again. Now why don't you tell me where you are."

Her mind quickly ran a few calculations. "I need my Visa reinstated to have my car repaired."

"Don't worry about the car. I'll arrange your transportation home."

That was when the truth hit her with a blinding realization. Once her father had her home and working for him, she would be under his thumb. And that would only be the beginning. He would arrange her life the way he'd wanted to since she turned eighteen. She would never have a chance to break out and find what she was truly meant to do. He'd even be back to finding the appropriate husband for her. He'd been making noises for some time now that he'd like to see some grandchildren before he was too old to enjoy them.

"Where are you?" Sean asked again, his accent strong with his agitation.

"No, I don't think so," she said slowly.

"You don't think what?"

"No, I don't think I'm going to come back and work for you, and, no, I don't think I'm going to tell you where I am." She took a deep breath. "Don't worry, Daddy, I'll be all right." With careful deliberation, she slid the phone back onto the hook, disconnecting the call and her father's orders.

Cori leaned against the rough boards, uncaring they were snagging her delicate silk top. At the moment, all that mattered was the understanding that by cutting herself off from her father she had literally stranded herself in some small town, in some corn state—she wasn't sure which one.

"Ma'am?" Jess looked uncertain as he walked toward her. "What should we do about your car?"

She took a deep breath. "How much are the parts?"

He handed her the work sheet. Cori winced when she read the figures. She knew she didn't have that much cash in her wallet, and after her talk with her father, she wouldn't be surprised if he found a way to close her checking account, too.

Why had she started this crazy drive to nowhere after her fight with her father? All the stress from the past hour had done was leave her head pounding and her stomach churning. Right now, all she wanted was to sit down in a cool place and not have to think about anything. She closed her eyes against the tiny feet wearing combat boots marching through her head. She opened her eyes and looked at the men still watching her as if waiting to hear what she would say next.

"I think..." was all she got out before her eyes rolled back in her head and she slid gracefully to the ground.

"SUCH A PRETTY little thing. Do you think that hair's her natural color? It's got to be a dye job. No one can have hair that color of blond. I wonder if she uses Clairol or L'Oreal."

Cori's hearing returned first. It took a moment for her to realize she was no longer lying in the dirt but on something slightly padded. A hand, slightly calloused, was curved around her wrist, a thumb pressing against the soft inner skin. She wasn't sure, but she had a vague idea the person holding her wrist was taking her pulse. At least she knew she wasn't dead.

"Enough about her hair, Ella. It looks as if she's coming around." A male voice seemed to roll around in her head.

A faint memory of a chocolate mousse she'd once consumed at a ski resort in Gaastad came to mind. His voice sounded the way it tasted: rich, smooth and sinful. She slowly opened her eyes. He looked the way he sounded. About as sinful as a man could get.

She blinked several times, frowning as the face in front of her seemed to ebb and flow like the tide. When she shifted her body, the paper underneath her crackled.

"Who are you?" she whispered, now recognizing the man's face as the one she had seen at the garage. The one in the sexy black T-shirt. Except now, he wore a white lab coat over it.

Only doctors wore lab coats, whispered a little voice in her mind. Except he didn't look like any doctor she'd ever dealt with. And no doctor she knew had deep brown eyes. Not brown puppy eyes, either, but "it's a hot time in the old bed tonight" brown eyes. She blinked several times.

He smiled. "Welcome back, Miss Peyton. How do you feel?"

Cori started to sit up, then moaned as the earth tipped on its axis. She flopped back before it tipped all the way. "Like I've been set down in the middle of the Bermuda Triangle. Who are you?"

"I'm Dr. Ben Cooper," he explained. "You fainted over at Cal's. Jess was afraid you were sick and brought you over to the clinic." He frowned and looked carefully into her eyes. "He didn't think you had hit your head."

She sat up, swinging her legs over the side of the examination table. This time her balance remained stable.

"I'd be luckier if I had. No, I'm just fine. My car is broken down, I have no idea where I am and my father canceled all my credit cards." She looked at him suspiciously. "What do you folks do here, drag in people so you have patients to examine? Isn't this town big enough to give you enough business? How do I know someone didn't slip knockout drops in my Diet Coke?"

The nurse, standing behind the doctor, gasped at the slur. He merely grinned.

"Hey, a doc's gotta do what he can when business is slow." He picked up her cap and handed it to her. "Sophie said you only ate a salad for lunch. What did you have for breakfast?"

"I assure you I have very good dietary habits," she said huffily. Ever since she started receiving injections, she had hated doctors. They were synonymous with pain. She shifted her body experimentally. At least he hadn't tried to give her a shot while she was unconscious.

"What did you eat?"

Cori could see he wasn't going to move back until she told him. And she couldn't get all the way up until he did. "Toast, grapefruit juice and coffee. Are you happy now?"

He shook his head. "Not with your idea of food. Sweetheart, I suggest you head over to Myrna's and tuck yourself into a real meal before you pass out again. It's only a guess, but I'd say you're a good fifteen pounds underweight. I know that thin is supposedly in, but, honey, you're asking for trouble."

"I don't need a meal. I need a way out of here!" Cori could feel the heated moisture behind her eyes and hated the idea she was going to cry in front of total strangers. If she wasn't so damn stubborn she'd call her dad back and beg him to take her away.

Ben, sensing her distress, glanced over his shoulder.

"Ella, why don't you put Ricky in exam room two," he suggested. "I'm sure he's more than ready to have that cast taken off."

She looked at Cori suspiciously as if the young woman would suddenly abscond with the good doctor. "Are you sure?"

He nodded. "I'd say Miss Peyton is fine now. I'll be there in a minute."

She paused a moment, then turned around and walked out, pointedly leaving the door ajar.

Ben grinned at the nurse's notion of propriety before he turned back to Cori. His grin dimmed as he saw the woe etched on her features.

"Hey, I'm not that bad a listener."

"Terrific. Do you act as the town shrink when medical emergencies run low?" She sniffed. "But then, I guess in a place this size you'd have to do what you can, wouldn't you?"

Most men would have lost their temper with her petulance by now, but Ben Cooper wasn't like most men.

"Fine, you're hurting right now and, since you obviously threw a tantrum to dear old dad, you're also in big trouble," he stated. "Now, I admit we may not have all the features of a big city, but we do pretty well for ourselves. Tell you what, there's a guest house out back that's not being used. You're welcome to stay there until you can straighten things out."

She narrowed her gaze. Suspicion was strong in her mind at his kind offer. "Why?"

"Because the town doesn't have a proper hotel and I don't think you have the money for the motel we do have. And since it's not even close to a five-star resort, I doubt you'd want to stay there," he stated bluntly. "But let's be honest about this. I'd hazard a pretty good guess you don't have a lot of money on you and no credit cards, so you don't have a lot of choices, do you?"

Cori squirmed under his direct gaze.

"I hate doctors," she muttered, sliding off the table and looking around for her purse.

"Yeah, but we do have our good points."

Cori shook her head in surprise. "Why are you doing this?"

"Because you obviously need a place to think things out, and if you go back over to Myrna's, even for a cup of coffee, you'd be spilling your life story to Sophie within five minutes. Trust me, she's better than any police interrogator when she wants to know about a person."

"What about the unlucky four?"

When Ben laughed, Cori hadn't expected to feel a warm feeling course through her veins at the rich sound.

"They'd love that." He chuckled. "Just slip out the back door and you'll be fine."

Cori still hesitated. "People don't do things like this without a reason."

Ben still smiled. "You've been living in L.A. too long, Miss Peyton. Out here, people help one another and don't expect a thing in return. If you want, I'll stop by Cal's and pick up your things later."

She gave a jerky nod. "Please call me Cori."

"There're cold drinks in the refrigerator," he told her, escorting her toward the end of the hall and opening the rear door. He gestured toward the small house at the end of a flower-edged path.

She started to step out, then turned. "What about a key?"

Ben smiled and shook his head. "We don't lock up all that much out here."

He waited, watching her walk down the path, with head downcast, shoes scuffing the dirt.

"That girl is pure trouble," Ella pronounced from behind.

Ben looked over his shoulder. "Think so?"

She nodded. "She's from a big city where sin is their idea of fun. Why, for all we know, she's into drugs and wild sex." Her pale blue eyes widened in horror.

Ben resisted smiling. He knew his nurse's idea of the big city came from the movies she watched via her satellite dish. But Ella meant well. Nowhere could he find a woman with a bigger heart. And as a nurse, she was worth her weight in pure gold. She had worked for his father until his death, and when Ben returned home to take over the practice, she showed up the day he reopened the clinic. Not once did she ever say something should continue being done a certain way because his father had always done it that way. And when he talked about expanding the clinic in hopes of starting a small hospital, she told him she'd make sure any additional nurses were properly trained.

He shook his head. "No, I think she's all right. In fact, maybe we're the best thing that's come her way. It's obvious she's rich and spoiled. Maybe she just needs to learn about the real world."

Ella clucked under her tongue. "Now you sound like your father. He never believed anyone was bad, either. Mark my words, that girl is trouble with a capital *T.*" She started to walk away. "Are you taking off Ricky's cast or shall I? He's figurin' on gettin' in that softball game later today."

"And probably break his other arm this time. Wait till he hears getting it off doesn't mean he can go out and pitch today." With one last look at the tiny cottage's closed front door, he walked back inside with Ella and closed the clinic's rear door.

CORI DROPPED HER PURSE and cap on a chair and proceeded to study her surroundings. The room may have been small, but it had a cozy feeling with a blue floral love seat and easy chair that looked out the multipaned window. She examined the crocheted doilies topping the chair arms and the pictures decorating one of the walls. None of the artwork could be considered valuable, but the country scenes fit the room perfectly.

She wandered on to poke through the other rooms. She inspected the tiny kitchen that didn't invite serious cooking; good thing, since she could barely boil water. The bathroom boasted fluffy rose and blue towels, a lovely deep old-fashioned claw-foot tub next to a modern frosted-glass shower cubicle. In the bedroom, the bed was covered with what looked like a handmade quilt. She admired the old-fashioned design, then tested the mattress and flopped down on it. She barely bounced as she stretched out on top of the covers.

Cori couldn't figure out why she felt so tired when it was barely the middle of the day. Usually her energy level was high from the moment she woke up until she dropped into bed in the wee hours. Lately, though, weariness seemed to be the order of the day. After that fainting spell, she only hoped she wasn't coming down with something.

"Even if this town does have a more than adequate doctor," she said throatily, kicking one leg upward.

She closed her eyes, but couldn't find any solace there. Not with the image of the good doctor imprinted in her mind.

"One thing for sure," she murmured just as she slipped into a deep sleep, "Dr. Marcus Welby, he's not."

Chapter Two

Farrington Pharmacy and Gifts

Ben tried posting strict hours when he first reopened the clinic. It hadn't taken him long to realize that emergencies didn't take business hours into consideration. Which was why he was still working at eight o'clock. Thankfully, Ella called home, told her husband to eat without her and stayed to help when Lorna Reeves showed up. There was no question the pregnant woman was in labor.

"You shouldn't have been driving. Why didn't you have Ray bring you in?" he chided as he and Ella helped her into an examination room. "Or call me?"

"It was easier to just come in," she panted, allowing doctor and nurse to assist her onto the table. "Ray's cellular phone must be dead 'cause I couldn't reach him and, no offense, but I wasn't going to wait out there until you showed up."

"You just start your breathing exercises, darlin'," Ella advised, helping the young woman out of her dress. "I'll have my Henry try to get ahold of Ray for you. Meanwhile, we're going to bring that baby into the world."

"You won't get any argument from me on that." She gasped as another contraction hit.

Much later, Ben had to smile as a stunned young husband raced into the clinic just in time to greet his new daughter. Ben didn't argue when Ella insisted she'd take care of things and for him to get himself something to eat.

While the idea of a hot meal sounded appealing, Ben thought of his unexpected guest first. Even though the gas station closed promptly at six, he wouldn't have any problem retrieving Cori's things. Not when Jess lived in a trailer behind the garage and was even known to work late on a truck or car if the owner needed it right away. Sure enough, he found the young mechanic bent over the front of Isaac's ancient truck.

"Why don't you just tell old Isaac he needs a new truck?" Ben called out.

"Hey, Doc." Jess straightened up. He grabbed a rag and wiped his hands. "Nah, if I did that, I wouldn't have a steady customer." He grinned. "I heard Miss Peyton is out in your guest house. She okay?"

He nodded, not surprised the town grapevine had already targeted Cori's destination. Secrets weren't allowed in Farrington. "Just overtired, I think. I thought I'd come by to pick up her things from her car."

"No problem." Jess led the way toward the rear of the garage and out a back door. "I put a cover on her car to protect it." He folded the tarp back and lovingly caressed the rear fender. "I asked one of the guys in Wichita about these cars. He said you take care of them the way you'd take care of a baby." He looked at the sports car as if it were a beautiful woman. "She's pretty, isn't she?"

"That she is." Belatedly, Ben realized Jess meant the car, not the woman. He watched Jess open the trunk, then stepped back and whistled. "Will you look at that?"

Ben peered into the interior. "I never knew a person could cram so much luggage into one trunk," he muttered.

"Then take a look in the back seat. There's even more there." Jess chuckled. "Maybe you better drive your truck around back here. It would be easier to load up that way. 'Course, if she's only stayin' the night, she might need only one suitcase, although I don't know which one you should take."

Ben looked at the designer-insigniaed suitcases and tote bag. "I better take them all."

Jess helped him unload the car and settle the bags in the back of Ben's truck.

"You tell Miss Peyton I'll keep her car safe until she can get it fixed," he told Ben.

Ben smiled. He wondered if Cori would realize that in L.A. she wouldn't be this lucky with a mechanic. Jess, as good as his word, would keep her car covered and safe until it could be repaired.

"I'll tell her. Thanks." He climbed inside his truck.

"Oh! I saw Ray speeding past a while ago. What'd Lorna have?"

"A girl."

Jess whooped. "He'll be gray with worry by the time she's sixteen!"

Ben waved as he drove off.

His first thought when he pulled up in front of the cottage was that she had taken off, since the building was dark. Except he knew she had no transportation and doubted she had braved Myrna's again so soon. He grabbed one of the smaller cases that he had set next to him and climbed out of the truck. He walked inside and switched on a lamp near the door.

"Cori?" he called out softly. It didn't take him long to find her stretched out on the bed, sound asleep.

The lamplight from the living room shone softly through the doorway and highlighted her form with its golden glow. She lay on her side, one hand curved under her face while the other curled across her waist.

Ben sat carefully on the side of the bed.

His doctor's mind told him she was about five feet six inches, short golden blond hair, blue eyes and had a slender build. Other than her too-thin state, she appeared very healthy—obviously had the best of health care, and teeth that were a dentist's dream. Her hair had been pampered by experts, her nails shaped and polished a pale rose and her skin golden from the sun. But an analytical mind couldn't describe the way her hair seemed to glow like a rare sun, how her eyes were such a rich navy blue they didn't appear real and why her skin was like silk to the touch.

"Cori," he spoke softly, gently shaking her shoulder. Her bare skin was warm to the touch and had him thinking about touching more than just her shoulder. "Hey, sleeping beauty, time to return to the present."

She rolled onto her back, murmuring a protest at being awakened. She opened her eyes and blinked several times. Her expression was confused as she looked around, obviously trying to figure out where she was. Her eyes widened when she looked up at Ben.

"Oh, it's you. Not a bad dream, after all." She sat up, brushing her hair from her face. "What time is it?"

Ben was impressed with her lack of vanity at being caught at a vulnerable time. Her hair was mussed from her nap and her make-up slightly smudged, but she didn't seem to notice or care. And here he thought she was lovely before. But now, looking sleep tousled, she seemed even lovelier.

"Eight-thirty," he replied. "Are you hungry?"

"What is this obsession you have with food?" she grumbled, not so carefully pushing him to one side so she could swing her legs over the edge of the bed.

"I didn't have any dinner and I bet you didn't, either. Myrna's will be open for another half hour." He stood and held out his hand.

Cori allowed him to pull her to her feet. "Sure, the condemned ate a hearty last meal," she muttered.

Ben grinned. Obviously, she wasn't one of those who woke up perky and cheerful. A disgruntled Cori was a sight to see.

"Let me make sure I don't look like a total mess." Cori pushed her hair away from her face, picked up her purse and went into the bathroom.

"I brought over your suitcases," Ben called out to the closed door. "You must think you're going to need something if you have to travel with your entire wardrobe."

"Oh, that's just some things I threw together for my trip to England," she said, coming out of the bathroom. Her hair was brushed and a rose gloss colored her lips.

"You know most people find it's easier to fly to England than drive."

Cori shot him a droll look. "Ha, ha." She headed for the front door, confident he would follow.

Ben watched the gentle sway of her hips, the way her denim skirt hugged her rear, and decided following her was the best place to be.

"What kind of doctor are you?" Cori asked once he had her settled in the cab of his truck after tossing his medical bag behind them along with a small box of other medical supplies.

"General practioner."

"No GP does all this. Maybe I should warn you that I may not be able to pay your bill," she told him. "Although I can't imagine he would cancel my medical insurance."

"Who said anything about charging you?" Ben said cheerfully, switching on the ignition. "It's not often we get a California girl in town."

Cori studied her surroundings as Ben drove down the main street. All the stores were closed except for the restaurant where lights were still blazing.

"They stay open late on Thursdays because the city council meets tonight and they like to stop by here for pie and coffee afterward," he explained, parking the truck in front of the restaurant, getting out and walking around to help her down.

"Hi there, Doc," a man who looked more like a grizzly bear than a human being called out from the rear of the restaurant. "Hey, darlin', you feelin' better? Heard you took a dive out at Cal's."

"Is there anyone who doesn't know?" Cori muttered under her breath as she kept a smile firmly pasted on her lips.

"Mrs. Tweedy," Ben said promptly. "She's out of town visiting her sister."

"I'm fine, thank you," Cori told the man. She guessed by his food-spattered apron he was the cook. And by the variety of tattoos adorning his arms, he had done quite a bit of traveling.

"Cori, this is Ralph, owner and cook for Myrna's," Ben introduced. "Ralph, meet Cori Peyton, who's still not too sure about us, so be nice."

"Hell, I'm always nice," the man growled. "Take one of the rear booths. Council meeting won't be over for another half hour or so. Fred's bitchin' about that new bond issue and you know how long-winded he is when he's got a bee in his britches. How about the stew?''

"Make it two," Ben replied, guiding Cori to a booth.

"Maybe I'd prefer something else," Cori whispered.

"Maybe I'd prefer you eat something substantial instead of passing out again," he whispered back, waiting until she slid into the booth. "What do you want to drink?"

"Diet Coke."

He nodded and walked over to the machine, expertly pouring two drinks and bringing them back to the table. Instead of taking the seat across from Cori, he slid in next to her, his denim-covered thigh brushing against her bare one.

Cori looked pointedly from where he sat to the empty seat across from them.

"Is there something wrong with the seat across from us?"

"Not a thing." He handed her a straw along with her glass. "You'll like Ralph's stew. He throws just about everything in it but the kitchen sink. He serves it with homemade rolls that are better than my mom's, although you'll never hear me say that around her. Not if I want to keep my butt in one piece."

His grin sent a shaft of heat straight to Cori's middle. In an effort to defuse the attraction she felt, she quickly unwrapped her straw and dunked it in her drink.

She was grateful for Ralph's interruption when he brought over two shallow bowls filled with stew and a basket filled with warm rolls emanating a warm yeasty aroma. She mentally counted the calories as she stared at the bowl's contents: chunks of beef, potatoes and carrots swimming in a rich brown gravy.

"Don't you ever think about your patients' health if you encourage them to eat like this all the time?" she mumbled. "I hate to think of the fat content in this meal."

"I only worry if they have dietary problems, but I don't see that too often around here." He dipped his spoon into the stew. "I have an eighty-year-old patient who's drunk a pint of corn whiskey every day for the past sixty-five years and smoked since he was twelve. He has the heart and lungs of a teenager. According to his medical history, his weight hasn't varied more than three pounds over the years, yet fried chicken is one of his favorite meals. At the same time, I have another patient who claims she can eat a peanut and gain ten pounds. I think the fudge surrounding said peanut has something to do with that claim."

Cori shook her head. One mouthful of stew tempted her taste buds so much she dug in hungrily. She hadn't been all that hungry for the past few days, so she knew she shouldn't be surprised by the return of her appetite.

"So tell me, Cori Peyton, what do you intend to do now?"

She swallowed the bite of butter-drenched roll she had taken and half turned to face him.

"Do as to what?"

"Your car, your dad canceling your charge cards. That. Jess figured out what was going on after Dan and Zeke told him about your phone call to your dad."

She grimaced. "Is there no privacy around here?"

"Not really."

Cori muttered a curse regarding Ben's cheerful manner. "Then let me give you the whole story. I'd hate people to get it wrong since I have a pretty good idea it will be all over town by tomorrow morning." She set her spoon down. "I was discussing a business proposition with father. He didn't like it and basically said his only daughter was nothing more than a mindless flake. I got angry and took off. The clothes in the car were meant for my trip to England."

"But you didn't go to England," he prompted.

She grimaced. "I guess you could say I strayed off course. I got in my car and just drove. Pretty soon, it was easier to keep on driving. Before I knew it, I was here and my car refused to go any farther."

"You know, there're easier ways of handling a situation than going to England."

"I wasn't going there for fun. I had a chance to buy a country manor over there at a steal of a price."

"What do you consider a steal?" He whistled under his breath when she told him. "*That's* what you consider a steal?"

"Of course! The house has been family owned for centuries, but they can't keep up the taxes and wish to sell it." Her face lit up with animation. "It's in a wonderful location outside of London. Tourists travel that route on a regular basis. Admittedly, there are repairs that will have to be done and landscaping and such, but it should pay for itself within a year."

Ben nodded. "So you've worked in the hotel industry?"

"Well, no," she admitted, uneasy with the direction he was taking.

"A bed and breakfast?"

She shook her head.

"A cheap motel?"

"What does that have to do with it?" Cori demanded.

"A lot. How can you know the place will pay for itself if you've never worked in the hotel industry?" he said with more logic than she wanted to hear. "Do you have a business degree?"

She shifted uncomfortably. "Actually, I majored in fine arts and I've taken some business courses. There is nothing wrong with fine arts!" she said hotly in her own defense.

"Nothing whatsoever. So tell me, since it's obvious you're not getting your bed and breakfast and you don't have the money to get your car fixed or get yourself out of town, what do you expect to do?"

Cori opened her mouth, fully prepared to inform Ben she wasn't at all worried. Except that would be a major lie. She lifted her chin.

"I'll find a job."

Ben was grateful he hadn't taken a bite just then. He probably would have choked. Looking at Cori Peyton he would hazard a guess she hadn't worked a day in her life. But he knew he could be wrong. Still, this could prove interesting. And the chance of keeping the lady in town for a while was tempting.

"Then I'll help you in any way I can. What can you do?"

Cori seemed to look inward. "Clothing, hair, consumerism," she said promptly.

"Fine. I'll find you something tomorrow." He returned to his meal.

"Thank you, but I can find my own job."

"Not around here. Farrington is a small town and people tend to stick together. A reference from a local would be a good idea. You're more than welcome to use the guest house rent free. Just remember you're not in California. Salaries are a lot lower out here."

Cori stared at him, still stunned by his more than generous offer.

"Maybe you're more like Marcus Welby than I first thought."

"That's a new one for me." Ben chuckled. "Now eat up. Passing out your first day on the job won't look very good."

When Ben later drove Cori back to the guest house and walked her to the door, she fully expected him to make a move. Take her hand. Put his arm around her shoulders. Try to kiss her. Ask to be invited inside for coffee. Instead, he didn't move any farther than outside the front door as he pulled a key off his key ring and offered it to her with a warm smile before saying good night.

"There's food in the refrigerator," he told her. "Feel free to take whatever looks good. I'll ask around and should have something for you by late tomorrow morning."

"You still haven't explained why you're willing to do this for me," Cori said in her own attempt to keep him there a moment longer.

Ben paused. He smiled the smile that sent waves of heat through her.

"Could be for a lot reasons. One, you obviously need some help to get your car up and running again. Two, you can't seem to count on your dad right now. Or maybe it's three."

"And what's three?" she whispered, mesmerized by the warmth reflected in his eyes. Oh, yes, they were definitely bedroom eyes.

His smile sent another jolt through her. "Three is, maybe it has to do with those pretty blue eyes that say a hell of a lot more than you probably intend for them to say," he murmured before taking his leave with nothing more than a brief squeeze of her hand.

Cori stepped inside and stared at the lamp for several moments before she realized it needed to be switched on. Most of her luggage had been left in the living room while a few of her suitcases had been placed on the bed.

She couldn't remember the last time she had eaten in a restaurant like Myrna's. If, indeed, she ever had. And tomorrow, with luck, she would be starting a job. She had no idea what she would even be doing! But that didn't matter to her. Not when she realized this was her chance to prove herself to her father.

"I'll show Dad I'm more than worthy of running that inn," she muttered, carrying her cosmetics tote into the bathroom and pulling out a variety of jars. "Working at anything around here will be a snap."

"THAT GIRL IS CAUSIN' quite a stir over at Elliott's," a grizzled man wearing patched overalls and a faded red plaid cotton shirt informed Ben.

"What girl, Dan?" he asked absently as he studied the man's blood pressure.

"The pretty little blonde who showed up yesterday in that danged foreign car," Dan insisted. "The one you talked Elliott into hiring since Marcelle wanted a few weeks off to go up to see her niece in Sioux City. Elliott's about ready to bust a gut. He says she's ruining his business."

Ben looked up. "All she's doing over there is ringing up sales at the register and stocking shelves just the way Marcelle did. What's so dangerous about that?"

"Why, she's tellin' people they don't need to use any of those over-the-counter drugs Elliott sells," Dan explained, trying to peer over the edge of the paper. He was always interested in what Ben wrote on his chart. Probably because he was convinced he didn't have high blood pressure or heart problems—only that Ben wrote them down to make him think he did. "Reba Murphy went in to pick up some of those sleeping pills she takes when Larry is on one of his long hauls, and the little missy tells her she shouldn't be putting stuff like that in her body. That she should be eating roots. Now you tell me, what person in their right mind would be wantin' to eat roots?" He puffed up.

Ben shook his head, still unclear what Dan meant. Then it came to him. "Are you talking about valerian root?"

"Don't know what kind of root, just that she's supposed to be takin' roots. That's pure nuts." The older man grumped. "Now what are you writin' down there, boy? I don't have to take those danged pills anymore, do I?"

"You most certainly do," Ben replied. His mind raced with questions. What was Cori doing over there? When he talked to her this morning, he explained the job at the pharmacy was only a few hours a day, but it would help. He also tactfully suggested she wear something a little longer than the skirt she wore the day before. Although, he had to privately admit looking at her legs wasn't that much of a hardship. He turned his attention back to his patient. "Of course, if you'd follow the diet I gave you and slowed down a little, you could have a chance of getting off the blood pressure medication, but as it stands, you're still on them."

"Your pa didn't believe in all this modern medicine."

"Yes, he did. He just said it differently." Ben made a few notations in the chart. He opened his mouth, fully prepared to begin his monthly lecture on how Dan should slow down, when there was a knock at the door and Ella poked her head in.

"Elliott's on the phone," she told him. "He said you talk to him right now or else."

Ben filled out a prescription slip and handed it to Dan. "You take these on schedule," he instructed. "And no sneaking out to Isaac's for some of his corn liquor."

Dan took the slip. "Maybe I should talk to the girl about what roots I should eat," he said slyly.

Ben held his gaze. "You want to travel the eighty miles to see Doc Jackson?"

The older man shuddered. "No way! The last time I saw him, he had me takin' something that kept me close to home for three days." He slowly got to his feet and shuffled out of the room. "Think I'll go over to Elliott's and get this filled now. So I don't forget."

Ben muttered a curse that would have earned him a mouthful of soap as he walked back to his office and picked up the phone. The moment he heard the agitation in the pharmacist's voice, he knew there was trouble.

"You got her in here, you get her out," the man ordered.

"What are you talking about, Elliott?" he asked, deciding to opt for innocence.

"That California girl," the man blustered.

Ben shuffled the few message slips on his desk. "What has she done?"

"She's losing me customers," Elliott told him. "She's out there telling everyone not to buy aspirin or cold medicine or whatever they're in here for! I should have known she was dangerous."

"How can one woman be dangerous?" he asked, mentally recalling that lush mouth he had wanted to kiss and skin he wanted to touch. Come to think of it, she was pretty dangerous—to his peace of mind!

"Simple. She's from California, isn't she? That's where the hippies came from. And now she's telling people about herbs. She'll have them smoking funny stuff next! Get her out of here, Ben, before I throw her out." He slammed the phone down.

Ben looked at his watch. "She was only there for two hours," he mused aloud, shrugging off his lab coat.

As if on cue, Ella looked in. "You going down to Elliott's?"

He nodded. "What have you heard?" Ella opened her mouth to inform him, but Ben held up a hand. "Don't tell me. I'd rather not know." He muttered another curse. "How can she create so much havoc in only two hours?"

Ella's laughter was the last thing he heard.

Since the pharmacy was just down the street, Ben reached it in a few minutes. After what he'd already heard, seeing several people milling outside the door wasn't a surprise to him.

"Elliott thinks she's one of those hippies who's here to turn us all into druggies," one silver-haired woman told Ben, clutching his arm.

"Now, Sarah, you know better," he chided, patting her on the shoulder. "I will personally vouch for Cori."

"Saw something like that in a movie once," one of Dan's checker-playing cronies intoned. "The government used a small town as a test. And we'd be the perfect town for somethin' like that."

"I saw somethin' like that, too," one of the women said, her eyes dilated with fear and eagerness to be involved. "Who knows what she's really here for? Maybe she's part of the mob and she's hiding out from the godfather because she stole something of his or killed one of his dons. I saw something like that on TV just last week."

Ben bit back a curse. The last thing he needed was a case of mass hysteria to deal with. He went into the pharmacy

and noted the people milling around, unashamedly eaves-
dropping on the argument emanating from the back of the
store.

"I am not a pusher!" Cori said hotly. "I am merely
trying to give people alternatives to some of the drugs."

Ben hurried his pace.

"Alternatives, my foot. You're from L.A., aren't you?"
Elliott demanded. "That's where all the druggies come
from. For all we know, you're planning to plant a mari-
juana field outside of town."

"I suggest you read your newspaper more often than
once every thirty years," she argued. "You'd discover drug
addicts live everywhere, even in small towns."

"We don't have any druggies here!" he shouted.

"I didn't say you did!" Cori yelled back, placing her
hands on her hips and pushing her face into his as she deliberately stepped forward into his space. "I merely said
they live everywhere nowadays. You really should try to
come into the twentieth century, Elliott. You might learn
something!"

"I read the *Enquirer* just like everyone else," he said
huffily.

Cori rolled her eyes.

Ben noted the hectic flush coloring Elliott's face and
knew it was time to step in.

"All right, you two." He deliberately walked between
them. He turned to Elliott first. With his short, stubby
legs, round belly and carrot-red hair sticking up from the
times he had run his fingers through the strands, Elliott
looked like an agitated rooster. Especially since his voice
always turned into a squawk any time he got upset. Right
now, he would have been a perfect alarm clock at dawn.

"The man has no idea the strides modern medicine has taken in the past fifty years," Cori pronounced in a haughty voice. "Homeopathic medicines are widely recognized."

"And where did you receive your pharmacology degree, missy?" Elliott demanded.

Ben turned to Cori. He held up his hand, forefinger raised to indicate he wanted silence. Ordinarily, she would have ignored him, except the expression on his face warned her that one word would bring his wrath down upon her.

"I'll make this easy for all of us," Ben said quietly with just enough menace in his voice to keep the combatants quiet. "Elliott, we've discussed homeopathic medicine before. You don't believe in it. Fine, that's your opinion." He turned back to Cori. "Cori, you obviously do. Sometimes it is helpful, other times it's not. Do yourself a favor—if someone doesn't agree with your opinions, keep them to yourself."

"Get her out of here." The pharmacist looked at Cori as if she had sprouted horns and a tail.

Ben took Cori's arm and ushered her down the aisle toward the door.

"Wait a minute!" She shook herself free and stalked back to Elliott with Ben rapidly on her heels. "You owe me for—" she looked up at the clock hanging over the pharmacy counter "—two hours and forty-seven minutes." She held out her hand.

Elliott's scowl would have flattened a lesser person. He walked over to the register, punched the No Sale button and pulled out some bills and a few coins. He slapped them in her hand and walked away.

Cori's mouth dropped open as she scanned the meager lot. "Four dollars and twelve cents!"

Elliott spun around. "Taxes," he said succinctly.

Ben grasped her arm in a firm hold and hustled her out of the building. By then, the small crowd outside the pharmacy had grown and he pushed his way past them.

"It's all over, folks," he informed them as he pulled Cori up the street.

"That is so unfair," she muttered, jamming the money in her pocket. "The man has no concept of modern technology!"

Ben gritted his teeth, determined not to say a word until he was sure they were alone. At the moment, it was difficult not to throttle Cori. She went on incessantly, like a yapping dog. Didn't she understand the meaning of "silence is golden"? His jaw muscles flexed.

He jerked on the cottage's front doorknob, swore when he found it locked and turned to Cori. She met his blazing scrutiny with unflinching calm.

"I know. Out here, you don't bother locking doors." She pulled the key out of her pocket. Before she could step forward to fit it in the lock, he took it out of her hand, opened the door and pushed her none too gently inside.

"How do you do it?" he demanded, pacing the length of the room. "Within the space of a couple hours, you turned one of the calmest, sanest men into a raving lunatic. Is it a gift?"

"Me?" Cori was affronted at the blame being placed on her. "I was told I was hired to help out."

"Help, not create a war!" He stopped short and took several breaths to calm a pulse he could tell was racing. "All you had to do was familiarize yourself with the merchandise and ring up purchases."

"This sweet old lady came in to complain the sleeping pills she had been taking weren't working. I suggested a more natural method of dealing with her problem," she explained. "What was so wrong with that?"

What could he say to that?

"Nothing." He closed his eyes and pinched his nose.

"Do you have a headache?" she ventured.

"Only in the past ten seconds," he muttered.

"Sometimes headaches are due to restricted blood flow to the brain. A neck massage would work wonders for that." She stepped toward him with her hands raised.

"No!" Realizing how panicked he sounded, he quickly lowered his voice. "No thanks, I'll be fine in a minute." He took several deep breaths to calm himself. "All right, I'll make a few more calls and come up with something else for you. But—" he held up a warning hand "—no more talk of herbal therapy."

Cori bobbed her head up and down.

He took that for a yes and headed for the door.

"Ben."

He looked over his shoulder.

"I *am* willing to work," Cori said softly. Her deep blue eyes were dark with sincerity. "I didn't know he'd get so angry."

"I suggest you stay out of there for a while."

As Ben walked back to the clinic and what he was certain would be an influx of questions from Ella, he realized something else hammered at his brain.

All the time he wanted to put his hands around Cori's neck and squeeze, he also wanted to cover her luscious mouth with his own and see what she tasted like. Trouble was, once he started he knew he wouldn't stop there, because he also wanted to see if her skin was silky all over. And after that, anything was possible.

By the time he reached the clinic, he found himself aroused. He stopped at the door and willed himself back to normal.

"I've always been a sucker for blue-eyed blondes," he muttered, pulling on the doorknob.

Chapter Three

Regina's Cut 'n' Curl

"Honey, that is the most gorgeous head of hair I've seen in a long time." Regina, owner of Regina's Cut 'n' Curl, lifted a lock of Cori's hair and examined it with the eye of one who has been in the beauty business for the past twenty-seven years. "What color did they use on you?"

"No color," Cori replied. "Just a weave every three months for added highlights. Tommy, who's done my hair for the past four years, is a genius." She wrinkled her nose in distaste against the strong odor of permanent-wave solution. She felt a little queasy from the smell and took shallow breaths through her mouth. She only hoped she would get used to the smell fast.

Regina eyed her closely. "Doc says you know hair."

Cori nodded briskly. "Oh, yes." After all the years she'd had her hair done, she couldn't imagine it would be all that difficult to do. Cut a bit, mix colors, shampoo; it would be a snap. "I learned everything I know from Tommy."

"He in L.A.?"

She shook her head. "Actually, he's in Paris. He has a second salon in London, but he prefers to work in Paris."

"Paris, France?" Lorraine Bradley's eyes popped open to the size of saucers. "You actually go to Paris to have your hair done?" Her bright apricot-colored hair was neatly wrapped around small pink rollers. The moment Cori had stepped inside the shop, her head popped out from under the dryer. Listening to the newcomer was infinitely more interesting than listening to Velma Perkins talk about her gall bladder surgery. After all, gall bladder surgery was nothing compared to her own health problems.

"You know how it is when you find a good hairdresser. You go where they go." Cori flashed a warm smile.

"Honey, before you do a thing, I want to see how your hair is cut." Regina pushed her into a chair and seemed to examine every strand of hair before letting Cori back up. "I can't believe it. How did he get this?"

"He uses very tiny scissors. He feels he can control his cuts better that way." Cori figured if they wanted to ask her questions, she'd ask a few of her own. "You have a very nice town here."

"We think so." Regina's beak of a nose was almost buried in Cori's hair.

"You know, when Jess first mentioned your doctor, I thought he would be someone like Marcus Welby. You know, that old doctor on TV?"

"That was a wonderful show!" Janet Stiller, one of the other hairdressers, chimed in. "Did you see the one he did on a woman suffering from menopause? I swear, he could have been talking about me!"

"I just meant I expected someone older than Dr. Cooper," Cori quickly inserted.

"He took over when his dad died four years ago," Regina explained. "Why, as long as I can remember we've had a Dr. Cooper in town. Before his dad, his grandpa was the town doc. Ben's dad treated everyone until he was called into the service. He served in the South Pacific," she said proudly. "My Fred wouldn't be alive today if it hadn't been for Doc Cooper keeping soldiers alive."

"Oh, he served with Dr. Cooper's father?"

"No, darlin', he saved Fred's daddy's life." She laughed. "If he hadn't, Fred wouldn't even have been a twinkle in his momma's eye. Ben's daddy served overseas, too. Came home with an Eyetalian wife. Folks weren't too sure about that, but Lucia is such a darlin' woman people soon fell in love with her."

Cori nodded. That explained the slight olive cast to Ben's skin and dark hair and eyes. Not to mention that aura of pure sex the man exuded.

"Ben's the youngest of eight and the only one who wanted to be a doctor," Regina went on.

Cori's eyes almost popped out of their sockets. *"Eight?"*

Regina nodded. "They sure loved having kids. Some say they had so many 'cause they didn't get a boy until they had Ben."

"Not to mention loving what it took to have all those kids." One of the women snickered.

For the next hour, as Regina instructed Cori in her duties, the younger woman also had another kind of education. At first, she thought women living in the Midwest would be a bit straitlaced. She soon found differently. Husbands' sexual habits, friends' and relatives' surgeries in graphic detail and gossip about anyone who wasn't present in the shop that morning—all were fair game. Nothing was said maliciously, but she was positive she picked up more information about the town's inhabitants than she would ever need to know—or want to. Except for one inhabitant, whom she quickly learned was a main source of gossip with the ladies. Ben Cooper's life and work were discussed freely. Ben's work: Never a better or caring doctor, they said. His family: His sister, Carla, married a stockbroker and lived in Chicago, where she was a member of a large architecture firm. Sister Maria moved to Italy to live with their mother's family for a year and study painting over there. Another married a local farmer. What the Coopers were known for was their tradition of doctoring the Farrington locals for the past four generations. The more Cori heard, the more she committed to her memory banks. It was soon becoming clear to her that any information on the handsome Dr. Cooper was important.

Yesterday, he had been angry when he left her. That was apparent. But that hadn't stopped him from checking on her last night and suggesting he take her back to Myrna's for dinner. Except she hadn't been as forgiving as he had— not after he had yelled at her. So she stiffly declined and settled for fixing herself soup. She only hoped the burned mess could be gotten out of the pot. And here she thought soup would be the easiest thing to cook. At least nothing had caught on fire.

"Tell me something, if you have your hair done in Paris and have such an expensive wardrobe, why are you in Farrington and why are you working here?" Valerie Townsend asked from the manicure table she resided over. At the moment, she was idly filing her nails and glancing at the assortment of nail polish bottles that ranged from fire-engine red to pale pink. "Why not just call Daddy and ask him to pay your car repairs, so you can go back to Beverly Hills and all your charge cards? I bet you go to lots of big parties out there, don't you? Did you ever date any celebrities? My, my, I can imagine you're already bored here in this itty-bitty town."

Cori looked at the woman. She wouldn't be surprised if the manicurist sported a healthy set of fangs to go with the claws she was presently painting bloodred.

"I like to handle things myself," she said calmly, pouring a dollop of shampoo in her hand and rubbing it into Belinda's hair. Belinda, whose husband owned the feed and seed shop, had asked Cori to be the one to work on her hair. Proud, Cori immediately draped a plastic cape around the older woman's shoulders and escorted her back to the sink. This wasn't so difficult, she thought as she shampooed the woman's hair. This she could do.

Cori found herself enjoying the easy conversation in the Cut 'n' Curl. She watched Regina cut hair, and Sonia deftly roll wet strands on perm rods, and she even mixed hair color under Regina's direction.

"I tell you this is the most important night of my life," Cori heard Thalia Roberts, Regina's client, confide. "I just know Rawley's taking me to dinner at the Easton Inn because he's going to propose to me."

"Oh, honey, we'll have you so gorgeous he'll beg you to marry him." Regina patted her shoulder before applying the color Cori had mixed. "Now this won't change your color a lot. Just brighten it up a bit."

"What kind of shoes are those? Italian?" Valerie pointed to the delicate black leather sandals Cori wore with her black linen walking shorts and matching weskit. A black-billed cap was perched on her head with her hair feathered around the edges. "Pretty expensive shoes to wear around a one-horse town like this."

Cori shook her head. "I honestly can't remember what they are. I chose them more for comfort than looks. I believe I found them at Neiman Marcus."

"Well, of course, it would be Neiman Marcus." The derision in Valerie's voice was unmistakable. "A fancy store for fancy shoes."

"You leave her alone, Valerie," Regina warned, waving a rattail comb at the manicurist.

"I just asked her a question," she defended herself, looking about as innocent as a barracuda. "What's so bad about that?"

"It's the way you're doing it."

"Regina." Thalia scooted to the front of her chair and peered closely in the mirror. "Is the color solution supposed to look like this?"

Regina, who now had been taking rollers out of another client's hair, walked back over to Thalia and took the plastic cap off her head. She slipped on her glasses that rode on top of her head and studied the colorful mess. "Cori, did you mix in color sixty-two with forty-eight?"

Cori had only heard part of the question. "No, you said sixty-four," she said absently as she dropped combs in the sterilizer jar.

"Sixty-four!" Regina hurried her customer over to the sink.

"What's wrong?" Thalia kept asking as Regina sudsed her hair. "Regina, what happened?" Her question later ended in a scream as she saw herself in the mirror. Her normally dark blond hair, better known as dishwater blond, was now a vivid shade of orange.

"YOU'RE NOT GOING to believe this." Ella cornered Ben when he finished seeing Marge Sinclair, now expecting her third baby.

He closed his eyes. "Don't tell me. Cori Peyton."

"All right." The woman lumbered off. "Billy Larson's in exam room one. That boy doesn't understand he can't eat six hamburgers without ending up with a bellyache."

Ben's eyes popped open. "Ella."

"You told me not to tell you," she said over her shoulder.

"Ella." His silent warning held no threat to the crusty nurse.

She stopped and turned around. "I can't believe you didn't hear Thalia screaming. Some say she cracked a few windows in town."

He resisted the urge to throttle his bullheaded nurse and calmly said, "Tell me what happened at Regina's."

"Regina had little Miss Cori mix the color solution. You see, Rawley's taking Thalia out to dinner over at the Easton Inn tonight. Word has it he's going to pop—"

"Ella," Ben interrupted. "Get to the point."

"Thalia's dark blond hair is now the color of a traffic cone you see out on the highway."

Ben uttered a pithy curse.

Ella's dark eyes danced with laughter. "Too bad it hadn't happened with that Valerie. She's the one who needs taking down a peg or two. She figures she can get her hooks in you, you know. Working as a manicurist is only her first step up to obtaining her goal as the wife of the town doctor."

"In her dreams," he muttered, pulling on his T-shirt neckline as if it had suddenly gotten too tight. Even his lab coat felt snug.

"You did take her to the last church social," she reminded him.

"And Brian Walters took her to the Valentine dance at the Elks Lodge. And Ed Farley took her to the Christmas social and—" Ella's hand over his mouth stopped his recitation.

"Go rescue your little project before Regina tears her hair out by the roots," she advised as she efficiently divested him of his lab coat. "And while you're at it, give Thalia a heavy-duty tranquilizer. I heard she's having major hysterics. She's now convinced Rawley will never ask for her hand." She held up a small envelope.

Ben looked inside the envelope and easily identified the capsule. "This could put her out for the next month."

"Might be a good idea." She pushed him toward the door. "I can't wait to see where you send the lady next."

"Neither can I," he muttered.

"Just remember one thing, Benjamin. We're a small town and there's only so many businesses you can blackmail into taking her," she called after him.

"You're telling me."

Ben realized how quickly the story spread as he walked down the sidewalk.

"Hey, Doc, I hear that little girl you've taken under your wing turned Thalia Roberts's hair orange!" a man called out, on a wave of laughter from his cronies. "Think maybe Rawley otta wait until Halloween to take her out again?"

"I heard it looks as if she dumped ten bottles of iodine on her head," another man quipped.

"Hey, Frank, next time you get that nasty heat rash around your privates you can go over to Milton for treatment," Ben called back. He smiled to himself as he heard the joke now on someone else. His smile quickly disappeared as he approached the beauty shop. The small crowd milling about in front was a repeat of the scene at Elliott's.

"But, Doc, Milton's a hundred miles away!" Ben was certain Frank's wail could be heard that far away.

"Yeah, a nice long bumpy ride," Ben muttered to himself with no small amount of satisfaction as he walked into the beauty shop. Just before he stepped inside, he halted and speared his glance in the direction of one of the women in the crowd. "Good morning, Mrs. Rebus," he cordially greeted the dark-clad woman. "Why, I'm real surprised to see you here today. Especially after your husband's stirring sermon last Sunday about the evils of gossip." He inclined his head in a respectful bow and walked in.

"How would he know?" the woman sputtered. "He wasn't even there!"

Ben grinned. He knew the minister's wife was more chagrined at getting caught being part of this gaggle of gossipy hens than he was at not being in church. He'd driven out to Hale Branson's farm to stitch up the man's leg after he cut it on a piece of machinery.

"My life is ruined!" he heard as he entered the shop.

"Now, darlin', don't you worry. We can fix your hair," Regina was heard soothing her distraught client.

"Then fix it!" Thalia wailed.

"I just can't do it today." Regina wrung her hands. "If I try it now, the chemicals could make it all fall out."

"I'd be better off with no hair!"

"I honestly thought that was the color number you said!" Cori apologized, looking as upset as the others.

Thalia raised her head. Tears ran down her cheeks along with smears of black mascara, making her look like an orange-haired raccoon.

Ben winced. Thalia wasn't a pretty woman to begin with. That hair only worsened what few good looks she had.

"Anyone need a doctor?" he spoke up, hoping a light-hearted approach would help. He immediately stepped back from the glares directed his way.

"You give this girl a hearing test!" Regina shouted at him. "I tell her to mix number sixty-two and she mixes sixty-four and we come up with this!" Her outstretched arm directed his gaze toward Thalia's brilliant orange hair.

Ben winced at Regina's screech. He figured Cori's hearing was just fine when she also made a face.

"Now, Regina," he placated, "you can't tell me you haven't made a mistake in all the years you've done hair."

Her stony gaze could have turned him to concrete. "I have *never* made a mistake when it comes to my client's hair," she haughtily declared, throwing her head back with an equally dramatic gesture. "They are too precious to me."

Another mistake he'd made. "Well, I'm sure you can do something," he ventured.

"What do you suggest I do?"

Ben thought of suggesting it all be cut off, but he already knew it wouldn't be appreciated.

"You could tell Rawley it's a new craze." He winced when Thalia's high-pitched wail assaulted his ears again.

"He'll never propose now! I'll be single all my life!" She buried her face in her hands.

Regina stared at Cori as if she wanted to take her scissors to *her* hair.

"Get her out of here."

Ben didn't waste any time. He grabbed Cori's hand and dragged her out of the shop.

"I heard bleach rots the brain," a woman muttered as they made their way through the small crowd. "Maybe that's why she screws up so much."

"I heard that, too," another one chimed in.

Cori's face mirrored her outrage. "I do not bleach my hair!"

"Do yourself a favor and be quiet," Ben whispered, picking up his pace.

"I don't care what she said. She told me number sixty-four," Cori went on, now almost running to keep up with him. "It's because she tries to do too much and I just bet she *has* made mistakes in the past."

Ben stopped short and spun her around to face him. "Cori, shut up." He threw his head back and sought answers from above. Unfortunately, at that moment, the lines must have been busy.

Cori blinked her eyes furiously to keep the tears from falling. "Look, I'm sorry Thalia's hair ended up that way. I tried to apologize, but she only cried more."

He shook his head and started walking down the side of the clinic until they reached the cottage in the back.

"Let me explain something to you," he said quietly, now that he figured he'd regained his composure. "You probably noticed that Thalia isn't exactly a raving beauty. But that doesn't matter, because Rawley isn't that much of a prize, either. But that's beside the point, because they really care about each other. Rumor has it Rawley's taken the past month to get up his courage to pop the question. Thalia's afraid if she postpones this dinner date, he'll lose his courage. And it's all thanks to you."

The moment he saw her stricken face, he should have regretted his sharp words. But they were necessary. Right now, he was about ready to pay for her car repairs himself and send her on her way before she did any more damage.

Cori's chin wobbled dangerously. "I didn't do it on purpose," she whispered. "She sat there, so excited about tonight . . ." The tears began falling fast and furious.

Ben cursed himself for sounding so harsh with her and immediately folded her in his arms.

"Hey, it's okay," he murmured, stroking her back in an effort to calm her. Except, while he was busy trying to calm her, his own system was racing. She was soft and fragrant in his arms. A light floral scent wafted from her hair, just adding to the dream he was convinced he was having.

"I don't want to hurt anyone!" she sobbed, linking her arms around his neck and unconsciously pressing herself closer against him.

"I know." Taking deep breaths didn't help when all he wanted to do was find out how she tasted.

Cori sniffed several times as she tipped her head back.

"You're very good looking," she murmured, as if it suddenly occurred to her.

He smiled. "In hopes I don't boost your ego too high, let me say you're not so bad yourself."

Cori stared up at him. While most women's faces looked red and blotchy when they cried, hers glowed. Her tear-glazed eyes appeared covered with luminescent stars and her lips were damp from her tears.

Ben was only human. He instantly lowered his head, covering her mouth with his.

He was lost the moment his lips touched hers.

She tasted of salt. She smelled like rare spring flowers, and she felt like heaven.

Cori moaned softly, allowing his tongue access into her mouth. Even that was like an experience he'd never felt before. She tasted of hot nights on cool sheets. Of the feel of silky skin against hair roughened skin. He knew she would wind herself around him like a sheet, but infinitely more arousing. She would match him move for move and once he made love to her, he sensed once wouldn't be enough.

Ben had kissed more than his share of women during his thirty-six years, but no woman aroused him as instantly as Cori Peyton did. Nor instilled feelings he couldn't comprehend. Part of him was afraid to even try to explain them. Right now, he was more than content to stand here with Cori in his arms and her lips against his.

Cori was the one to break the embrace. She looked up at him with the same stunned expression he was sure mirrored his own face.

"I can't—" She held up her hands in a helpless gesture and turned her back on him. And then she ran.

* * *

"ARE YOU EVER going to return to earth?" Ella demanded, barging her way in the office where Ben was busy making notes on several charts. It had been a long day for him, starting with the incident at the Cut 'n' Curl and definitely not ending with the kiss. Cori's incredible kiss lingered with him all afternoon. As well as her reaction. He hadn't even tried to stop her from running away; he'd been too busy trying to make sense of his own jumbled emotions. Right now, all he wanted to do was go home and watch TV.

He looked up at Ella. "Excuse me?"

"You heard me, lover boy. That little blonde has your tail wagging, and if anyone should know what to do about it, you should." She grinned.

"Before or after the townspeople lynch her?"

Ella shook her head. "Guess who I saw go into the cottage about an hour ago?" She purposely waited.

Ben sighed. "I hate guessing games."

"Too bad."

He dropped his pen on his desk. There would be no peace until Ella had her say. "Fine, I give up. Who?"

"Thalia."

Ben jumped to his feet. "And you didn't try to stop her?"

"She didn't look as if she was going to commit murder but I stayed by the window just in case," she told him, hot on his heels as she followed him to the door.

"I can't believe this," he muttered, charging out the back door and almost running to the cottage. Without bothering to knock he ran in.

"Are you sure it isn't too much?" Thalia could be heard asking in a hesitant voice.

"Are you kidding? You look gorgeous! I'm talking very elegant," Cori assured.

Both women were walking into the living room when Ben ran in, with Ella right behind him.

"I don't believe it," Ella said in an awed tone as she stared at Cori's companion.

"You and me both," Ben muttered, his mouth agape.

Thalia Roberts stood in front of them—a completely transformed woman.

Thalia's skin seemed to glow, her eyes had been discreetly and expertly made up to show them off as her best asset and her lips were colored a lovely soft red. Her hair was wrapped in a black silk turban with what looked like a diamond clip at the center and drop earrings sparkled with the same expensive lights. She wore a black slip dress that was perfect on her gangly frame, a lacy bolero jacket and high-heeled pumps.

"Doesn't Thalia look wonderful?" Cori practically beamed. "We were real lucky we wear the same size shoe."

Thalia literally glowed. "She called me and asked if I would come by. She said she wanted to make up for what happened to my hair." Her fingers fluttered near the turban. "Well, I wasn't too sure I wanted to see her again, but she sounded so sorry for what she did and Regina couldn't do anything. When I came over, Cori suggested I wear this turban. She said it's the rage in Hollywood."

Ben stepped forward and picked up Thalia's hand. "Darlin', if Rawley doesn't propose to you, I will," he drawled, pressing his lips against her hand.

"Wow," Thalia said breathlessly, wide-eyed at the gesture. She turned back to Cori. "I really want to thank you. Even if everybody's wrong and Rawley doesn't propose, I know tonight I do look pretty."

Cori hugged her. "Pretty?" she argued. "You look gorgeous and you remember everything I told you!" She gently pushed her out the door. "And don't run in those heels unless you want to break something!"

She closed the door and turned back to her unexpected visitors. "May I be blunt and ask why you're here?"

"I wanted to make sure Thalia wasn't turning your hair orange," Ben replied.

Her lower lip quivered, then she quickly shored herself up with a high-voltage smile. "I thought about what happened and how she was looking forward to tonight. I hoped I could do something and was glad she allowed me to."

"If I thought I could come out looking so good, I'd have you take a crack at me," Ella interjected.

Cori's smile suddenly dimmed. "If you'll excuse me—" She quickly bolted to the rear of the house.

There was no mistaking she was in the bathroom and what was going on.

"I bet she didn't eat a thing all day," Ella clucked, hurrying into the bathroom to be of assistance.

"I hope I don't have the flu," Cori fretted, allowing Ella to help her onto a chair. "I hate being sick, and this throwing up at the toss of a hat isn't all that fun."

"Maybe I should look you over," Ben offered. "You did faint the other day."

"I'm fine," she told him, only to grimace and bolt for the bathroom again.

Something was niggling the back of Ben's mind and, for once, he hoped he was wrong.

"Bring her to the clinic," he instructed Ella. "I'm examining her whether she likes it or not."

"Something tells me she won't."

By the time Ella ushered a protesting Cori into the examination room, Ben was ready for her.

"Why don't you get undressed? I want to give you an exam," he told her, handing her a gown and walking out of the room, closing the door behind him.

"Exam?" She stared at the nurse. "What kind of exam?"

"Don't worry," she soothed, reaching for the gown. "Doc's the best around. He just wants to make sure you don't have a nasty stomach virus."

Cori groaned. "No wonder they warn you to always wear clean underwear." She started to unbutton her vest. "Although, I do wish doctors would come up with more attractive gowns."

For the next ten minutes, Cori was alternately stunned, shocked and mortified as she lay on the examination table and answered Ben's intimate questions. Considering she was attracted to him, she found them embarrassing and difficult to answer.

"You know more about me than most men I've dated," she quipped, although the joke fell flat.

Ben stood and pulled off the latex gloves. The expression on his face was wry as he faced Cori. "Why don't you get dressed and we'll talk in my office."

"What's wrong?" She tried to grab his sleeve and almost fell off the table when she missed.

"In my office."

"In my office," she mocked, pulling on clothes with shaky fingers. "Doctors are the same everywhere. They have to do everything their way."

By the time she had dressed and then entered his office, she was convinced she was dying from a rare disease.

"All right, just give it to me straight," she ordered. "It's a tumor, right? Or some exotic parasite is tunneling its way through my body. Or something equally gruesome. I'm not going to give birth to one of those creatures they had in *Alien,* am I?"

Ben started to smile at her questions, then sobered. "Not exactly."

"Then what?"

"All right, I'll give it to you straight. I'd say you're about ten weeks' pregnant."

If Cori hadn't been sitting down, she would have fallen to the floor.

"No, I'm not," she quickly denied, even as the truth wormed its way into her mind. "I can't be. I'm on the pill and I believe in totally safe sex. So you see, Dr. Charm, you're wrong."

He shrugged. "Admittedly, we can run a test, but it will show up positive."

She shook her head. "No, I am not pregnant. Because if I was pregnant that would mean Rufus is the father and I will not allow him to be the father of my baby!" Her voice rose in agitation. "He's an idiot! He was a major mistake in my life! I don't want to think of him as a father! No baby should be born with his lack of common sense!" She jumped to her feet and paced back and forth.

Ben eyed her closely. While she was upset she wasn't hysterical. Not yet, at least. He had an idea it hadn't truly sunk in yet.

Odd, he hadn't bothered to think that she probably had a lover back in L.A. Although it sounded as if the man were well and truly out of her life. All he had to do was wait and see what she would do now. Still, for a man who hadn't thought much about a family, the idea of this little blond vixen pregnant wasn't all that bad.

Cori turned on him with blazing eyes and outstretched arms. "Don't you have anything to say?"

He settled back in his chair. This, he could handle. "After your reaction, I figured you didn't want to hear anything more from me."

"I can't be a mother! I don't know anything about babies." She waved her hands in the air around her as she resumed her frenzied pacing.

"Don't worry, it will come to you." He prayed she wasn't thinking of alternatives.

Cori dropped into the chair and stared at Ben. A strange calm seemed to overtake her as the truth sank in with the impact of an atomic bomb. "Then I hope the baby comes with a complete set of instructions or we're both in a lot of trouble."

Chapter Four

Dr. Benjamin Cooper's Clinic

"Well, Benjamin, what do you intend to do for that little girl?" Ella advanced on Ben with the force of a Sherman tank.

Ben was still reeling from Cori's erratic reaction and her sudden departure. She had simply announced she needed to think things over and left. Ben looked up with a pained expression he was rapidly coming to think of as a permanent fixture on his face.

"I didn't think I needed to do anything for Thalia. She looked fine to me and I bet Rawley'll be knocked on his butt when he sees her."

She shot him a threatening look. "You know very well I'm talking about little Cori."

"'Little Cori,'" he repeated. "Isn't she the person you almost considered a jinx to the entire town? Someone you thought would bring us down? A flighty twit, a real airhead?"

Ella was horrified by his implication. "Benjamin, I can't believe you said such a thing! That little girl is going to have a baby. It's clear she doesn't intend to tell the father, and it doesn't sound like she can expect her daddy to stand by her. She needs emotional support."

Ben sat back, eyeing his nurse with a speculative gaze. "I didn't expect to hear all that from you, Ella. After all, she's not a member of this town."

She drew herself up. "We are a town of God-fearing folk who were put on this earth to help those in need. I'd say Cori is most definitely in need of our help."

He laced his fingers behind his head, looking very comfortable as he gazed at his nurse. "Do you realize that in the space of two days she's ticked off three-quarters of the population and almost destroyed two businesses? Considering her track record, I don't think they'd be all that eager to help her out."

"They don't hold grudges. Well, maybe Elliott will," she amended her statement, "but he'll come around. I'll make sure he does."

"God help Elliott." Ben looked down at the pad of paper he had been doodling on while he first talked to Ella. Tiny pictures of pudgy babies smiled up at him.

He had already delivered a great many babies in his career. Even had a few named after him. So why should the knowledge of Cori's pregnancy affect him so? A woman he was attracted to; a woman he had only known for a few days; a woman who was driving him nuts. And the baby wasn't even his.

"You look like something even the cat wouldn't drag in. You haven't had a decent night's sleep for the past month. Why don't you just head on home and get some rest," she suggested. "By morning, you'll be refreshed and come up with an idea to help her."

He knew she was right. He felt like hell.

"I should check on Cori," he argued. "She hasn't been taking care of herself and she had quite a shock today." He could still see her stunned reaction as his diagnosis sunk in. "It's bad enough she's stranded a good fifteen hundred miles from home, but for her to find out she's pregnant..." Not to mention he had kissed her, only to discover he wanted to do it again.

"I bet the guy seduced her. Those Hollywood types do that kind of thing, you know." Ella clucked, shaking her head. She patted her hair, but not one strand from her French twist had dared stray. "I think what she needs right now is a mother figure, not a man who's been looking at her as if she's a rich dessert and he's still hungry after a full meal."

Ben looked at Ella as if he had never seen the woman before. First she wanted him to do something about Cori, then she wanted him to keep his distance. And now what did the woman want? "What did you just say?"

"You heard me. You're showing too much interest in that girl. While you should be in here treating your patients, you've been on the phone trying to find her a job. Then going out and interfering when she had trouble."

"Wait a minute. You're the one who wanted me to go over to Regina's! You're the one who thinks I can solve all of Cori's problems. You're the one who..." He stood and shrugged off his lab coat. "Okay, enough, Ella. I already have one mother who lately has been lamenting the fact that her only boy and husband's namesake doesn't have a wife or any babies. Maybe if I turn Cori over to Mama, she'll get so involved with Cori she'll leave me alone."

"Or—" Ella ambled toward the door "—she'll decide Cori needs a husband. And who better than you?" She tossed her verbal bomb back to him as she left.

Ben looked at up at the ceiling for divine help. "What did I do to deserve this?" he demanded to know.

Unfortunately, no answer was forthcoming.

CORI THOUGHT ABOUT fixing herself another bowl of soup even if it meant sandblasting the burned pan.

She stood at the sink, using a steel-wool pad on the burned crust. In between scrubs, she alternately sniffled and mumbled to herself.

"I can't believe that one time with Rufus ended up this way," she muttered, her movements becoming more savage the longer she thought about her condition and how she got that way. "He was one of the biggest mistakes I've made in my life. So how come one of his lousy sperm manages to break through and swim upstream?"

"The school's science teacher has a great video on the subject. I'm sure I could borrow it for you, so you could find out exactly how it happened."

She spun around, the pad she still held sending droplets of water flying. "How did you get in?" She gasped, pressing one hand against her chest.

"The door was unlocked."

Ben, looking about as sexy as a man could get, was standing in the doorway, leaning against the jamb, his arms crossed in front of him. His faded jeans molded to his muscular thighs with a lover's ease and the faded denim over the fly unerringly drew Cori's gaze.

"So what was this Rufus like?" he asked. "Other than not having any common sense and having strong sperm, that is. Not to mention getting you pregnant that one less than memorable time."

Cori could feel her face burning with embarrassment. She was positive her color was a bright tomato red. She had never thought of it as a good color for her.

"Look, you've seen parts of my body even I haven't seen. You've asked me intimate questions I hated answering." She tossed the scrubbing pad into the sink. "And you expect me to stand here and tell all? I don't think so."

Ben straightened up and walked over to the sink. It was admirable he held back his grin when he saw the pan and brown suds.

"Having a problem?" he asked with an amicable nonchalance. He tsked at her less than polite reply. "You know, sometimes all you need is a little muscle." He rolled up his shirtsleeves and plucked the scrubber out of the sink.

Cori had no choice but to stand back and watch Ben apply said muscle and soon had the pan sparkling clean.

"It was problems like this that had me eating more often at Myrna's," he explained, rinsing out the scrubbing pad and pan. "In fact, how about some dinner?"

A ghost of a smile flitted across her lips. "Trying to feed me again?"

He looked her over with a clinical eye. "I'd say you're a good fifteen pounds underweight and now you have someone else to look out for."

Cori flinched. "Sorry, it's still pretty new to me." She looked off in the distance. "I don't know a lot about small towns, but after the past couple of days I can see that the residents love to talk about friends and neighbors. Not necessarily maliciously, but just about everything. It's as if they feel gossip is better than daytime television. If we show up at the restaurant again, people will start to talk and I can't imagine that dining with an unwed mother from California would be good for your image."

"Cori, I'm not eighty and I don't think anyone will throw stones at you," he said gently. "Especially after they hear what you did for Thalia."

She grimaced. "I made her promise not to say anything."

"For Thalia, that's easier said than done since she has one of the biggest mouths in town. Not to mention Ella, who's on your side and will now let anyone who will listen know that. Now—" he rubbed his hands together briskly "—why don't you do whatever you feel you need to do before going out in public and we'll head over to Myrna's for some of Ralph's chili. I can guarantee you'll find it better than anything you'd find in Texas."

Cori couldn't argue she didn't want to spend time with Ben.

"Why are you willing to do all this for me?" she questioned him. The cottage, the jobs, upholding her reputation. It seemed she got more from a stranger than she did her own family.

Ben shrugged. "I guess I'm just a sucker for a blue-eyed blonde."

She didn't believe his flippant answer, but had an idea she'd never hear the truth from him.

"Why is it called Myrna's if the owner is Ralph?" Instead she asked the question that had bothered her from the beginning.

"Because Myrna was Ralph's mother and after her death he decided the name should stay. She was the one who opened the place and gave the people not just a place for a meal but for company. We have a lot of retirees in the area. The men like to get out of the house and out from under their wives' feet. Myrna's offers that. They usually take up a couple rear booths where they can have their coffee in peace and figure out how to change the country."

"You're right, a nice idea." She walked out of the kitchen and stopped in the bathroom long enough to make sure her hair wasn't too mussed. She fluffed it up and added a quick spritz of her favorite perfume.

As she applied her lipstick, she suddenly recalled Ben's mouth on hers. A wave of heat swept through her body, leaving her weak at the knees.

What was wrong with her? She had been kissed before. Kissed by men who viewed lovemaking as an art and kissing as a part of that art. Not that it meant she allowed them to kiss their way into her bed. Just that they knew what they were doing. So what was so potent about Ben's kiss?

"Whatever it is, he should bottle it," she murmured, walking out of the bathroom. She flashed him a smile. "I'm ready."

The warmth in his smile signaled he liked what he saw.

Cori still wore the outfit she had on earlier and settled for a quick freshening up. That impressed him. As if she needed anything more to enhance her beauty. He would have told her that, but he was afraid she'd think his words were corny. They sure as hell sounded corny to him.

"Is something wrong?" she probed, confused by his silence.

He shook his head. "No, I'm just thinking that you're sprucing up this old town." He walked to the front door and opened it for her, waiting until she passed by him. Ben inhaled the springtime fragrance that wafted after her and instantly thought back to that kiss. And wondered if there was a chance they could repeat it.

"I would think after the day you spent at the clinic, you'd be too exhausted to go anywhere," Cori commented as they walked toward Myrna's.

He should have been, but oddly, since seeing Cori, he found his energy renewed. He just wasn't sure that was something to tell her.

"Today wasn't so bad," he admitted, hiding his grin as he noticed the interested glances directed their way from shopkeepers as they passed various town businesses. If it hadn't been close to the dinner hour, he was certain there would have been more people around to watch their progress down to the restaurant.

The same interest Vivian was showing as she stood just inside her dress shop at the display window. Then there was Homer, pretending to be changing the display in his hardware store window, except he hadn't changed the display in the past ten years. He figured plumbing supplies, particularly a toilet, would sell year-round.

"Compared to what?"

He didn't have to think about it. "Compared to Saturday night when there's a full moon out and every lunatic in the city is bleeding in the middle of the ER."

Cori wrinkled her nose. "Sounds like something you'd see on TV."

"Unfortunately, TV doesn't prepare one for what goes on in real life."

"Are you speaking from experience?" she asked.

Her question went unanswered as Ben opened the door to Myrna's and ushered her inside. He waved to Ralph and guided Cori toward one of the rear booths.

"Evenin', Doc." A waitress Cori hadn't seen before walked up to them. The woman smiled at Cori. "That was a really nice thing you did for Thalia. She hasn't had it easy since her mom died last year, and Rawley's been the only bright spot in her life. I heard that he took one look at her and about proposed right then."

Cori shifted uncomfortably under the woman's praise. "I just wanted to make things better."

"Well, honey, you did a lot more than make things better." She turned to Ben. "I suppose you know Kevin figures you patched him up so well the last time there's no reason why he can't go out joyriding every weekend."

"Then tell him the next time he rolls that car of his over, I'll let Ella patch him up," Ben advised with a grin. "Cori, this lady who never stops talking is Charlotte, Ralph's wife. And if you think I like to feed people, you wait until she gets going."

"You're looking for trouble saying things like that, Benjamin Cooper!" She planted one hand on her hip while the other slapped his shoulder so hard he would have pitched forward if he hadn't braced himself. She suddenly turned to Cori. "Of course, darlin', you do look a bit peaked—" her voice lowered "—and in your condition you need your vitamins. And I don't mean that crap they call vitamin pills, either. Ralph!" Her voice boomed as she turned toward the kitchen. "How about ladling up some of your vegetable beef soup for Cori?"

"You so busy flirtin' with the doc you can't do it yourself?" the cook growled.

Charlotte sighed. "The man can't get along without me," she confided before ambling off to the kitchen.

Cori looked back to Ben. Her eyes were navy blue saucers.

"And I thought it was bad the first time I was here," she whispered. "She really isn't bringing over vegetable beef soup, is she?" He nodded. "I hate vegetable beef soup."

"It doesn't matter. You'll eat it or she'll want to know why and you can't tell her it's because you don't like that kind of soup. She considers anything her husband makes a work of culinary art."

"Ben, darlin', you want the chili tonight, don't you?" Charlotte called out.

"You got it, and something cold with it," he called back.

"And Cori, darlin', after you finish your soup, I'll bring out the meat loaf platter. You need some meat on your bones. A glass of milk, too."

"I hate milk!" she whispered fiercely.

Ben couldn't stop grinning. A panicky Cori was a treat to watch. "Too bad, because Charlotte will make sure you drink every drop."

"Here you go." Charlotte set a bowl in front of Cori. She turned to Ben, saying, "I'll bring your chili with her meat loaf." She returned a moment later with a large glass of Coke for Ben and Cori's glass of milk.

Ben reached across the table and swiped a packet of crackers.

Cori dipped her spoon into the soup and tentatively tasted it. "It's good."

"Told you."

She took several more spoonfuls. "So I assume the whole town knows about me and my 'condition'?"

Ben shrugged. "There may be one or two people who haven't heard yet," he deadpanned.

"How can you live in a town where there's no privacy?"

"Very carefully." He quickly raised his hands in mock surrender. "Okay, I'll be serious here. As a kid you hate it. If you accidentally break Mr. Walters's window, your mom will know about it within five minutes. You can't skip school because the school nurse is best friends with your mom and wouldn't think twice about calling home to see how sick you are. If you borrow the car for a midnight drive, your dad will find out from one of his poker buddies who's coming home from a lodge meeting."

"It sounds stifling but wonderful at the same time," she admitted, wrinkling her nose as she sipped her milk.

"Spring," he said suddenly.

Cori blinked in surprise. "Excuse me?"

"Spring." He grinned sheepishly. "Your voice. It's light and almost airy and your perfume has the smell of spring to it, so I figured out your voice has the sound of spring, as well."

Cori's laughter rippled out like gentle waves on a pond. "Well, that's a new one."

"You mean, spoken like a hick," Ben said wryly.

She reached across the table and covered his hand with hers. "No, I think it's lovely because you mean what you say. I've had my share of compliments, but they were never spoken as sincerely as yours. It makes a big difference."

Ben's eyes blazed with dark gold lights. "I can't imagine anyone giving you a line."

"No? Think about the popularity of blond jokes. When you're blond, pretty and have an eclectic educational background, you expect to hear every manner of lines," she said without any malice toward the opposite sex. "Sincere ones without a hidden meaning are very rare and need to be cherished."

"Is that what Rufus did—hand you a line you thought was sincere and turned out not to be?"

Cori suddenly exhibited a great deal of interest in her milk. "Is it true I'll have to drink gallons of this for the next seven months?"

"You're not answering my question, Cori."

"No, I'm just ignoring it." She took a deep breath, picked up her glass and drank two-thirds of the contents.

"Good girl," Charlotte approved, snatching up the glass for a refill. "I'll be bringing along your meat loaf."

Cori stared at the refilled glass with dismay. She glared at Ben whose lips were twitching with restrained mirth. "It's not funny."

"You ought to be flattered. Charl doesn't take just anyone under her wing," he replied.

"Don't you scare her with those untrue stories about me," the waitress scolded, setting laden plates in front of both of them. She turned to Cori. "Obviously, you're going to need a job after what happened over at Regina's. Sophie, my morning waitress, is moving since her husband got a job in Kansas City. Show up here at six and wear somethin' cheerful." With that, she bustled off.

"Another job I can screw up," Cori muttered, stunned by the woman's offer.

"Maybe not. Maybe you're made to be a waitress."

"I don't know what I'm made to be. I have one semester in business administration, another in psychology, another in fine arts." Cori stared at the biggest slice of meat loaf with gravy she'd ever seen, a creamy mound of mashed potatoes dotted with pure butter and a healthy pile of green beans off to one side. "Not to mention two years in a Swiss finishing school my father thought would be a good idea."

"Finishing school. I'm impressed."

She giggled. "Don't be. I was expelled for sneaking out after-hours. I was going through my rebellious phase then."

Ben shook his head. "Has there ever been a time you haven't been rebellious?" He scooped his spoon through the thick chili.

Cori thought about it. "Not since I entered puberty." She found her meat loaf tasty and one bite quickly led to another. She swallowed before continuing. "Please don't get me wrong. My father is a wonderful man and I love him dearly, but he has this thing about control. Perhaps things would have been better if my mother had lived. During my psychology phase I came up with the theory that he was protecting me. He felt I had two chances in this world—I could either marry someone who would take care of me or I could learn to deal in his world. That meant I needed a heavy-duty business education. But it was soon apparent business administration wasn't a strong point for me, so my father viewed marriage as my only option. Since then, he's brought around a large number of eligible men who he felt would be appropriate for the Peyton empire." She tried the mashed potatoes next. She couldn't remember ever eating anything so good. "It didn't seem to matter to him that there might not be any sparks between us."

"Was one of them Rufus?" Ben shook his head in wonder. "You know, I'm sorry, but Rufus sounds more like a dog's name than a man's."

She chuckled. "That's what my father said, and, no, Rufus was very definitely not on his approved list."

"So you decided Rufus was a good way to rebel?"

Cori shifted uncomfortably. "I really don't like discussing Rufus."

Ben leaned across the table slightly. "You could go to bed with the guy, but you can't discuss him?"

Immediately, Cori felt herself blush. "It was one time and I regretted it instantly," she whispered heatedly. "I thought because he was an artist and had a sensitive nature, he was what I needed in my life. When I realized he figured my money—or rather my father's money—would finance his artistic endeavors, I knew I had been duped and I let him know I didn't like it."

"Is that when you decided buying an English country manor and turning it into an inn was better?"

She nodded. Barely a third of the food had been eaten and she already felt full. She set her fork down. "It was a wonderful opportunity."

"Which is why you're stuck in Farrington, Kansas."

Cori looked at Ben and felt that falling-in-space sensation in the pit of her stomach again. "Maybe I was supposed to end up here," she murmured. She was right. The man had major bedroom eyes. The more she looked at his eyes, the more she thought about bedrooms. The more she thought about bedrooms, the more she envisioned Ben naked. Quickly, she grabbed her glass, almost spilling the milk she drank to soothe her dry throat. "Maybe fate stepped in and decided I was meant to come here instead of going there. I've never been one to argue with fate."

Ben started to say something, then realized where they were. He looked up to find most of the tables in the restaurant filled and the occupants watching them without any pretense. "This is one of those times I hate the lack of privacy."

Cori was a little more subtle in checking out their surroundings. Jess smiled openly at her. Elliott scowled at her and Regina eyed her with distrust. One elderly man she remembered as part of her entourage at the garage was seated with a silver-haired woman. He nodded and smiled.

"The way they look at me you'd think your town doesn't get very many visitors," she commented.

He shook his head. "More departures than arrivals. We're not exactly a town booming with prosperity."

"Why?"

"We're off the main highway and we have nothing that would bring in the tourists. And that means we're slowly dying. I was one of them that tried to escape. I hadn't intended to return after I got my residency."

"What did you do?"

"I worked as a trauma surgeon in a Chicago ER," he answered, sadly examining his now-empty chili bowl. He looked up with a hopeful grin. "Char, think I can have seconds?"

She was there to retrieve his bowl. "You mean Ralph's chili hasn't burned your stomach to a cinder yet?" she teased before turning her laser gaze on Cori. "Darlin', you've barely touched your dinner. Eat before it gets cold." She rushed off, filled Ben's bowl and slid it in front of him before bustling off as her name was called.

"I've eaten more in the past three days than I've eaten in a week," Cori confided in Ben.

"No wonder you kept passing out. You can't do that anymore, Cori," he said sternly. "You have more to think about than keeping yourself so thin a good stiff breeze could blow you away."

"That must be the doctor speaking, and since I didn't think the doctor was the one who asked me to dinner, I do believe I'll ignore that statement." She used her fork to cut another bite of meat loaf. "And he isn't to worry, since I would never do anything to harm a child. And I do not skip meals to stay thin."

Ben smiled. "So this is a dinner date. Are you sure you can handle that?"

Cori thought of Regina's statement that Valerie was after Ben. What if Ben had kept one secret from the townspeople—Valerie?

"I wouldn't call this a dinner date. Just two people who happen to be sharing the same table."

Ben shook his head. "No, I think I'd prefer to call this a dinner date. Makes it more official."

Date. A date meant going out with someone of the opposite sex. A date meant his taking her home afterward. And kissing her. And if she were lucky...

Cori resisted the urge to shake her head in rapid denial. How could she even think about a man in that sense? After all, she had just found out she was pregnant and *he* wasn't the father.

"Just two people having dinner together," she maintained.

Ben's knowing smile easily undid her formal manner.

"Most couples have dinner and then..." He left it at that, giving Cori a pretty good idea what his idea of "and then" was.

"I can't imagine 'and then' happens all that much in Farrington. Not unless the couple wants the story printed in the paper the next day," she smoothly countered.

He wasn't the least bit offended. "See, and you thought you didn't know anything about small towns."

After that, by unspoken agreement, they kept the conversation casual, light and entertaining for their avid audience.

"I can't believe we weren't thrown out." Cori giggled when they stood outside the restaurant. As they had left, Charlotte had reminded Cori what time to show up for work, then shot Ben a knowing look as if she figured out what he was doing.

"I can't believe you went along with it." Ben reached down for her hand, threading his fingers through hers.

"Discussing your favorite memories of dissecting Harold, your cadaver, had seemed a bit strong, although I notice no one else seemed to mind." She shook her head, amazed she had actively participated in a discussion centered on dissections. For someone who had been throwing up off and on lately, her stomach had stood up admirably during Ben's reminiscences. She wondered if the meat loaf had anything to do with it. "From now on I'll never be able to look at liver in quite the same way."

"I had classmates who turned into strict vegetarians because of that class," he recalled. "I figured once I'd eaten a hamburger I would be fine."

Cori wrinkled her nose. "Not exactly a lovely method."

"Maybe not, but a workable one. I went into the greasiest dive you ever saw. The hamburgers didn't even look like something that came from a cow." He smiled at the memory. "I even thought about taking some of their special sauce back with me. I thought it would make a great chemistry experiment."

"And?"

"I'm sure I barely escaped food poisoning, and figured if I could survive that, anything was possible."

Just as Ben expected, Cori laughed at his joke. The walk back to the cottage seemed even shorter than usual. He wondered what his mother would think of her. His mother was away visiting one of his sisters, but he knew that wouldn't stop the town's grapevine from letting her know everything that went on. In fact, he was surprised she hadn't called him yet for his version of the new girl in town.

He stopped short as he realized they had reached the cottage door. And chuckled as Cori dug in her pocket and pulled out the keys.

"I know, I know. No one out here locks their doors. But I'm from L.A. Out there, if we don't lock our doors we would come back to nothing. Including, probably, the front door." She showed surprise when he took the keys from her hand and inserted the proper one in the lock.

"Life here isn't always perfect," he countered, pushing the door open.

Cori stepped inside. "Somehow, I can't imagine this town having a major crime spree." She fidgeted under his amused gaze. "Would you like some coffee?" Her eyes briefly registered alarm at the expression on his face. "Oh, please don't tell me I have to give up my coffee! I can't live without coffee! No offense, but it's bad enough you don't have a coffee store in town. I used to pick up these wonderful beans flavored with French vanilla. They were the perfect way to start the day."

"I'm afraid around here you'll only find your typical brands. Besides, caffeine restriction is strongly suggested. Just drink decaf," he suggested, dropping into a chair.

"Decaf has no kick to get one started in the morning," she protested, taking the chair across from him. "All right, you may as well tell me all the bad news at once. What else am I going to have to give up?"

"Cigarettes."

"I gave up smoking in high school. I hated having the smell on my clothing."

"Salt."

"No problem." She wondered if she could find saltless pretzels at the small grocery store.

"Alcohol."

"My limit is an occasional glass of wine or champagne at a party." Cori slipped off her sandals and scooted back in the chair. She drew her legs up, sitting cross-legged.

Ben found himself unable to keep his eyes off the tantalizing length of golden tanned bare leg. Toes polished a bright pink coral peeped out. When was the last time he had ever fixated on toes? Had he ever?

He dragged his gaze upward. Cori's gaze was expectant, slightly questioning, as she stared back. But it was the light of amusement in her eyes he found unnerving. As if this form of glazed attention was nothing new to her.

"I'm not accepting all of this as well as you think I am," she told him. "Later on, when I'm alone and my thoughts keep returning to the—" she seemed to be reluctant to say the B word "—I'll suddenly scream with the realization that I'm responsible for a little person who would have been better off with someone else as a mother."

"There are alternatives," he muttered, even hating to say the words.

"Not as far as I'm concerned," she said firmly. "For some insane reason those chromosomes came together in my body because they felt I needed to have a child at this time in my life. Let's just hope I don't botch it up the way I've been botching up jobs."

"I wouldn't say you've botched them up." He searched his mind for the right description, but everything that came up was found wanting.

Cori shrugged. "I would."

"What kinds of jobs did you have while you were in college?" He threw up his hands at the look of disbelief directed his way. "Sorry, I don't know what I was thinking of."

She bestowed on him a sweet smile. "That's all right, you didn't know. I carried a heavy class schedule. I'll have you know I had a very high grade point average," she said proudly.

"Don't worry about tomorrow at Myrna's. You'll do fine. You already have champions in Jess, Zeke and Dan."

"Terrific, I have my own fan club." Cori watched him with an unblinking gaze that was unnerving. "Why did you kiss me earlier?"

Her blurted question was so sudden, it stunned him, even though by now he knew nothing about Cori should surprise him.

"Because you looked as if you needed a kiss," he answered simply.

She uncoiled her body from the chair with the grace only a gold-star pupil from Madame Reshanka's Ballet Academy would have.

Cori bent at the waist and looped her arms around Ben's neck. Her face was close to his, her breath warm on his skin.

"Dr. Cooper," she whispered, "would you mind prescribing that medication again?"

Chapter Five

Myrna's Diner

"Now, darlin', you tell Ralph I want my hash browns fixed the usual way with the bacon piled on top of them." Zeke waved his finger at Cori as she stood before him, order pad in hand. "And I like my eggs real runny. Ralph knows that, but I want you to make sure he does 'em right. He's got to ladle the grease over them, too."

"Mr. Corrigan—"

"Zeke, honey."

She nodded. "Zeke, do you realize how much fat and cholesterol you're consuming in this one meal? You're shortening your life by years! And runny eggs? They should be fully cooked to kill any bacteria. If I were you, I'd have a nice bowl of oatmeal and some fresh fruit."

Zeke leaned across the table. "Sweetheart, I'm seventy-two and I've eaten Ralph's breakfasts since my Edna died four years ago. My body ain't complainin', so don't you worry, neither."

Cori winced at the double negative as she turned to Dan, waiting for his order, which was identical except for a request for ham instead of bacon. "I really wish you gentlemen would think about your diets," she murmured.

"You kids think too much about what you eat and too little about how to enjoy it," Dan told her as she turned away.

Cori yelped as a heavy hand connected with her backside. She spun around, staring at the men with blazing eyes. Zeke, Dan and their other two cronies all grinned, daring her to figure out the guilty party.

"Just remember who refills your coffee cups." This time she was more cautious when she left the table.

"That's telling them," Charlotte congratulated Cori as she gave Ralph the order. "I tell you, the older these men get the more they get like little boys. Those four are about the worst in town. Unless you count..." Her voice drifted off and her expression sobered as another customer walked in. "I'll take this one for you."

Cori looked over her shoulder and saw a man who could have doubled as a mountain in a dark blue suit seat himself at the counter.

"Hey, Pudge!" One of the town's silver-haired marauders, as Cori was coming to privately call them, shouted, "What's wrong? No one to harass today?" The four men chuckled.

The man settled for a scowl before turning back to the coffee cup Charlotte set in front of him.

"Hear you got new help in here." His eyes tracked Cori with sharp scrutiny. "Considerin' how careful you are about your girls, I'm surprised you'd hire her."

"She's a friend of the doc's," Charlotte explained. "And good people."

"Yeah, well, my Marla's good people, too, but you wouldn't hire her. Yet you'll take on this little California blonde here. You know what they're like out there. Hot tubs. Orgies." His upper lip curled. "No morals at all."

Cori clenched her teeth as she carried a plate over to one of the other tables. It was bad enough everyone could hear him.

"Is that what you do, honey? Splash around in a hot tub out there in Hollywood? You wear clothes in those fancy hot tubs, honey?"

Cori walked over to the man with head held high, shoulders back. Posture was always something she excelled in. "You know, most people can call me *honey* and *sweetheart* and I don't mind hearing it one bit. And if they want to give me a bad time about where I come from, that's all right, too," she said conversationally, "but I've changed my mind. I don't like hearing it from you."

Beady eyes the color of faded chambray looked at her as if they could see through her bright turquoise tank dress. Her leather flats and jaunty-looking silk visor matched the bright pink scarf that doubled as a belt. She had chosen it today with the idea of showing off her waist as long as she had one. Not to mention the bright color was definitely cheerful, and after crawling out of bed and losing all her breakfast twice, she needed all the good cheer she could get. When she had walked into Myrna's at six, Charlotte had taken one look at her and made her sit down long enough to down two slices of dry toast, some juice and a glass of milk. Once assured her stomach was back to normal again, Cori let Charlotte show her the ropes.

Luckily, her first customers hadn't been Dan and Zeke. By the time they ambled in for breakfast and talk, she felt as if she were an old hand at shuttling filled plates to the customers and refilling coffee cups with ease. Her confidence had grown by leaps and bounds. She had found something she excelled in. Until this Neanderthal clumped in and ruined her day.

The man merely grinned and spat out something obscene.

Cori's smile didn't waver. "You really need to learn some manners," she commented. "Not to mention, you emit the most atrocious smell. Perhaps you forgot your morning shower. No problem. I can help with that." She picked up the nearest pitcher and spilled water over his head.

Pudge's shocked bellow was punctuated by chuckles and snickers from the other diners.

"Feel better?" Cori sweetly asked.

From the kitchen, Ralph stared out at the scene with disbelief. "She's gone and done it now."

Charlotte's mouth dropped open. For once, words escaped her. "Oh, my," was all she could finally manage.

"You little bitch!" Pudge climbed off the seat and advanced on Cori.

But she refused to back down as she brandished the heavy glass pitcher. "Don't even think about it, buster. I know how to protect myself."

The war was on.

"GUESS WHAT?"

Ben looked up. The expression on his nurse's face said it all. If he hadn't been with ancient Mrs. Weatherby, he would have muttered the mother of all curses.

"Cori."

Ella nodded. "It seems she dumped ice water over Pudge Mason's head, then threatened to bean that nasty noggin of his with the pitcher."

Ben couldn't help it. The curse just slipped out.

"Benjamin!" Mrs. Weatherby fixed him with the same look that had kept him in hand when he was in her fifth-grade class. "You know I do not appreciate that language from any of my boys."

"Sorry, Mrs. Weatherby," he muttered.

The elderly lady's faded eyes twinkled. "But it's understandable you forgot yourself when we're talkin' about that nasty ole Pudge. You better go over and make sure that little girl is all right. You know how he gets when he's riled. The boy never did learn how to handle that temper of his. I kept him after class countless times, but it never mattered. He only misbehaved again the next day."

"Great," Ben muttered, almost running down the street.

"Heard that girl of yours went after Pudge," Vivian commented from the open doorway to her dress shop.

"I heard she shot him!" one of her customers exclaimed.

Ben mumbled around a smile he didn't feel like giving.

"What happened to the nice sane life I used to have?" he asked no one in particular.

He rushed inside the restaurant and found himself falling backward as his shoes slipped in a puddle of water.

The scene that greeted Ben was even worse than the other two. A red-faced Pudge loomed over Cori as if engaged in a battle of wits. Considering the combatants, he figured the man was losing. She looked about as cool and collected as anyone could when a man with the proportion of an army tank was trying to threaten one with his size. Ben only had to look at her face to know Pudge's idea of intimidation wasn't working.

"You are, without a doubt, the most arrogant, disgusting, demeaning human being who doesn't even deserve that description," Cori coolly stated, looking down her nose at him. Which wasn't all that easy since he was a good seven inches taller than her. Somehow Cori managed it with style.

"And you are a slut."

She narrowed her eyes, clearly prepared to wage war with a vengeance. "You belong in the Neanderthal period."

"You probably do drugs."

Cori crossed her arms in front of her. Her posture was ramrod straight, her foot tapping a merry beat on the tile floor.

"Restaurants carry a right to refuse service," she reminded him.

"No one would dare do that to me," he said smugly, looking around, as if daring anyone to argue with him.

"Morning, Pudge." Ben thought it was time to step in. He purposely didn't look at Cori as he walked up to the man. "How're you doing?"

"I was doing better until I was attacked by this insane waitress," he snarled. "I'll be pressing charges."

"For what? Pouring water on you couldn't be considered assault with a deadly weapon unless the water happened to come from a toxic waste dump," she countered. Her upper lip curled. "What a shame I couldn't find one."

"Cori," Ben said in a low voice. "Not a good idea."

"The man insulted me and verbally attacked me." She turned her ire on Ben. "No one gets away with that."

"You better tell her who I am, Ben," Pudge told him, glaring at Ralph, Charlotte and the other patrons before spearing Cori with a deadly stare. "I don't put up with the kind of crap she's dishing out." He pushed himself off the stool and lumbered his way to the door.

"What in hell happened?" Ben demanded the moment Pudge was gone.

"He was rude," Cori stated. "I don't care what he says, he deserved getting that pitcher of water dumped on him."

"You missed a real sight, Benny boy." Zeke cackled. "This gal cooled ole Pudge off real fast."

Ben groaned, burying his face in his hands. "Why did you have to do it to Pudge?"

Cori was confused by his question. "Because the slime deserved it!" She looked around to get the others' reactions. "You all heard him. He made statements that can be considered sexual harassment."

"I don't know about that," Dan replied. "But I can say that Pudge did say some pretty raw things to the girl," he told Ben. "I'm surprised Pudge went outta here as calm as he did."

"Calm?" Cori threw up her hands. "You all act as if he could put me in jail."

"He could, Cori," Charlotte was the one to tell her. "Pudge has a mean streak and a lot of power in this town. He could put you in jail."

"Are you saying he's a cop? Is this how bad off your town is? That you have to put up with someone like *him?*"

"He's not the sheriff, Cori, he's the district attorney."

A wave of cold passed through Cori's body. "District attorney?" she parroted, blindly reaching behind her for a chair. She dropped onto it in an ungraceful heap. "A district attorney is a lawyer with the county, isn't he?" Heads bobbed up and down in agreement. "And he would be mean enough to have me arrested." Again, they nodded. She looked at Ben. "I blew it again, didn't I?"

His nod was a great deal more solemn.

Cori blinked furiously. "But he was disgusting."

"That's just the way Pudge is," Charlotte explained. "We've grown to ignore him over the years."

Her chin wobbled. "But he called me a slut."

Ben closed his eyes. He knew Pudge was a sleaze, but he had no idea he would deliberately insult a woman he didn't even know.

"Pudge likes to tromp on people before they tromp on him," he muttered. "Come on, Cori." He cast Charlotte an apologetic look.

"But I haven't finished my shift yet," Cori protested.

"Honey—" Charlotte clamped her lips shut. But the sad look in her eyes said it all.

Cori was stunned. "Do you allow your customers to come in and say those things to your waitresses?"

"Pudge can."

"But it's not right." She dug in her heels.

Ben tightened his grip on her hand and pulled harder. "Come on, Cori."

Her eyes blazed deep navy fires. "No."

He could feel a burning sensation deep down in his stomach. He feared a few days' exposure to Cori was giving him an ulcer. He kept his grip on her hand as he turned back around. He leaned down, putting his face next to hers.

"Cori, do not make a scene," he said between clenched teeth.

"I am *not* going to leave here without having my say," she whispered fiercely.

"Yes, you are, because I think you've said more than enough." He yanked on her hand. He was stunned when she didn't budge an inch.

Cori freed her hand and turned back to the waiting audience. She swept her arm across in a dramatic gesture.

"A person who allows another person to rule them by intimidation doesn't deserve to call themselves a human being," she declared in ringing tones.

"Oh, hell," Ben muttered. He stepped forward, bent down and picked up Cori, flipping her over his shoulder in a fireman's carry. "Goodbye, all," he shouted over her screams of outrage.

"You bastard, put me down!" she yelled, pounding her fists against his back.

"Not yet."

"You can't carry me all the way back!"

"Oh, yes, I can," he stated, nodding pleasantly at each and every person he met along the way.

"How come a refugee from the Cro-Magnon period can say horrible things to me and get away with it," she shrieked, "but if I deliver one little protest I'm punished?"

He shook his head. "Honey, you're getting off easy."

"I'll go to the public defender! He'll see what an atrocity of justice this man is."

"That's Yale Pearson and he's as scared of Pudge as everyone else is."

"Just like you?" she jeered, pummeling his back with her fists.

"Sorry, but I'm very secure with my inner self," he quipped.

Before she had a chance to utter a comeback, whispered voices reached her ears.

"There's that girl living in Doc's cottage! I wonder what she did now."

It was followed by another comment from a group of shoppers on the corner.

"Did you hear she poured some horrible concoction on Thalia's head and turned it purple?"

"I heard it was green."

"I heard that she tried to perm her hair and burned it all off!"

"Don't forget she also attacked Elliott."

"You heard that, too? Maybe she needs psychiatric help."

Cori moaned as the comments flowed fast and furious around her. "Do something," she shouted at Ben.

"They'll talk no matter what. Don't worry. Eventually, the real story will get out. Thing is, they don't feel it's as interesting as what they're coming up with now."

Cori was grateful when Ben approached the clinic. But she couldn't help remembering the last time they walked down this path. He had kissed her then. This time, he held her like a sack of oatmeal.

A second image flashed in front of her. Her on the phone to her father. She could see it clearly: She'd tell him she was pregnant and he'd have her on the next plane home. By the time she arrived, he'd have a complete nursery set up in the house and a nanny on standby. He'd also probably take a whip to Rufus. The latter idea, at least, sounded very appealing.

"I hate all of you," she mumbled against his back. The cotton of his shirt was warm against her face and smelled of him, all male and musky. Not like Rufus who had smelled of that godawful cologne she equated with flea spray. And Ben was hard, all muscle. Oh, wow, it was not a good idea for her to even think about that.

Ben's voice broke her fantasy. "You're just getting a fast education in small-town living."

She hated his amused laughter. "Anyone named Pudge deserves even more than I gave him."

"Yeah, he does, but you just can't do it." He put her on her feet, opened her door and pushed her inside.

"Fine, I lost another job." Cori struggled to regain her composure. "I can live with that." She walked into the bedroom.

Ben followed her in—and every muscle in his body went into immediate paralysis. He stood in the doorway, staring at a lilac confection doubling as a nightgown tossed across the unmade bed. The same intoxicating fragrance Cori wore on her skin lingered in the air. Perfume bottles, body lotion jars and pieces of jewelry were scattered on top of the dresser. The room had taken on a feminine air with Cori's personal touch.

It was the shell-pink lace bra tossed over a chair in the corner that was his undoing. He felt himself start to sweat and he raised his hand to pull on his collar—but he wasn't wearing one.

"That was a horrible thing you did back there!" Cori sat on the edge of the bed and looked up with her lower lip trembling, her deep blue eyes glistening with tears.

"I was getting you out of there before you caused any more trouble." He looked at his two choices of where to sit—the bed or the chair. He chose to stand. Ben walked over and squatted down in front of her, taking hold of her hands between his. He found them cold to the touch and briskly rubbed them.

"Why do people have to bow and scrape to a disgusting individual like him?" she demanded.

"Because Pudge has been a bully from the day he was born."

"Then how did someone like him become district attorney?"

He discovered by looking an inch past her left shoulder, he had a good view of her nightgown. And wondered how she looked in it. "His family owns a lot of land and a lot of politicians."

She wrinkled her nose. "I thought small towns meant togetherness."

"They do. Pudge is just someone we put up with." He glanced at the clock and winced. "Look, I've got to get back to the clinic. Are you going to be all right?"

She nodded. "Will you do me a favor?"

His idea of a favor was rapidly turning sensual. "Anything."

"Don't try to find me another job. I don't want everyone here hating you." She leaned over to press her lips against his cheek.

Ben had the presence of mind to turn his face so her lips met with his mouth. For a moment, their mouths clung.

"You really do prefer getting your own way, don't you?" she murmured.

"You got it." He grinned cockily as he stood. "Just take it easy. Something will come up."

Cori remained sitting as Ben left the cottage. She realized he had taken with him the energy that had raced through the room when he was there.

"This is crazy!" she told herself. "You're barely out of a relationship with one man and practically lusting after another one." Her lips curved in a smile. "Although this one certainly is a big difference from Rufus." Her upper lip curled at the name. "The snake. The slime." She dropped back against the pillow. As she did, her gaze fell on the phone.

The man may be a snake and slime, but he's also the father of your baby. Call him and tell him.

Cori hated her conscience for always being right. She hated it even more that she still remembered Rufus's telephone number. She quickly punched out the numbers and waited, hoping he wasn't home.

"Yes?"

She took a deep breath. "Rufus?"

"Cori?" he almost shouted her name. "Where the hell are you?"

There's was nothing more that could ruin her good mood than a demand like that. "What do you care?"

"I care when your father comes by here and threatens to take me apart unless I tell him where you are. He didn't believe me when I said I had no idea," the man accused.

Where had that whining come from? she wondered. Had he always sounded like that?

"I called for one reason and one only." She took a deep breath to shore up her defenses. "I thought you should know I'm pregnant, but I don't expect anything from you for the baby. We'll do fine on our own."

"You're pregnant?" he exploded. "There is no way you're pinning this on me. We only had sex that one time and you couldn't have gotten pregnant then."

"True, it wasn't one of the highlights of my life," she countered, "but I did get pregnant."

"You can't pin any paternity rap on me," Rufus argued.

By then, Cori was seeing red. "You know, you're right. You aren't the father. Silly me, it must have been someone else, so I'm hanging up now."

"Where are you if your father comes by again?"

"You don't need to know. One suggestion, though. I'd think about moving real soon. Daddy might not be as pleasant on his next visit." She slammed the phone down and glared at it. "I hope Daddy tears him apart."

Cori gently rubbed her tummy. "Don't worry, baby," she softly assured. "I may not be the greatest mom you could have gotten, but at least you won't have to worry about having Rufus for a father." She stared at the phone and thought about picking it up again.

All she had to do was call home.

But, this newfound freedom was invigorating. For the first time, she was truly on her own, and she found that, regardless of the disasters, she was having fun at her jobs. Still, her fingers itched to pick up the phone and call her father, even if it meant she would be under his thumb until he found her a husband with the same domineering attitude.

"ET might have wanted to call home," she said finally, "but personally, I think it's a bad idea."

"YOU'RE ALREADY FALLING for that girl, aren't you?" Ella asked the instant Ben had a free moment. Being the only doctor in a hundred-mile radius meant all kinds of emergencies at all hours. This last one was Matt and Tricia Patterson's four-year-old, Matt Jr., who answered his older sister's dare by swallowing a rock. Luckily, it was small enough they could get it out without having to resort to surgery.

"Nope, she's just another of those lame ducks you say I'm always helping the way my dad always did."

"None of the other lame ducks looked like this one does. And your father's never did, either."

"True. I did get lucky this time." He grinned at her.

"Is that how your mother will look at it?"

His grin disappeared just as quickly. "Mama." The word held a wealth of meaning. "I'm surprised she hasn't called me."

Ella's smile was his first warning. The pink message slip she held out was the second. "She and I had a lovely talk about Farrington's newest resident. Mainly, I cleared up what she already heard. I think the best story had to do with Cori being a porn film star hiding from her Mafia lover."

Ben groaned. "I don't even want to know who related that one to her."

"Good, because I didn't ask. Although—" she tapped her finger against her chin in thought "—it sounds like Wilma Farris. She's always watching those shows on criminals. Remember when she was positive Warren Tyler's nephew was a serial killer they had highlighted on 'America's Most Wanted' the previous week? It was a good thing she couldn't convince the sheriff to arrest him." She cocked her head at the sound of a small bell ringing in the reception area. "That's probably your one o'clock. If I were you I'd call your mama before she hears any more stories."

Ben didn't reply. He was already picking up the phone.

"Hey, Mama, how's it going?" Ella could hear him ask as she softly closed the door.

As she walked down the hallway to the reception area, a broad smile wreathed her face. "All it took for him to fall was a pair of blue eyes." She chuckled, then raised her voice. "I'm coming, Mrs. Patton! You don't need to wear your arm out ringing that dratted bell! I'm not deaf, you know."

CORI DECIDED the rest of her day was markedly uneventful. After a nap, she straightened up the bedroom.

"He must think I'm the sloppiest person alive," she murmured, gathering up the scattered clothing and putting it away. She looked at the clothes and realized she was going to have to keep a job long enough to pay her dry-cleaning bills. She sat down, clothes draped over her arms, and considered her problem. She snapped her fingers and picked up the phone.

"This might not be the kind of town I would ever have thought to be stranded in, but it's what I've been given and

I intend to make the best of it," she murmured to herself, quickly dialing. "Yes, I'd like to make a collect call. From Cori." She crossed her fingers until she heard the phone on the other end pick up and a woman's voice accepting the charges. "Dina, hi!"

"Cori! Where are you?" one of her best friends asked. "Your dad has called here several times. He seems to think I know where you are, even though I told him I don't. I think he finally believed me the last time. And why are you calling collect?"

"I don't think you'll believe me when I tell you," Cori said. "And I'll pay you back for the call, I promise."

"I'm not worried about the call. Just you. What's going on?"

Cori related the story to her friend, pausing each time Dina asked her a question.

"So what do you need?" Dina asked when Cori finished.

"A small loan would help. I wouldn't be asking, but I'm down to very little money. I have no idea how, but I'm going to somehow earn the money to get my car fixed. In the meantime, I don't have enough money for any essentials. I'd really appreciate a loan."

"Give me the name of the bank there and I'll wire it to you. What else?"

Cori looked at her closet. "Clothes. Just tell Esmeralda I said you could borrow a few things. She won't tell Dad you were there. Most of the time she's mad at him, anyway. I'll give you a list of what I want." She ticked each item off on her fingers as she relayed the requests to her friend.

"So what's this town like, anyway?" Dina asked after assuring Cori she would pick up the needed items and ship them out to her care of Ben's clinic address. "Maybe I'll just fly out and rescue you."

"It's like Mayberry without the Southern drawl."

"And what about this doctor you're sort of staying with. What's he like?"

Cori didn't have to think about that. "He's the type of man we wish we would meet and never do."

"Really? Are there any more like him there?"

"No."

"Too bad. Are you sure you don't want me to fly out and rescue you?"

Cori thought of Ben. Especially that kiss. "No, actually everything is fine." She gripped the receiver. She wanted to blurt out the news about her pregnancy, but she found she couldn't. The sensation was still new to her and she wasn't sure she was ready to admit it to others, even one of her closest friends. "I'm starting to learn a little bit about myself here."

"Learn about yourself?" Dina laughed. "Cori, you are one of the most together people I know. What could you possibly learn in some Podunk town?"

"If I'm lucky, I could find out who I really am. Look, I have to go. I really appreciate you doing this for me."

"I'll have the funds wired to you before the end of the day," she promised. "I probably won't be able to get over to your house until tomorrow."

Cori didn't bother extracting a promise from Dina that she wouldn't divulge her whereabouts. Her friend had never been fond of Sean Peyton, nor he of her.

"Just promise me one thing," Dina said before they said their goodbyes. "If you have any problems, you'll call me? I understand you don't want to call your dad, but that doesn't mean you can't call me."

"I will," she vowed. "Thanks."

Cori replaced the phone on the nightstand and stood. As she wandered aimlessly through the cottage she experienced a strong wave of loneliness she had never felt before. All the times she had been away at school or traveling, she never felt alone. But today, she felt very much so. She looked down at her tummy.

"Well, kid." She gently rubbed the still-flat surface. "I guess it's just you and me."

"I'LL NEED IDENTIFICATION," the bank teller informed her with the supercilious expression Cori hated.

From the moment she had walked into the bank she felt the teller's hostility. She had been grateful to her friend for not wasting any time in wiring money to the local bank for her. The moment she had been notified, she was out the door and up the street, heading for the bank.

"No problem." She pulled out her wallet and extracted her driver's license. She handed it over.

The woman barely looked at it. "This is an out-of-state driver's license. We require local identification."

"If I have a California driver's license it would be natural to assume I don't have a license for this state," Cori explained. "My friend made a wire transfer to this bank for me. I was informed by phone all I had to do was come in and pick up the money after showing ID. I'm here and I want my money. I have identification that states who I am. I can't imagine there should be a problem, can you?" She glared at the woman. She figured her reputation was already shot in the town. After what she had been through, what harm could it do to thoroughly intimidate the teller? Of course, with her luck she figured the woman would decide she was trying to rob the bank and call the police. With the district attorney already against her, she would only be in prison for a minimum of a hundred years.

Cori drew herself up to her full height. The expression she fixed on her face was the one she recalled her father using when a business deal wasn't going the way he wanted it to. It had never failed him.

"If you cannot handle a simple transaction, perhaps we should have someone come over who can," she said in her frostiest voice.

The teller was a good six inches shorter than Cori, and possibly a good six inches rounder, but that didn't deter her from swelling up to her full height.

"I am the head teller."

"Good. Then you won't have any problem releasing my money, will you?"

The teller silently counted out the bills and handed them over to Cori after Cori signed the appropriate paperwork.

"My husband said you were one of the pushiest women he had ever met," she commented. "Now I see he was right."

"Oh? Who's your husband?"

Her narrow lips curved into a nasty smile. "He's the district attorney."

Not by a bat of the eye did Cori show her dismay at the woman's news. "Oh, really?" She tucked the money into her wallet. "Well, then, I must say you are a perfect match. Thank you so much. Have a nice day." She smiled briefly at her and sailed out of the small bank. She waited until she was outside and a few buildings down before she allowed her shoulders to droop. She looked around, spied a grocery store sign and headed in that direction.

"One nice thing about small towns. You don't need a car to go shopping."

Chapter Six

Stop and Shop

Cori couldn't remember ever being in a grocery store, so this one was a revelation for her. She grabbed a cart and began strolling down the aisles, inspecting produce and buying what looked good. Every so often she noticed people looking at her curiously and a few whispering among themselves.

"Milk," she decided, picking up a carton.

Mindful the money Dina sent her wouldn't last forever, she was careful with her purchases, but a few nonessential items made their way into her cart.

"Ma'am, would you like us to drop that off at the doc's cottage for you?" the checker, a young woman in her twenties, asked after totaling her order and taking her money.

"You mean you deliver?"

The woman nodded. "For some, we will. This could be a heavy load and, in your condition, you might not want to overdo it."

Cori's eyes widened fractionally. "Does everyone know?"

She smiled cheerfully. "Probably."

If she planned to stay here for a while, she knew she would have to get used to it. "Any reason why everyone has to know I'm pregnant?"

The woman blinked, not understanding why news like that could be kept a secret. "But you are."

"Silly me in thinking it couldn't be important to everyone in this town," she murmured, turning away. "I think I'll take you up on the delivery offer. I admit the idea of carrying those bags back to the cottage wasn't my idea of fun."

By the time Cori returned to the cottage, she felt so weary she could barely drag herself inside. Luckily, within ten minutes of her return her groceries were delivered by a freckle-faced young man who reminded her of a friendly puppy.

Too tired to do much, she settled for storing the perishables, then went into the living room and collapsed on the couch.

"Where did all my energy go?" she moaned just before she fell asleep.

BEN ASSURED HIS MOTHER that Cori wasn't a member of the Mafia. Explained that, no, Cori didn't attack Elliott in the back of the pharmacy. And, yes, she did pour a pitcher of ice water over Pudge's head. And, yes, Ben would bring her over for dinner when she returned to Farrington. By the time he got off the phone he felt as if he had been interrogated by experts.

As he treated patients that afternoon, he heard about Cori's trip to the bank. Her dealings with Loretta, Pudge's wife, and how Loretta lost the battle. He wondered who sent her money. Had she broken down and called her father? Maybe he'd sent the money for her car repairs. The idea she could be leaving town in the next few days left an oddly empty sensation inside him.

Naturally, the news regarding Cori didn't end there. He also learned about her trip to the grocery store. What she bought. Even that Chuck Mayfield delivered the groceries.

"Is there a reason why there's a Cori alert going on?" he asked Ella once the last patient had been ushered out and the door locked. "I doubt she's taken one step without my hearing about it."

"They felt you would be interested."

Ben narrowed his eyes. There was more to her explanation, but it was obvious she wasn't going to tell him. Not until she was ready. While Ella was a talkative sort, there were also times when she could have been called the sphinx.

"Why would I be interested?" He cursed himself for asking when he knew he wouldn't get an answer.

Ella smiled. "Maybe it has to do with the interest you've shown in her since she's arrived. People can't recall the last time you'd shown that kind of attention to a woman. Of course, you never did say what you did at that medical conference a few months ago." She eyed him speculatively. "What did you do there?"

"Listened to boring talks on new methods in family practice." He affected a yawn by patting his palm against his open mouth. "I did hear how a nurse can be replaced by a computer."

"In your dreams, Cooper." Ella picked up her purse and draped the straps over her arm. "No computer can do what I do."

He cocked his eyebrow. "Oh, yeah?" He figured one of his favorite pastimes was yanking his nurse's chain.

"Yeah." Ella gave him the same look she would give one of her own sons if she felt they were getting out of line. "You get yourself a good night's sleep. You're starting to look a little ragged," she said over her shoulder as she walked out. "Good night."

"Night, Ella."

Ben stayed in his office long enough to look over the latest medical journal and scan his mail. By then, he hoped Ella was home. He had started to walk out the back door when his beeper went off. Smothering a sigh, he turned back to the phone. The idea of relaxing that evening was off to a rocky start.

Before Ben left, he headed for the cottage. Since he knew Cori had to be there and she didn't answer his knock, he tried the doorknob. And smiled when he found it twisted easily under his touch. He found a light burning in the kitchen, sending a soft glow over the woman asleep on the couch. He crouched down by her head and ran the backs of his fingers across her cheek.

Soft velvet, he thought, touching her cheek again as he whispered her name. "Cori."

She frowned at the intrusion into her dreams. "Go 'way," she muttered, flicking her fingers at his.

"Sorry, babe, nap time's over," he continued to speak quietly. "I have to make a call outside of town and thought you might like to ride along."

Cori squinted her eyes as her mind rose slowly from the depths of sleep. Ben hid his smile. A smile that abruptly disappeared when she licked her lips, which were dry from her nap. His gaze focused on her mouth.

"Are we talking about something that involves blood?" she murmured.

"No, but I might have to give a shot."

She slowly sat up. "As long as I don't have to look." She arched her neck and stretched her arms over her head. The action thrust her chest forward, molding the fabric of her dress against her breasts.

"You, ah, you might want to wear something a little more casual," Ben said hoarsely. He stood.

Cori nodded woodenly as she stumbled to her feet. She mumbled a thank-you when he grabbed her arm to steady her.

"I'll just be a minute." She yawned widely. "I never sleep during the day!"

"You forget. Your body is changing. Hormones are taking over, and for a while when your body wants to sleep, it will sleep whether you want to or not."

"Oh, goody." Cori disappeared into the bedroom, closing the door after her.

Ten minutes later, she came out looking remarkably alert, considering her state when she first woke up.

Heeding his suggestion, she had put on a pair of jeans and topped them with a bright coral T-shirt that she had tucked in. A narrow black leather belt circled her trim waist. She had brushed her hair and added a pair of coral earrings. Her idea of casual was a bit dressier than his, but he enjoyed what he saw.

"Come on." He held out his hand.

"Wait a minute. I slept through lunch." She ran into the kitchen and returned with two apples. She threw one to Ben and munched on hers as she walked out ahead of him.

"A woman giving a man an apple," he murmured, biting into his. "What a concept."

"I heard that, Dr. Cooper," she called over her shoulder. "And I know what you meant."

"I sensed you were a smart lady, Miss Peyton." He trotted over to pull open the passenger door to his truck for her.

Cori settled in the seat, tucking one leg under her. "Can I ask you a question?"

"Has that ever stopped you before?" he explained, starting up the truck and pulling around to the front of the building.

"No, not really," she agreed, "but I thought I'd be polite and ask first."

"Go for it."

Cori finished her apple in a couple bites, grabbed a tissue from the box on the truck's floor and carefully wrapped the core before continuing. "How come you don't live in the cottage?"

"It's always been used as sort of a recovery area for patients who needed hospital care but didn't want to stay a hundred miles from home," he explained. "My dad set it up. The family could bring in food and the spouse could stay and help out. It also saves them having to put out hospital and nursing fees. They pay a small fee for the use and everyone's happy since they know there's a doctor at all times across the yard. The upstairs of the clinic is fixed up as my living quarters. Dad stayed there sometimes, such as when we had a bad outbreak of influenza. I stay there now. He wanted to set up an operating room upstairs, but it meant putting in an elevator and he didn't have the funds. Someday, I'd like to build a small hospital that can serve the neighboring towns. Maybe then we could keep a few more kids in town if we had more jobs to offer."

"Except building a hospital isn't cheap," she said. "I've worked on fund-raisers just for a new hospital wing and the figures for that were astounding."

"Out here, we wouldn't need a hospital the size of Mount Sinai," he countered. "Just a facility where I can handle any heavy-duty emergency that comes up without having to call in for a medical helicopter. Where I don't have to worry that a patient will die before real help comes." His voice turned pensive. He concentrated on the road so hard it took a moment for him to realize a hand rested lightly on his arm. He looked down, saw the slender fingers curled around his forearm, the polished nails gleaming in the dusk light.

"You'll have your hospital, Ben. I know you will," Cori said softly. "Just in the short time I've been here I've seen your dedication to your patients. I would think they would be more than willing to help you get that hospital started."

He shook his head, the wry smile on his lips telling her she couldn't understand.

"Cori, we're not an affluent community. More leave every year because the jobs aren't here. The day after graduation, the kids leave either for college because they were lucky enough to get a scholarship and want to make something of themselves, or because jobs are so scarce around here they have to move to a bigger town. It's a fact of life."

"If you feel the town is dying, why did you come back?"

"Because my dad had been their doctor for more than forty years and they needed someone to take his place," he said without hesitation. "Besides, I was getting tired of the politics and the pressures in a big city hospital. Here, if an afternoon's slow, I can take off and go fishing. People can reach me through my beeper. I make house calls. That you don't see in the big city. My nurse reminds me every day she knows more than me and I better not forget that. Most of my patients either remember me as a snot-nosed kid or went to school with me." His arm flexed under her touch as he turned the wheel, steering the truck down a dirt road. The vehicle lurched as he negotiated past potholes.

"But the town isn't all that far off the highway. And you've spoken of neighboring towns. How far away are they?"

He thought for a moment. "There're three within a ten- or fifteen-mile radius. One carries the status of having one of the very few drive-in theaters still operating. Another has a nice little strip mall."

"But nothing that could lure the tourists off the highway," she mused, sitting back. "It seems like a shame. When I think of all the towns that have some sort of gimmick or tourist attraction. You know what I mean. Like towns that have these twenty-foot dinosaurs kids can climb or caverns with odd rock formations. I even heard of a town motel where the rooms were actually built to look like Native American tepees. But I guess that wouldn't work here, would it? What kind of Native Americans lived in Kansas? I guess it was Plains, wasn't it? History was never a strong subject for me."

Ben braked to a stop. "Cori."

She was engrossed in her ramblings, her hands moving in expressive gestures. "What about famous Civil War battles? No, I guess they all happened on the East Coast, didn't they? We have a town in California that's Danish. I mean the buildings! They look like they came from Denmark. People love to visit there. Or maybe..."

"Cori!"

She stopped and turned her head, cocking it to one side.

Ben placed his fingers over her lips. "How often do you go off like that?"

She looked upward in thought. "Whenever I get excited about something."

His lips twitched. "This could prove real interesting. But for now, we're almost at the Williams house so let's not let them think all those rumors about you floating around are true, okay?"

She wasn't the least bit offended. "Whatever you say. Although I do think I'm on the right track. I find that the more I talk, the more things fall into place for me."

Ben shook his head, bemused by her breezy reply. He put the truck in gear and started forward.

"What kind of emergency are you out here for?" Cori asked.

"It's not exactly an emergency," he answered, soon parking in front of a sprawling two-story house. "Just checking on their kids."

"House calls. How quaint," she murmured, opening the door and hopping out of the truck.

"Hey, Doc," a man, around the same age as Ben, greeted them. He looked at Cori with little curiosity.

"Stan, this is Cori Peyton. Cori, Stan Williams."

"It's nice to meet you." Cori smiled, putting out her hand.

Stan smiled shyly and took her hand. "Pleased to meet you."

She felt the rough calluses on his palm, but didn't draw away. "It's all right. I'm sure you've heard all the nasty stories. Please be assured only half of them are true." She stepped inside. She turned around and frowned in thought. "Unless you heard I was an alien."

"Now that's a new one!" A lilting voice exclaimed, walking into the kitchen. "I hope that story's as good as the others."

Cori turned to see the woman she assumed to be Stan's wife. Shoulder-length dark red hair was pulled back into a braid and tiny wisps of hair framed a face that couldn't be considered textbook beautiful, but no one would have noticed, or cared, due to the warm smile on her lips and in her bright green eyes.

"Hi, I'm Denise Williams," the redhead said. "I'm afraid to say you don't look anything like an alien." She turned to Stan. "Wasn't it Claude Fielding who claimed to have been abducted by aliens?"

Stan nodded. "'Course, they sent him back. Can't blame them. The man has the intelligence of an aardvark."

"He also said he saw Elvis at some truck stop when he was in Tennessee," Denise added.

"And that's only in the past three months." Ben grinned.

"And people say we Californians are Looney Tunes," Cori spoke up. "All I can contribute is knowing someone who believed some kind of rare Asian oil was going to keep her looking twenty-five forever."

"Did it?" Denise asked.

She shook her head. "She conveniently forgot that using the oil meant no tanning. Her skin is already looking like leather."

Denise looked at Ben. "She'll fit in just fine." She turned toward the stove. "Coffee for anyone?"

Cori turned to Ben. "I thought this was a house call for you," she said, confused by the almost festive air.

"In a way, it is. Their youngest is diabetic. I come by to check on him and make sure he's doing what's necessary."

"I heard you're expecting," Denise said to Cori. "Congratulations."

Cori winced. "I'm still in the shock phase."

"That's natural." Denise patted her arm. "Come on, the coffee's decaf." She ushered her over to the kitchen table. "Stan and Ben can handle Ronnie."

"We're dismissed," Stan said, giving Ben a wry grin.

Denise waited until she heard the two sets of footsteps climbing the stairs.

"Until I saw you I had no idea someone could look gorgeous wearing jeans and a T-shirt," she said, shaking her head.

Cori's spirits sank. She had hoped Denise wouldn't see her the way everyone else seemed to. "Since I arrived here, people act as if I'm a species they've never seen before. They follow me and make fun of me."

Denise set a mug in front of her, gestured for her to help herself to coffee creamer and sugar. "We're not all that way, hon. Sure, we have a few, but I'm sure you do out there in Beverly Hills, too."

"I've known my share," she admitted.

Denise sat down across from Cori, cupping her chin in her palm. "So what do you think of Ben?"

He's a fantastic kisser was the first thing that came to mind, although Cori would have died before admitting it out loud.

"He's very nice," she said instead.

Denise made a face. "Nice is something you say about the weather. Not when you're talking about a hunk like Ben." The freckles on her nose seemed to dance as she grinned. "Stan and I grew up with Ben. He was Stan's best man at our wedding. You won't find a better man than Ben, and his family is wonderful."

"That's a lovely recommendation, but there isn't anything between us."

Denise's smile broadened. "Easy for you to say."

"I am saying it!"

"Now where are my manners?" Denise jumped up. "I made a pie today since I knew Ben was coming over." She opened a cabinet and pulled out plates. She looked over her shoulder. "Do you know if he had any dinner? More times than I'd like to think he'd skip dinner and show up here and never say a word."

"No, he didn't. He said he came over to get me after he finished with his last patient. He didn't expect to find me asleep. But then, I didn't expect to fall asleep, either."

"Don't think anything about it. I took at least four naps a day during my pregnancies." Denise looked at her sharply. "Wait a minute. Didn't he feed you? That rat!" She changed direction for the refrigerator.

"No, I didn't mean you had to feed me!" she protested.

"Nonsense, I usually feed Ben when he shows up. You having problems with a queasy stomach? What I'm asking is if you think you can handle a roast beef sandwich?"

Cori's mouth was already watering. "With mustard?" she asked in a soft voice.

"No problem."

"And pickles."

Denise pulled jars out of the refrigerator.

By the time Ben and Stan returned, Cori was happily munching on a sandwich she could barely fit her mouth around.

"Don't get that hangdog look," Denise chided, gesturing to a filled plate next to Cori. "I made you one, too."

"I can see Cori made herself right at home," Ben teased, pulling out the chair next to hers and sitting down. "The kid's fine," he told Denise. "The little hustler tried to get me to play Super Nintendo with him, but I reminded him what a sore loser I am."

"How many children do you have?" Cori asked.

"Three, but sometimes I think I have four. Such as now." Denise slapped Stan's hand, which hovered over her sandwich. "Just wait for your own, buster."

During the next few hours as they graduated from roast beef sandwiches and potato salad to peach cobbler for dessert, Cori learned Stan and Denise were married the day after they graduated from high school and their three children were all boys—seventeen, twelve and six. Denise had had two miscarriages and was hoping to have another child.

"I want a girl this time," she told Cori. "I feel so outnumbered at times!"

"Yeah, and guess who rules this family!" Stan laughed.

Cori felt a sense of loss when Ben stood and announced it was time to go.

"Some people have to get up at the crack of dawn," he kidded Stan.

"Yeah, but I don't get called out in the middle of the night to deliver babies and stitch up people."

"It's the glamour of the job. Bye, gorgeous." Ben dropped a kiss on Denise's cheek.

"Ha! After seeing Cori, that name won't mean a thing to me." She hugged him before turning to Cori and hugging her, too. "Next time I get into town we'll meet for lunch. And don't worry about any of the gossiping biddies."

"At the rate I'm going, they'll soon have something new to say."

Cori was quiet as she and Ben walked out to his truck.

"Stan and Denise are very nice," she commented as he started driving down the road.

"I've always thought so." He turned on the radio to a golden oldies station, keeping the volume low. The warm sound of the Association filled the cab. Cori hummed along.

"Hard as this is to believe, my life isn't all filled with parties and charity events," she murmured. "Sometimes a bunch of us would go out to dinner, then to a club for the evening."

"Your idea of a quiet night isn't anything like the quiet nights around here." Ben had a quick flash of Cori wearing one of those formfitting dresses that adhered to the body like an adhesive bandage and were short enough to show off those spectacular legs of hers. Black, he decided. And the club would have those glittering balls overhead, sending sparklers of light down on her. Just like in the movies.

"But the club scene isn't what it used to be," she chattered on, oblivious to his wandering thoughts that heated up with each mental picture of her dancing wildly.

Pretty soon he had her dancing only with him on a deserted dance floor. By then, her formfitting dress had mysteriously disappeared and she wore a bra, panties, thigh-high stockings and high heels he'd once seen in the lingerie catalog Ella had brought to the clinic one day when she was shopping for a bridal shower gift for a niece. Except they looked even better on Cori than they had on the model.

"Most go to the clubs to be seen. I go to dance," Cori went on. "I love to dance."

Ben shifted uneasily and his hands gripped the steering wheel even tighter as his fantasy Cori seemed to prance across his vision. "Yeah," he said without even listening to her.

What the hell was wrong with him? He was in his thirties. A settled man. A professional. He even remembered being a reasonably sane man.

Until Cori drove headlong into his life and turned it completely upside down. And this was only after a week.

"It is amazing, isn't it?" Her question intruded on his thoughts.

"What? That you like to dance?"

Cori had half turned in the seat so she could face him. The frown on her face told him he'd given her the wrong answer.

"Dance? I was talking about how clear your sky is out here." There was a trace of impatience in her voice. "Back home, smog can be so bad at times the stars look more like smudges. While out here—" she tipped her head back to look up and out the passenger door "—they're like diamonds."

He smiled at her whispered reverence. "I guess living out here and seeing it every night, we take it for granted."

"But you shouldn't," she insisted, leaning forward, sending a soft wave of her perfume in his direction. "This is so natural, so beautiful."

"You're the one who's beautiful."

His murmured declaration brought a wave of color to her cheeks. The more he saw her reaction to compliments the more he wondered just how she got pregnant. Or didn't a man look beyond the lovely face and deep blue eyes?

"Out here, you see me as beautiful. Back home, I'd look like any other woman."

Ben pulled over to the side of the road and shut the engine off. He turned, resting his arm along the back of the seat.

"You could be among hundreds of beautiful women and you'd still stand out."

"Why, Doctor, you sound positively poetic."

He moved closer. "Maybe because you make me think poetic."

Her lips curved upward. "Really?"

"Not completely, but it sounds better than if I told you what I had really been thinking." Unable to resist, he reached out and fingered her hair, savoring the silky strands slipping between his fingers.

"Tell me what you were really thinking, Ben," she whispered.

He leaned forward a bit more. "You, dancing."

She smiled as she leaned in his direction a fraction. "Just dancing?"

He moved that last needed fraction. "Oh, a lot more than dancing." His mouth captured hers in a kiss that left nothing to the imagination. He grasped her shoulders, pulling her up against him. Her breasts pressed warmly against his chest. Her breath was heated against his mouth. But what he noticed most was her reaction. She opened her mouth to his thrusting tongue as naturally as if they had been lovers countless times. She softened against him, twining her arms around his neck.

"Ben," she breathed the sound of his name into his mouth.

"Hm?" He grew engrossed with the shape of her ear and the gold-nugget-shaped earring in her lobe.

Cori settled herself more firmly in his arms. "Did anyone ever tell you your kisses should be considered illegal?"

"No." He nipped the lobe, smiling at her exhalation.

"They are. They could be used as a secret weapon." She ran a hand along his denim-covered thigh, feeling the muscles flex under her touch.

He drew in a sharp breath when her hand started wandering a little north, but stopped short of where he wanted it to be. "You are a wicked woman, Cori Peyton."

"You make me feel wicked." She almost purred, nibbling her way along his jawline.

Having more than a few wicked thoughts of his own, Ben gripped her chin and raised her face to his. Kissing her soon proved not to be enough. He thought of the bed back at the cottage. Even the small bed he used in the clinic. Either would be fine. He even started wondering if he had any blankets in the back of the truck. He slipped a hand under the hem of her T-shirt and upward until he reached the lace edge of her bra. He edged a finger underneath the fabric, feeling the satiny skin of her breast. He realized how sensitive her breast was when she flinched.

He murmured reassuring words as he lightly traced the rounded perimeter. He felt her rapid heartbeat under his fingertips, delighted that it was his touch that caused it.

The knock on the driver's window brought Ben coldly back to earth.

"Any problems in there, Doc?" a male voice growled.

Cori moaned, reaching between them to pull her T-shirt back down.

"Hi, Andy," Ben greeted the town's sheriff in a false voice. "No, everything's fine. We're just having a talk."

The broad grin on the man's face told him he knew just what the conversation consisted of.

"Well, maybe you'll want to move along before someone else stops by," he suggested, tapping his flashlight against the top of the truck as he walked back to his vehicle.

"I don't believe this," Cori moaned, burying her face in her hands.

Ben laughed. He hadn't realized she could look so appealing when she was embarrassed.

"I wouldn't worry. Andy's seen a lot during his years as sheriff."

"But it could have been worse!"

"Hopefully, we're adult enough to hold off." Ben noticed the sheriff's vehicle didn't move until he started up his truck and pulled onto the road. Andy then blinked his headlights twice and drove off in the opposite direction.

Cori was silent during the rest of the drive back to the cottage. Ben was also, except his thoughts were centered on continuing what they had started. His body throbbed with arousal as he thought of the soft bed awaiting them.

He parked the truck near the clinic's rear door and hopped out. He noticed Cori seemed a little stiff as they walked toward the cottage, but he put it down to shock at being caught by the town sheriff.

"Andy won't tell anyone what he saw, Cori," he told her as he unlocked the door and followed her inside.

She spun around. "It's not that." She took a deep breath. "I know that what happened in the truck meant something should happen here, but it can't."

His arousal took a nosedive.

"It can't?"

She shook her head. "I'm pregnant by another man!"

"A man who means nothing to you."

She winced at his statement. "A mistake I wish I hadn't made. All I'm saying is I'm strongly attracted to you and it's obvious you're attracted to me, but I don't think it would be a good idea."

Ben stared at her so long she began to fidget.

"Say something!"

He stepped forward and dropped his hands on her shoulders. Before she could ask what he planned to do, he pressed a light kiss against her forehead.

"You know, having someone want to protect my reputation is new to me," he murmured. "But it's entirely unnecessary. Believe me, our time will come, Cori. Good night.''

A wide-eyed Cori watched Ben walk out, making sure the door lock was engaged.

''Whoever said country boys were slow hadn't met Ben Cooper.''

Chapter Seven

Vivian's Boutique

"I don't believe this." Cori looked up after she leafed through the pitifully thin yellow-page section of the telephone book.

"Don't believe what?" Ella asked absently as she alphabetized the files.

"There is no health club in the area. What do you do for exercise?"

The older woman chuckled at the question. "Guess we figure walking's good enough exercise. I read walking's the up-and-coming popular exercise. Don't they do that in L.A. since they're all so health conscious?" Ella said with tongue planted firmly in her cheek.

Cori shook her head. "You don't walk in L.A., unless of course you're on a designated walking trail or using the track at a health club. Except here, you don't have either!"

Ella patted her comfortable bulk. "Sorry, dear, I guess none of us ever felt the need for one of those exercise places."

"Well, I do." She hopped onto the desk, swinging her legs back and forth, her heels knocking against the side. "I've gained six pounds."

Ella looked at Cori over the top of her glasses. "Where? She frowned. "Where what?"

"Where did you gain the six pounds? Because I can't see one extra ounce on that scrawny body of yours."

"I do not have a scrawny body! As for where, I've gained everywhere!" She looked down and pinched her still-nonexistent stomach. "It's a good thing my friend Dina sent me clothes with looser waistbands or I'd be out of luck!"

Cori smoothed down the full legs to her turquoise cotton shorts. Topped with a bright sunny yellow tank top and a lightweight fuchsia jacket on top of that, she was a living modern painting. As if that wasn't enough, she wore a turquoise crushed hat and swung between her fingers a pair of fuchsia framed sunglasses by one of the temples.

She frowned at the beam scale standing like a silver sentry in the hall by the door. "Do you think that monstrosity could be wrong?"

"Honey, if I could look like you I wouldn't worry about a measly six pounds, and, no, the scale isn't wrong. As for you needing looser clothes, those boxes your friend sent you kept people talking for a week while they tried to figure out what arrived here for you."

Cori couldn't think about the delivery of her clothing without a few pangs of sorrow. Her friend had also included a hastily written note that there had been no problem in her picking up the clothing Cori requested since Sean was in Europe for a few weeks. So much for her father missing her, she'd thought sadly.

Her shoulders lifted and fell as she took a deep breath. "I'm positive I felt the baby move today."

"Much too soon," Ella told her. "It was probably gas."

"Gas? That's a lovely thought." She picked up the file folder marked with her name. "I guess it's a good thing my dad didn't cut off my health insurance. It's embarrassing enough to go through these examinations without Ben getting paid for it." She suddenly frowned. "Somehow that didn't come out quite right."

Ella plucked the folder out of Cori's hands. "That is not for your eyes, missy. And you're right, that didn't come out right. Makes it sound as if the doc's getting paid for more than checking on that little one you're carrying."

"It's *my* file!" she protested.

"It's the clinic's file." Ella pulled open the file cabinet and dropped the folder inside. She turned to the younger woman with a trace of impatience. "Don't you have something to do?"

"Not since my day of helping out at Vivian's dress shop. You know, if I had my car, none of us would have to worry about these episodes happening."

"Lots of people survive without a car," Ella countered.

"Not when you're from California. Why, out there, living without a car is like—" she tapped her forefinger against her chin "—well, it's like the Pacific Ocean going dry. Impossible!"

The older woman shook her head. "You are something else. Now why can't you go back to Vivian's?"

"I don't think you want to know." Cori picked up file folders and started putting them in alphabetical order.

Ella took the files out of her hand. "I can't believe you've insulted every major person in this town."

"I didn't insult the woman!" Cori argued. "I merely pointed out a few helpful hints to her. I don't care if she is the mayor's wife. That color and style were much too young for her. Not to mention trying to wiggle into something that was obviously two sizes too small! I don't know how she managed to get into it. I have a spandex dress I love and getting into it was a battle when I was thinner." Cori held one hand out in front of her. "I miss the manicures, but even if I had the extra money, I'm afraid Valerie would make sure I ended up with a few less fingers."

"She hasn't been happy since Ben stopped seeing her."

Cori stopped twirling her sunglasses and dropped them on the desktop. She looked down, pretending a great deal of interest in a medical journal lying by her hip.

"Were they very close?" she asked, as if she couldn't care less about the answer.

"They've dated off and on since he came back to take over his father's practice." Ella was busy filing that day's patients' records.

"Did they ever...?" She waved a hand back and forth in silent communication.

"Not that anyone knows." Ella looked up. "Why are you asking? Are you interested in the doc?"

Cori straightened up. "I'm just curious, that's all."

The older woman smiled knowingly. "Uh-huh."

"She is pretty." She picked up a pen and began doodling on a pad of paper.

"So she thinks." Ella shook her head. A restless Cori was a sight to behold. "You never did tell me what happened at Vivian's."

Cori made a face. "You probably heard at least twenty versions of the story before I even walked out of the store, so mine shouldn't make any difference."

"Yes, I did, but I haven't heard yours."

"Vivian asked if I would be willing to help out in her shop this morning since it was the first day for her annual spring sale," she recited. "If there was a job I couldn't screw up, it was working with clothing, so I accepted. I suggested Vivian take the dress out of the window and put in a gorgeous peach suit she had just gotten in. We added a straw boater with a peach scarf tied around the brim and a taupe purse. The new display looked great. Quite a few people stopped to watch.''

"What does the suit in the window have to do with Margaret?'' Ella asked, by now growing impatient.

"That's what brought her into the shop,'' she explained. "She saw the suit in the window and decided she wanted it. Pale peach, Ella!''

"Go on.''

"I was in the back unpacking a box for Vivian when I heard the woman come in and ask to see the suit in a size twelve.'' Cori rolled her eyes. "I could see her and went out and suggested she might like to try another color that would be more flattering to her complexion.''

Ella sighed and shook her head as if she knew what was coming next.

"Not only is her complexion completely wrong for peach, but her hair is the strangest color. She claims it's red and it's not even close,'' Cori confided. "It's this sickly pinkish orange, and even if she'd worn the suit in her true size, she would have looked like a joke. The style was also meant for a much younger woman.''

"Margaret prides herself on being eternally thirty-nine and a size twelve.''

"She has to be sixty if a day and at least a size sixteen. She told me I didn't know what I was talking about and Vivian tried to referee.''

Ella shook her head. "What you're saying is you interfered again?''

"Vivian told me I have no sales sense. Perhaps I'd do better at buying than selling, but I do feel I know what looks good on a person." Cori shook her head. "Let me tell, you, Ella, a peach sausage is not a pretty sight!"

Ella bit down on her lower lip, but it didn't help. The laughter just rolled out.

Cori laughed, too. "You should have seen it."

When Ben stepped into the office, he found the two women laughing so hard tears were streaming down their cheeks. Cori lay back on the desktop, her legs kicking upward while Ella was sprawled in a chair, her body jiggling. He stood in the doorway a moment, taking in the scene before him.

He knew there could be only one reason for their hilarity. If only he hadn't been out on a house call.

"What did she do this time?"

Cori turned. For a moment, Ben was blinded by her dazzling smile.

"Did you have fun?"

"No, but I'd say you did. What did the two of you do? Go over to the dentist's office for a whiff of laughing gas?" He set his medical bag on the desktop as he nonchalantly brushed her off his desk. "You sit in the chair, not on my desk. Or did you eat funny food at Myrna's?"

Cori opened her mouth to reply, then looked at Ella and burst into laughter again.

Ella could only wave her hands helplessly.

Ben shook his head. "I'm glad to see the two of you are enjoying yourselves. Anything interesting happen while I was gone?"

"Cori met Margaret Holloway," Ella managed to get out.

He thought of the mayor's wife. Officious, full-of-herself Margaret. He knew he didn't want to hear it, but he couldn't stop asking, anyway.

"In what capacity?"

"As a sausage!" Cori's reply ended on another wave of laughter. She held her sides. "*She* was the sausage!"

"You two are nuts."

"There's nothing like a medical opinion." With a great deal of self-control, Cori was finally able to stop laughing. "Do you want the long version or the short version?"

"Let's go for the short."

Cori launched into the story, oblivious of the pained look on Ben's face. "You know," she said, "if the town had a health club I wouldn't have this problem."

He closed his eyes. He knew he was going to ask. "Why?"

"Because I'm very good with aerobics. And with the way my stomach is pooching out, I need a regular workout."

Ben eyed her slim figure. "You're fine. You could actually gain more weight without any problem."

"Maybe now, but it won't last. I need to do something more energetic," she protested.

"I can think of something more energetic," he murmured, glancing at his message slips.

Cori smiled to let him know she'd overheard him.

"I'm off for that walk everyone has suggested I take," she announced.

"You might want to stay away from Vivian's," Ella suggested.

"I'm rapidly running out of places where I can go," Cori grumbled good-naturedly. "It would be a nice idea if the town could experience a healthy growth spurt in the next few days."

Ben shook his head in bemusement. "Don't worry, you've got a dinner invitation to look forward to. My mom wants us over for dinner tonight after I close the clinic."

Her eyes widened. "Me? Why?"

He shrugged. "She was out of town when you arrived and now that she's back she wants to meet you."

A soft moan escaped her lips. "But we don't know what horrible stories about me she might have heard."

"Then going out there for dinner is a good way to find out, isn't it?"

"Don't worry about Lucia, darlin'," Ella assured her. "She's one of the loveliest, most down-to-earth women you can meet. She's lived in Farrington so long that I doubt anyone remembers she had come here as one of those war brides."

"The only idea of a war bride I can visualize is Cary Grant wearing a WAC uniform and horsehair bangs," she muttered, walking out.

Ben chuckled at Cori's reference to the movie *I Was a Male War Bride*.

"I'd say you're way off base with your description," he told her, still chuckling. "But I can guarantee Mom would love the comparison."

"Then let's allow her to continue thinking the worst about me, shall we?" she playfully blew him a kiss. *"Ciao."*

Cori hadn't been walking for more than two minutes before she found Dan, Zeke, Carl and their crony, Alex, walking behind her. But then, they were never far from her, she noticed. She spun around and planted her hands on her hips.

"Why are you following me?"

As if orchestrated, Dan looked at Zeke with a silent question in his eyes. Zeke then looked at Alex and Alex looked at Carl. Then they looked at her.

"'Cause it's a good idea," they said in unison.

"I thought you spent your mornings at Myrna's."

"Mornin's over."

She took a deep breath. "All right, the morning is over. And then you spend the afternoons on the bench in front of the city hall because it's shady there and you can play liar's poker without anyone bothering you." She was pleased to recite the schedule known to all who remained in Farrington more than twenty-four hours.

"Now we're only over there the days you're not out here." Dan appeared to be appointed the group's spokesman.

Cori could only ask. "Why?"

"Because you're pretty to look at and you give us more entertainment than television."

Cori wondered why she didn't feel insulted. But she looked at the elderly men, dressed in their well-worn jeans, plaid shirts, billed caps and work boots and saw four men who, for some reason unknown to her, actually liked her.

"Well, you might not look like the kind of male entourage a lady would wish for," she finally said, flashing them her brightest smile, "but I don't think I could ask for anyone better."

"We'll make sure Pudge won't bother you," Dan told her.

"Sounds fair to me."

"Were you ever in Wichita not all that long ago?" Dan asked.

"Does it make a difference?"

All four grinned. "It could," Zeke answered this time, then asked hopefully, "Did you ever meet Sharon Stone?"

Cori shook her head. "Sorry, I never met her."

"Michelle Pfeiffer?" Dan asked.

She shook her head again.

"Meg Ryan?" was Alex's request.

"Bette Davis?" Carl asked. "Now there was a lady who had a mind of her own."

"Bette Davis?" Zeke turned on him. "She's dead!"

"Maybe she met her when she was a little girl!" he argued before turning back to Cori.

She looked apologetic. "Sorry."

They looked at one another again, as if debating something. "She's still better looking than Mavis, old Holloway's secretary," they decided before looking at her expectantly.

Cori took a deep breath. "Gentlemen, since your fair town doesn't have a health club I am forced to take walks." She dipped her head. "Shall we?"

She started up the street with the foursome not far behind her. As she walked, Cori realized they were already turning into a habit she didn't want to break.

"Oh, no," she whispered to herself. "I'm turning into a local!"

WHAT DID ONE WEAR when meeting a man's mother? Especially the mother of a man with bedroom eyes?

Cori had a few dresses to choose from, but she didn't want to overdress for the occasion. Since Ben tended to believe a doctor's attire consisted of jeans and T-shirts, she told herself she wouldn't have to worry.

In the end, she chose a pair of bright pink linen tailored pants and topped them with a dark blue V-necked weskit. Her chunky-style beaded choker and dangling earrings echoed the same two colors.

"You have a thing about bright colors, don't you?" Ben commented when he stopped by to pick her up, looking devastating in tan jeans and a cream-colored button-down shirt with the cuffs rolled back.

She looked down at her outfit, suddenly worried. "Is it too loud for your mother?"

He chuckled, shaking his head. "No, I wouldn't worry about that."

Ben helped her into the truck, but didn't close the door. He kept one hand on the door, the other flat on the top. "Looking at you brightens up a day," he said softly, just before he dipped his head and captured her mouth with his. His tongue traced the soft seam of her lips before delving inside. Cori was allowed only a brief taste before he lifted his head and looked down at her, noting her flushed features and glowing eyes.

"If we weren't expected at my mom's..." he murmured, running his thumb across her moist lower lip.

"Let's not think about that." She hastily turned around and fumbled for her seat belt. It didn't help when she realized she had two of the same. She dropped the driver's belt and hunted around for her own.

"Having a problem, Miss Peyton?" he asked silkily as he climbed in behind the wheel.

"Not at all, Dr. Cooper," she replied in an equally silky tone. "Why don't you tell me about your mother?"

"Ah, the change-the-subject ploy so I'll forget about that kiss."

"No, I call it the change-the-subject ploy so I won't think about the kiss," she muttered, staring out the windshield.

Ben didn't hide his triumphant grin as he started up the engine. "It's nice to know I'm so unforgettable," he murmured, guiding the truck up the driveway.

"Doesn't your mother live in town?" Cori asked as Ben drove toward the outskirts.

He shook his head. "No, she said she always preferred living away from the general populace. My brother-in-law took over running the family farm and my mom said the best way not to turn into an interfering mother-in-law was to have her own place. Mama had a house built on the edge of the property where she's close enough for baby-sitting and the grandkids to visit her, but far enough away to have her privacy.''

Cori thought of the Italian matriarchs she'd seen in movies—always laughing, bodies like large soft pillows and eager to mother anyone who came along. For someone who lost her mother at a young age, the idea was appealing.

''What did you tell her about me?'' she asked Ben.

''Didn't have to say a thing,'' he said cheerfully. ''Everyone else told her everything she needed to know.''

She moaned, covering her face with her hands. ''That isn't fair! She's going to think I'm worse than the aliens in the supermarket tabloids.''

''Have you been reading those things again?'' He shook his head.

''When you're standing in line for what seems like hours because Mrs. Murphy brought a bag full of coupons on double coupon day for her two weeks' worth of grocery shopping, you read whatever is in front of you,'' she defended herself.

Ben knew all about the frugal Mrs. Murphy, as well as all the other townsfolk Cori talked on about. But he delighted in seeing her amusement turn to genuine concern as she spoke about them.

Before Cori knew it, Ben pulled up in front of a charming white clapboard house. A black-and-white border collie jumped off the porch and walked, with tail wagging, toward the truck.

"Hey, Shasta." Ben squatted to pet the dog as he got out of the truck. "How're you doing, boy? Where's your mistress?"

"Where do you think she is? She's preparing a meal you will never forget." A husky voice with a trace of accent came from behind the screen door just before it opened and the owner of the voice stepped outside.

Cori's eyes widened to saucer shape as she stared at a woman she couldn't believe was Ben's mother—but judging by the way she was addressing him had to be. Lucia Cooper was about the same height as Cori's five foot six inches, but the similarity ended there. Waves of dark brown hair had been swept up in a loose knot, revealing a delicate-featured face that should have been immortalized in a painting. Dark brown eyes, like her son's, danced with the same laughter as her red glossed lips. Her slim figure was clothed in black linen pants and a red blouse.

"She could give Sophia Loren a run for her money," she muttered, still in shock. "Talk about aging gracefully."

"Yeah, I guess she could." Ben grinned just before he hugged his mother and dropped a kiss on her cheek. "Mama, this is Cori Peyton. Cori, my mom, Lucia Angiani Cooper."

"So you are Cori." The older woman smiled. She picked up Cori's hands and studied her. "You are much lovelier than the town grapevine said you were, although I do hear that Dan has a crush on you."

"I'm very pleased to meet you, Mrs. Cooper," she said numbly, then rushed on. "There is no way I can believe you had eight children!"

Lucia's laughter rippled in the air. "Thank you, my dear. And you must call me Lucia. Mrs. Cooper was my mother-in-law's name. Now come in and tell me all the nice things you've noticed about my baby." She smiled fondly at her son. She looped an arm around Cori's waist as they walked toward the house. "I guess you have already guessed that as the only son he was spoiled shamelessly."

"Bossy and pushy is more like it. He's always telling me what I can and can't do."

"Ah." Lucia nodded in understanding. "His father was like that every time I was pregnant. Doctors are bad enough, but when you are married to them—bah! They are even worse!"

"Thanks, Mom," Ben said wryly.

"You are and you know it." She reached over and patted his cheek. "But that is why I love you, my darling son. Because you remind me so much of your father. I hope you two are hungry because I couldn't stop cooking today."

"Nowadays, I'm always hungry," Cori confessed.

"That is natural when one is eating for two." Lucia led them inside the house and toward the room emitting tantalizing aromas that sent Cori's salivary glands working overtime. "Besides, my dear, you are too thin."

"That's what everyone says."

Lucia gestured for Cori to be seated at the table while she poured three glasses of iced tea.

"Do not worry, it's herbal lemon tea," she told Ben as she placed the glasses in front of them. "I made lasagna. Bennie's favorite," she confided in Cori.

"Bennie?" Cori repeated in an undertone.

"Only to my mother," he warned her. "Otherwise, I don't answer to it, so don't even think about using it."

Lucia placed a large green salad in the center of the table and a basket filled with warm bread.

"This all looks so wonderful," Cori enthused, buttering a piece of bread.

"Now tell me why you would leave California and travel to Kansas," Lucia asked Cori.

"Mama," Ben warned her.

"That's all right, Ben." Cori placed a settling hand on his. "I honestly don't know how or why I ended up here," she told Lucia. "I just got in the car, started driving and here I am."

"What does your papa think of you being pregnant?"

Ben muttered a curse.

"Bennie, you know better than to say those words at my table!" She raised a cooking spoon in a threatening manner.

"My father doesn't know," Cori confessed. "And if he did know, he probably wouldn't be very happy to hear about it. He feels I don't handle my life very well."

In an instant, Lucia was out of her chair and engulfing Cori in a hug. "Don't worry, my dear," she soothed. "You have more than enough family in this town, eh, Bennie?"

"She has the best medical care in the state," he said flippantly, aware of what his mother was trying to say.

"Of course she does!"

For the balance of dinner, Lucia efficiently interrogated Cori and learned just about anything there was to know about her. It wasn't until they were relaxing over decaf coffee and the lemon chiffon cake Lucia had made that the older woman dropped her verbal bomb.

"I understand your pregnancy is about three months along."

"That's right."

"How interesting. Bennie was in Wichita about three months ago," she commented. She turned to her son first, then smiled at Cori. "Perhaps that is why the town is convinced he is the father of your baby."

Ben, who had just forked a piece of cake into his mouth, coughed, sending the bite of cake across the table. Cori, who had picked up her glass of ice tea to drink, immediately lost hold of the glass.

Lucia, calm and serene, smiled at the couple amid the disaster her comment triggered.

"I guess this means they're right!" She held up her arms in a victorious gesture and beamed.

Chapter Eight

Cori's Cottage

"You must come back and see me again when Bennie isn't here to stifle our talk," Lucia told her, more an order than a request as Cori and Ben took their leave later that evening. She reached out and hugged Cori tightly. "And when you do, I will tell you all about my baby boy." She bestowed a fond smile on her son.

"Terrific," Ben muttered. "She's going to drag out those damn baby pictures where I'm holding the diaper I should have been wearing."

Cori laughed. "I'd love to come again, Lucia, but I don't have a car."

"Then take Bennie's truck," she insisted before turning to her son and hugging him tightly. She said something in Italian to him, which he answered in the same language. "You are too handsome for your own good." She patted his cheek. "I am so glad that Valerie didn't get her claws in you. I never liked her. This one—" she smiled fondly at Cori "—I like."

"Be careful," Ben cautioned Cori, taking her hand and pulling her toward the truck. "Next thing you know you'll be adopted." *Or married,* his inner voice intoned.

Ben put the casserole dish holding leftover lasagna and a plate filled with cake on the floor of the truck's cab, then helped Cori inside.

Lucia remained outside, with the dog by her side, as they drove down the narrow lane.

"I like your mother," Cori told him.

"She is one in a million." Affection warmed his voice.

"Do you think she'll be able to stop the rumor that the baby's yours?"

"No, because people will believe what they want to. The timing happens to be right in their eyes." He turned onto the main road. "Does it bother you?"

"N-no," she stammered. Why did she suddenly feel so overheated? It couldn't be the thought of Ben as her baby's father. Still, she couldn't hold back the fantasy of her and Ben in bed together, wrapped in a jumble of silk sheets, his eyes looking into hers as his body pleasured hers and— *Get a grip, girl!* "I'm only concerned about you," she finally said. "I don't want people to think less of you."

Ben reached over and took Cori's hand. He was surprised to find it icy cold to the touch. He kept it cradled in his, hoping his warmth would sink in. He lifted it to his lips and pressed a soft kiss in the tender center of her palm.

"I wouldn't worry about it. It seems they're happy to have proof I'm human." He tugged on her hand, urging her closer to his side.

She unfastened her seat belt and slid across, refastening the center seat belt when he gestured toward it. When Ben's right arm dropped around her shoulders, she snuggled up against his side.

"This is all so crazy. I end up in a town I've never heard of. My car is under a canvas tarp because I can't get it fixed. I've been fired from pretty much every business in town—"

"You haven't worked at Ed's Video Rentals yet," he suggested. "And there's the hardware store and the post office and—"

She shot him a look. "May I finish, please? In this town, I meet a man who's—" She waved her hand back and forth as if trying to come up with the description she wanted and ultimately forgoing it. "And I'm not only pregnant by another man, but the man I met is now my doctor. It sounds like a soap opera!"

"I'd say it's better than anything you'd read in a supermarket tabloid," he teased, turning his head briefly to drop a quick kiss on the top of her head.

"Dan did say I'm better than television," she said with a soft sigh. "I guess he's right."

"You're what?"

She explained to him about her four followers during her afternoon walks and their revelation that day.

Ben chuckled. "No wonder you feel off-balance if you're dealing with those four. It's said that the only reason they're out and about is because their wives won't put up with them during the day. Dan's wife said when he retired from the county she didn't expect him to sit home all day and do crossword puzzles. When Zeke retired the following year, the two started hanging out by city hall. Their numbers have steadily grown. Now, word has it they, along with the mayor, get together in the city hall basement one night a week for a poker game."

"Sounds exciting."

"They think it is because they believe their wives have no idea they're doing this."

She chuckled. "But the wives know."

Ben tipped his head to the side just enough to catch a whiff of her perfume. The image of Cori lying in a bed of brilliantly colored spring flowers instantly came to mind.

Just as quickly, the image of Cori lying in a bed, his bed, countermanded the first mental picture. He instantly felt his body tighten and his respiration labored.

"Ben," Cori said in a small voice. "I don't want to end up like a soap opera. Those people are either deliriously happy or viciously unhappy. I'd like to find a happy medium. Especially for the baby's sake. As long as he or she doesn't expect me to turn into June Cleaver, because I don't think it's possible. But do you think it's possible to find that happy medium?"

"I'd say it's possible for you to have anything you want," he told her. "Hey—" his voice lightened "—I see a side road up there."

She got his meaning instantly. "Oh, no! Not after the last time! If that sheriff caught us again, I know this time I would die of embarrassment."

"What if I could show you a place he doesn't know about?"

She paused. "Really?"

He grinned. He could tell he was tempting her. And, oh, how much he wanted to tempt her. "Yeah."

She looked at him out of the corner of her eyes. "Are you sure he doesn't know about it?"

"That's what all the kids say. And if anyone knows where to go for privacy, they do," he told her. One thing he wanted to share with the lovely woman was privacy. A lot of it.

Ben made a U-turn and drove a few miles before pulling onto a dirt road. He didn't stop until they reached the edge of a small lake.

Cori looked at the moonlight-dappled water with faint awe. "I can't believe teenagers willingly told you about this place," she commented, feeling more than a little suspicious.

"Not exactly," he admitted. "I was called out here a year ago when a couple of teenagers high on hormones got a little too adventurous and ended up needing some help."

Cori's eyes widened as her imagination took a fanciful leap. "I don't think I even want to know what happened."

"I know their parents weren't too happy with them." He switched off the engine and turned, unbuckling his seat belt. "C'mere, lady." He curved an arm around her shoulders and pulled her toward him after he unfastened her seat belt. She leaned willingly into his embrace as his mouth covered hers in a heated openmouthed kiss.

Cori's head was spinning as Ben's mouth seduced hers. His taste was just as wild as the feelings coursing through her veins. She knew if he hadn't been holding on to her she would have melted right into the seat. Instead, she let herself go and responded to his kisses with honest emotion.

How could she have ever thought Rufus was sexy? Or briefly thought her somewhat lack of response to Rufus was her fault? There certainly wasn't any problem with her response to Ben. She slid her fingers between his shirt buttons, feeling the heat from his skin against her fingertips. Eager for more, she unfastened two buttons. Warm skin covered with springy hair met her touch. He murmured encouraging words as she gently raked her nails across the slightly rough skin.

"I like you touching me, Cori," he whispered in her ear the same time his teeth gently tugged on the lobe. "I want you touching me more," he murmured as one hand covered her breast with a feather-light touch as if aware she was now extrasensitive there. Her nipple immediately stiffened in reaction, pushing insistently against his palm.

For the moment, she preferred to forget he was a doctor who knew more what was going on in her body than she knew. Especially when he touched her with knowing fingers and ignited wild sensations within her body. She closed her eyes, wanting to fully feel the small explosions already going off within her. Her weskit had been unbuttoned and her bra unclasped before she realized what was going on.

She threw her head back to take some air and felt his eyes on her. He looked at her with an intensity she sensed was mirrored in her own: sensuality mingled with stark desire. Her fingers trembled as she placed them over his mouth. His lips opened, inviting them inside. When they closed around her fingers, she felt an incredible shock of desire travel up her arm, but center in the middle of her body where it liquefied.

"Ben." She could only murmur his name.

He smiled. "Cori."

Unable to stop herself, Cori framed his face with her hands. She felt the slight roughness of stubble against her palms, the warmth of his breath as he turned his head to press a kiss in the center. She raked her fingers through his hair, feeling the silky strands curve around her fingers. She had never felt the need, the compulsion, to touch a man before. To imprint the feel of his skin on hers. To brand him with her touch. She wanted to do it all with Ben.

"My, my, Doctor," she whispered, pressing light kisses across his jaw. "Is this your idea of a physical examination?"

For a moment, he tensed as he pulled her onto his lap. "I'm not a doctor here, Cori. I'm only a man."

Her smile, even in the dark, was dazzling with its brightness. "Don't worry, that's something I'm not likely to overlook." The crowded confines of the truck didn't allow for much movement, but somehow Cori found a way to wrap her legs around his hips as she kissed him deeply.

She knew, deep in her soul, that she wanted this man. She was about to tell him so when a rap on the window shattered the moment. Ben turned his head and looked out the window. The pithy curse he uttered echoed in Cori's mind. She slid off his lap and turned away as she fumbled with her buttons.

"I don't believe this," she muttered between clenched teeth. "It's him again."

Ben started up the engine and hit the window button with more force than was necessary.

"Hi, Andy." He greeted the grinning sheriff with the same civility he would have offered the black plague.

"Doc." The older man nodded. His gaze briefly rested on Cori's back before returning to Ben. "Having trouble with your truck?"

"No."

The sheriff nodded again. "The kids think I don't know about this place."

"I guess they do tend to underestimate you," Ben agreed, wondering what was coming next.

"You know, as a medical man, you should realize better than anyone that the little lady here needs her rest," Andy said conversationally. "It is getting late."

"You got it."

As the sheriff headed back to his truck, Cori slid across the seat until she was almost hugging the passenger door.

Ben turned the truck around and started back up the road with the sheriff's truck's headlights reflected in his rearview mirror.

Cori sat upright, her back ramrod stiff as she stared straight ahead.

"I told you before that Andy doesn't talk," Ben said more to break the charged silence. "Even his wife can't get anything out of him."

"That is *not* a comforting thought," she snapped.

"Cori—"

"I must be crazy! This is a test and I'm failing miserably. Twice I've let my emotions take over where you're concerned and twice we've gotten caught!" The moment she spoke the words, she clamped her lips shut and remained silent for the balance of the drive.

As Ben drove, his mind worked at an incredible speed. He thought fate was on his side. His pager hadn't gone off. It was as if all medical emergencies had been put on hold for the evening. For a moment back there by the lake, he'd fantasized about making love to her in the lush grass at the water's edge. Boy, Andy sure had a knack of showing up when he was least wanted.

When they reached the outskirts of town, he opened his mouth to say anything to break the silence when his pager did it for him.

"You really should have a cellular phone," Cori commented, still refusing to look at him.

"I do have one. It's being repaired." He parked the truck along the side of the cottage. By the expression on Cori's face, she knew, as he did, his truck wouldn't be seen from the street there. She didn't wait for him to walk around and open her door. She pushed it open herself and hopped out.

"May I use the phone?" he followed her to the door.

"Of course. After all, it is yours." She opened the door and walked through the tiny living room and into the kitchen. She filled a glass with water and listened unashamedly to his half of the conversation.

"No, I can't imagine it's anything to worry about," he said in a soothing voice. "What? Oh, I had dinner at my mother's."

"How rude he is in not mentioning me," she murmured, sipping her water. She looked down and plucked an invisible speck of lint from her pants.

Luckily, Ben hadn't heard her. "No, Val, as I said, it's nothing for you to worry about, but if you're still uncomfortable in the morning, call Ella and have her schedule you in. No, you weren't disturbing me. Good night, Val."

"Maybe not him, but you're disturbing *me* a hell of a lot," Cori muttered, setting her glass down with a dangerous thump. She had regained her composure by the time he walked into the kitchen and was able to present him with a bland smile. "No emergency?"

"No."

She kept her smile firmly pasted on her lips as she walked toward him. "Good."

Cori grabbed Ben's arms and pulled him toward her. Her kiss was swift and hot: seduction personified. She wove a sensual spell around him with the kind of kiss that curled a man's toes. A spell she was going to make very sure wouldn't be easily broken, she decided as she seduced his lips into parting for her questing tongue. She had already discovered she enjoyed the way he tasted and was greedy for more.

This kiss was different from the one they shared by the lake. This one was pure sin. She aligned her body against Ben's, wrapping her arms around him so he could feel every inch of her. By the time she drew back, Ben's ragged breath matched her own.

He cleared his throat. "Is that your way of saying goodnight?"

She smiled as she sauntered to the front door with a deliberate sway of her hips. "No, that's my way of thanking you for a lovely evening."

Ben remained standing by the phone. "Lady, you have a bit of the tease in you."

Cori curled her fingers around the doorknob, but didn't twist it to open. "It hasn't taken me long to realize that small towns thrive on gossip. And after what your mother told us, I can see you and I are the main topic. I'm sorry to have dragged you into my mess." A flash of regret momentarily darkened her features.

"You could argue from now until doomsday that I'm not the father of your baby and they'd never believe you," he said quietly.

"Because they want to see you have a family and settle down?"

He nodded. "I think they're afraid someone will come along and lure me from the town."

"Why would they think that?"

"Because this town isn't exactly a mecca. When a town's population decreases, so does the number of a doctor's patients."

"It sounds as if something needs to be done to shore up the town," she replied.

"Interesting revelation coming from the only person who's been fired from ninety percent of the businesses here." Ben walked to the door and covered her hand with his. "Sleep well," he said, but his eyes asked a silent question. One she had no trouble understanding.

"You were the one who told me there was no privacy in this town," she replied. "And I'd hate to think I'd tarnish your reputation even more."

"Something tells me that's one tarnished reputation I wouldn't mind having." He dropped a light kiss on her cheek and opened the door.

"Ben." Her soft voice halted him as he stepped onto the walkway leading to the clinic. "I would like nothing more than for you to stay, but I'm just not sure it's right for us."

He turned his head and smiled. "I know. But I'm glad to see I'm wearing you down."

It wasn't until Cori closed the door that she expelled the deep breath she'd been holding. She slumped back against the door and inhaled Ben's scent that lingered on her blouse.

"Oh, you're wearing me down all right, Ben. If you only knew how much."

BEN COULDN'T BELIEVE the number of summer colds that hit Farrington overnight. By day, his clinic was overflowing. By night, he was out on emergencies. Just the way he liked it. When he worked himself into a stupor, he had no difficulty in sleeping at night. He needed the sleep—but not the dreams about Cori. He rubbed his eyes. They felt as if sandpaper had been rubbed against them.

"Do you realize we haven't seen Cori in the past two days?" Ella commented, staring out the window that overlooked the cottage.

"Hm?" He wondered if he could sneak upstairs for a quick nap. Last night, he'd traveled out to the Hendersons'. Ida Henderson had a habit of overreacting any time her husband ate something he shouldn't. She visualized him having a heart attack when it was actually heartburn and never failed to call Ben. And Ben never failed to go out there. He always had the fear the one time he might convince Ida it was gas or heartburn, Richard could be suffering a heart attack.

"Wake up, Benjamin!" Ella gave him a little nudge. He looked up and scowled. "I asked if you had seen Cori lately."

He frowned as he thought about it. "Come to think of it, I haven't seen her since the night we had dinner at my mother's." He pushed himself out of his chair. "Do I have anyone waiting?"

She shook her head. "You're finished for the day."

"Okay, then will you close up while I go over and see how she's doing?" He shrugged off his lab coat. "At least we haven't heard of anyone else firing her."

"You just go over and make sure she's all right," she ordered. "I don't feel right about this."

Ben smothered a yawn. "All right, I'm going!"

He walked over to the cottage and knocked on the door.

"Cori? Cori, are you all right?" He felt uneasy when no one came to the door. "Cori!"

"Ben!" Ella stood in the rear doorway. "I made a few calls. No one's seen her."

Ben tried the door and found it locked. It took him a moment to dig in his pocket for his key ring. He was grateful he'd kept a spare key in case of emergency. As far as he was concerned, this was most definitely an emergency. He stepped inside and looked around. What he first noticed was the silence.

"Cori?" he called out.

He started to think she wasn't there when he heard a faint moan. Not wasting any time, he hurried into the bedroom.

Cori lay in bed with her knees drawn up.

"Cori." Ben ran around to the other side of the bed and dropped onto one knee.

"Go 'way," she moaned between cracked lips. She closed her eyes as if not looking at him would make him go away.

"Are you in pain?" He wanted to check her, but he had a pretty good idea she wasn't going to let him near her just now.

A tear trickled down her cheek. "Look at me. I'm already a bad mother. I can't keep anything down," she whispered. "I can't even drink water without it coming back up."

"Why didn't you call me and tell me you were experiencing such bad nausea?" he chided gently. He reached out, brushing a lock of hair from her forehead.

"Because just thinking about throwing up made me throw up." She seemed to curl up in an even tighter ball against the pain in her abdomen. "I thought pregnancy only meant morning sickness. I never heard of all-day sickness."

"Sometimes it means morning, afternoon and evening sickness." He laid the backs of his fingers against her cheek, finding the skin warm and dry to the touch. "I'm going back to the clinic and get you something for the nausea."

"But they say you're not supposed to take drugs," she whimpered. Another tear trailed after the first.

"I'm your doctor and what I'm going to give you won't hurt you," he assured her. "You won't feel like running any marathons when it kicks in, but your stomach won't feel as if it's waging war against you, either." He started to stand, then hesitated. The last thing he wanted to do was leave her alone, even for a moment. He settled for walking around to the other side of the bed and picking up the phone. Luckily, Ella was still at the clinic. He quickly relayed what he needed. After hanging up the phone, he went into the bathroom and wet a washcloth. As he wiped her face, Cori managed a heartfelt thank-you.

"The poor baby," Ella commiserated as she bustled in within three minutes. She carried a drug bottle and syringe. "She had been doing so well, I guess we didn't think she could still end up with nausea."

Ben quickly filled the hypodermic.

Cori stared at him through pain-filled eyes. "I hate shots."

"Even ones that will make you feel better?" he asked lightly, tapping the syringe to make sure there were no air bubbles.

Ella stepped around Ben and lifted Cori's bed covers. "Don't worry, darlin'. You won't even see this one."

Cori moaned as she realized Ella was pulling down her panties. "Not there," she muttered. "Oh, please, another part of my body he's seeing. Is there nothing sacred?" She was so lost in her misery she didn't notice the faint prick of the needle.

"If people heard her now they'd think you just might not be the father," Ella murmured as she adjusted the sheet and lightweight blanket covering Cori. "Now, dear, I'm making you some broth. You'll feel better after you've had something in your stomach."

"Oh, please don't torture me," Cori moaned. "All my stomach does is get even when something comes near it."

"It shouldn't now." Ben crouched down by the bed. "By now you should start to feel a difference."

Cori silently took stock and noticed the rock-and-rolling motion in her stomach had started to subside. She took a shallow breath. Surprisingly, it didn't seem to hurt as much this time.

Ben smiled as he noticed a hint of color come back into her cheeks. "The miracle of modern medicine."

Cori started to cautiously sit up. Ben rushed to help her, adjusting the pillows behind her back. And as he did, he noticed the enticing dip of her nightgown's neckline showing the tops of her breasts. For a moment, the last thing he felt like was a doctor. He took a deep breath to bring himself back into control.

"It's just chicken broth, so you shouldn't have any trouble with it." Ella entered the room, carrying a mug. "Now you drink every drop, but drink it slow since you haven't had much lately. After two days, you have to be severely dehydrated." She shot a keen gaze in Ben's direction as she handed Cori the mug. "I have a husband waiting for me, so I'll leave you in the doctor's care." With a knowing smile on her lips, she took her leave.

Cori huddled under the sheet while Ben sat in the chair by the bed.

"Feeling more human?" he asked, taking her wrist and pressing his thumb against her pulse point. He was gratified to feel her pulse beating at a more regular rate. As a test, he gently stroked the soft skin and noticed her respiration pick up.

"Yes, thank you." She slid her hand from his and curled her fingers around the mug. She blew on the steaming broth and sipped the hot liquid cautiously.

"I'll prescribe something for you, so you won't have to worry about this again," Ben told her.

She soon finished the broth. Ben took the mug from her and set it to one side.

"I'm more trouble than I'm worth," she said softly. "If I had any sense, I'd call my father and tell him he could do whatever he wanted with my life. Even if it meant working for Peyton Consultants." Her lower lip trembled. "Damn, I hate these spurts of hormones," she muttered, swiping at her tears with the back of her hand.

Ben dug inside his jeans pocket and pulled out a hand-kerchief. He sat on the edge of the bed and dabbed at her cheeks.

"Is that what you want? Your father to fly out here and pick you up?"

"No." She said the word so softly if he hadn't been looking at her lips he wouldn't have known she replied.

"You don't have to worry, Cori. I'll take care of you."

She winced. "I left my dad for a very good reason. He tried to run my life and take care of me."

This time Ben winced. "And I'm saying the very thing you don't want to hear."

Cori nodded.

He pulled her toward him and wrapped his arms around her. She rested her cheek against his chest.

"What do you want to do next?"

Cori placed a palm against his chest, content to feel the warmth of his skin. "If they would have let me, I could have done any of the jobs I had."

"Honey, you couldn't even hold your job at the convenience store."

"I didn't like George calling me Sweetcheeks. He's lucky I didn't smack him with a sexual harassment suit."

Ben's shoulders rose and fell with a deep sigh. "Okay, take tomorrow to rest and I'll see what I can come up with."

Cori nestled closer to him. "Only on one condition."

Ben couldn't help laughing. "Only you, after obviously throwing up anything you put in your stomach and as weak as a kitten, could think to set conditions on your next job."

"This is important," she said forcefully. "I am willing to do anything."

"But—" he inserted.

She tipped her head back so she could look up at his face. She hadn't noticed before how tired he looked. She wondered what he had been doing the past couple days to have him looking so weary.

"Except work at that feed store. I refuse to smell like a cow."

He smiled as he kissed the tip of her nose. "No problem. Martin's already warned me about the limits of friendship."

Chapter Nine

Farrington Grammar School

"Are you really Dr. Ben's girlfriend?" a tiny elf of a girl, named Melissa, asked Cori.

She debated what answer to give. She sensed telling a five-year-old she was in lust with a man wouldn't be a good idea. "Not exactly."

When Ben first approached her about working as an aide at the kindergarten summer program for working mothers, she thought it sounded like a wonderful idea. Until he explained it wouldn't be a paying job, but he figured it would keep her out of mischief until something else came along. She didn't appreciate the latter notion, but she did know she didn't want to be housebound any longer now that the nausea medication had her feeling like her old self.

Cori had assured him she could do this. In fact, standing out here on the playground helping shepherd the kids and organizing games with them proved to be a lot of fun.

She hadn't expected to discover that five-year-olds were a lot more advanced than when she had been at that age. All she had cared about was finger-painting and playing games. These little girls asked her if they could wear her lipstick and the boys told her she was sexy.

"Did you ever see it?" Melissa insisted.

Cori grimaced. She realized she hadn't been listening to the little girl's rambling conversation. "Did I see what, pumpkin?"

"The cartoon about the swan and the duck? When the mean ole buzzard took the swan's babies, the duck got mad and flew in the air to get him, and when he did he turned into an airplane." Her eyes widened with excitement as she related the story. "And he gave the buzzard a thing of dynamite so he'd blow up. And the mama swan was so happy she let the baby duck stay with her baby swans. It was really neat. I like cartoons with babies in them." Melissa looked up and tentatively reached out to touch Cori's abdomen with her fingertips. "My mom says you're going to have a baby."

"That's right." As Cori said the words, she realized how matter-of-fact she had become about it. Which was surprising for someone who didn't have any prospects in her future.

Melissa frowned. "But how can you have a baby if there's no daddy?"

Cori swung the little girl up in her arms. "I'll tell you what. Why don't you ask your mommy that? I bet she'll tell you all about it."

"Okay!"

"That's the way to wiggle your way out of a problem."

Cori turned around. "Denise! What are you doing here?"

"I came to town to do some shopping and Ella told me you were over here." Denise looked over the playground and the children running around. "You're a braver person than I am. There're days when I feel I can't handle my three."

"Ben thought it would be good practice for me. I never had any idea they had so much energy or could ask so many questions." Cori wiped the back of her hand against her forehead and looked around. "By the way, Ben is not the father, Denise," she murmured.

"I might believe you, but most people won't. He's shown an awful lot of interest in someone he's not involved with."

She shifted from one foot to the other. "He feels sorry for me."

Denise continued looking at Cori's profile. "I don't think so. Ben's a caring man about people, but he's never been this caring about one person."

"I'm a novelty."

"Who are you trying to convince? Me or yourself?"

Cori could feel her lower lip wobbling. "Hormones are hell."

"Wait a few months when they go completely out of control," Denise said. "Stan used to say that my pregnancies were harder on him than on me since he was never sure what creature he was going to come home to."

"Oh, gee, I can't wait."

The other woman smiled at Cori's sarcasm. "Don't worry, the end result is worth it." She glanced across the playground and winced at a glare directed her way. "I can't believe Mrs. Timmerman is still teaching. I had her when I was in kindergarten and the boys have had her. She scared the hell out of me. Stan said she was all bark and no bite, but I noticed he dragged his heels when it came time for parent-teacher conferences."

"She is intimidating," Cori admitted. "The first thing she told me when I walked in was that her word was law here and she didn't care if Benjamin did recommend me. If she felt I didn't work well with the children, I'd be out of here."

Denise chuckled. "She always was tactful. I better get out of here before she comes up with a suitable punishment. Come on out to the farm Saturday afternoon. We'll barbecue." She suddenly grinned. "Bring Ben with you."

"Miss Peyton!" The teacher's voice rang out with the same authority. "You are here to help with the children, not to socialize."

"I'm out of here," Denise muttered, patting Cori's shoulder before she almost ran for the front gate.

"Coward," Cori called after her. She turned around, threw back her shoulders, pasted a bright smile on her lips and headed for the autocratic teacher, murmuring under her breath, "Coming, you dictator, you."

WHEN BEN GLANCED out the window in one of the examination rooms he noticed a chaise longue angled outside the cottage's front door and a slim body resting on it. A body wearing white shorts and an orange tank top. Oversize dark glasses covered most of the woman's face, obscuring her identity.

"But I'd know those legs anywhere," he muttered.

"Doctor, I suggest you worry more about Mrs. Wheeler's arthritis than the pair of legs out there," Ella murmured as she passed by him.

"This medicine you gave me isn't working!" the elderly woman shouted at Ben.

"It isn't working, Mrs. Wheeler, because you haven't been taking it on a regular basis," he reminded her. "You can't just take it whenever you think about it."

"Don't know why not." The woman thumped the carpet with her cane. She slowly rose to her feet.

"I'll need to see you next week," Ben called after her retreating figure.

"I'll see if I have any time to spare for you. Can't come in here whenever you want me to, you know."

"Go on and ogle your woman." Ella pushed him toward the back door. "Just don't do anything that could be seen by anyone who would tell your mother."

"Terrific. I live in a town filled with clones of my mother." He picked up his step as he walked toward Cori. As he got closer, he heard the throbbing beat of a sixties rock group coming from a small radio sitting next to a bottle of nail polish. A large glass of ice tea was set on the ground near the chair within easy reach. He had to smile at the picture of total relaxation she portrayed.

"How're you doing?" he asked, nudging her feet to one side as he sat down on the end of the longue.

"You are a horrible man to put me through such a sadistic time." She didn't bother taking off her sunglasses.

Ben picked up her glass and sipped. "I thought I told you no caffeine."

"I don't want to hear any lectures. If you put in the morning I just did, you'd insist on having it infused directly into your veins."

He concentrated on the rosy coral coloring her toenails. He noticed only two of her fingernails had been painted, as if she couldn't go on.

"I thought you'd have fun working with the kids."

"Oh, the kids were great." She took her glass out of his hand. "Get your own, Dr. Cooper. Admittedly, they asked questions I couldn't answer and expected me to know the plot of every cartoon made, but they weren't the ones who turned me into a mass of jelly."

"Mrs. Timmerman."

"You got it, Doc. That dragon lady is downright scary." She sucked on a piece of ice. "The kids are in awe of her, but adults are afraid she's going to put a spell on them, so they stay away. I'm sure she put one on me. I didn't think anything could ever scare me until I met up with her."

"A lot of us were convinced she was a wicked witch who would never die." He picked up one of her bare feet and began massaging her instep. Her skin was warm to the touch and he enjoyed the silky sensation between his palms. Along with the soft groans she emitted.

"Don't stop," she ordered. "That woman kept me running all over the playground. Do you know how hard a playground surface is? And how hot it was out there?"

He looked at her skin bared by the tank top. Her upper chest and shoulders glistened with moisture from the afternoon heat, but what had his temperature rising was seeing her breasts push against the soft cotton of her top. There was no denying her breasts had already become fuller. A cold shower for two suddenly popped into his mind.

"Why are you smiling like that?" Cori asked.

He figured he might as well be honest. "I was thinking about the two of us cooling off in the shower. Wanna see if it would work?" He was pleased to see a pink color travel up her throat.

She took her time answering by slipping her sunglasses up to the top of her head. "Somehow, I think the opposite would happen."

His eyes darkened with desire as he gazed at her. "Sounds interesting."

She smiled a slow, lazy smile. "I do declare, doctuh," she purred in a husky drawl that would have done a Southern belle proud. "Are you tryin' to compromise me?"

His grip slowly slid upward until his fingers circled her calf. "Yes, ma'am."

"Because you have a fascination with blue-eyed blondes?"

"There's only one blue-eyed blonde I'm fascinated with."

She tipped her head to one side. "Or maybe because you figure it's something I might be good at."

His lips curved. "We can always practice until we both get it right."

Cori bent upward from the waist and looped her arms around his neck. "Then, Ben, let's give the townspeople something to talk about." The tip of her tongue appeared between her parted lips and slid across his lower lip as her mouth brushed against his.

Ben's hands rested on her hips. He deliberately kept a slight distance so Cori would have to take the initiative. He didn't doubt she would take advantage of the situation. And she didn't let him down.

Cori discovered acting as the aggressor was fun. She nibbled his lips, whispered saucy suggestions in his ear and pressed her breasts against his chest. All she had to do was lay back and draw him down with her. It would be so easy. She couldn't say she didn't know Ben now after all the time they had spent together.

"If we went inside right now," she breathed the words in his ear as she traced the curve with the tip of her tongue, "how long do you think it would take for the entire town to know what we were doing in there?"

"Including outlying areas?" He sounded as if it was difficult for him to breathe.

"Uh-huh." She grazed her teeth along the soft skin behind his ear.

"Five minutes tops, since Ella's looking out my office window."

Cori didn't draw back at the news. She took her time unlooping her arms from around his neck and scooted back along the chaise. She leaned over and picked up a white hat reminiscent of a riverboat gambler's and settled it on top of her head.

"Then I guess I better go inside before we do something we shouldn't." She smiled at him to soften the blow.

"You're teasing me again." He also smiled.

"No, I'm very serious this time." She stood and quickly gathered up her things. "If you're feeling brave, come over tonight for dinner. I'll even cook."

He picked up her radio and handed it to her. "When there's a good doctor in town, one doesn't have to worry about food poisoning. What time?"

She thought for a moment. "How about when you finish up?"

"I'll be over a little after six."

Ben whistled as he walked back to the clinic.

"Should we have a talk about the birds and the bees?" Ella asked as Ben went into his office and changed lab coats. While he liked the idea of Cori's perfume on the cotton jacket, he wasn't sure his patients would understand. Or, if they did, they would be only too happy to comment on it in great detail.

"Should we have a talk about that night you went out with your buddies for a supposed bridge game?" Ben inquired.

The nurse glared at him. "That's blackmail."

"I know."

"You just remember that pregnancy enhances a woman's emotions. She shouldn't be toyed with."

In the process of shrugging on another lab coat, Ben looked over his shoulder. "Ella, the last thing I want to do with Cori Peyton is toy with her," he said seriously.

"Oh, my God," she said, shocked. "You're falling for that girl!"

"Damn straight."

Ella shook her head. "Oh, Ben."

"Why so unhappy about it? Everyone else seems to want to see a romance between us."

"Only because they think you're the father and hope you'll do right by her. I just don't want to see you heartbroken when she goes back to California."

Ben drew her to him for a hug. "Who knows. Maybe she'll decide to stay for good."

"I CAN DO THIS, I know I can," Cori muttered, settling on an easy casserole for dinner. At least, it looked easy in the cookbook she found in one of the cabinets. She didn't think she could ruin anything so simple. She hoped.

As she worked in the kitchen, she thought back to her and Ben on the chaise longue and she could feel her entire body tingle with anticipation. After all, tonight was the night she and Ben were going to become lovers. And after the pleasure of his earlier kisses, she had an idea that making love with him was going to be an experience she would never forget.

Humming along with Mick Jagger on the radio, she danced around the kitchen as she worked.

"Cori! Cori!" Ella stopped in the kitchen doorway. Her face was white as if she'd experienced a shock. "I'm picking up the spare blankets and sheets kept in the linen closet."

"What's wrong?" Cori followed her into the bedroom where the older woman opened a cupboard and pulled out the linens.

"There was a bad accident on the highway," she said quickly. "A bus hit a truck, which hit another truck and then plowed into several cars." She hauled the blankets into her arms. "Ben said for you to stay here. But I'd appreciate if you'd give Lucia a call. She has nursing skills and we could use her."

"Let me help."

She shook her head. "Honey, this is really bad. You just stay here."

Cori didn't listen. She grabbed half the linens, stopped long enough to turn off the oven and hurried out of the cottage. When she entered the clinic, she found Ben talking into the phone as he loaded up what looked like an overlarge tackle box.

"Look, we don't know what we have out here yet," he snapped. "But from what the sheriff said we're going to need a couple of choppers for the major cases. They can land in the school yard. The clinic's too damn small to accommodate the number of injured, so we're using the school gym. Just get them out here!" He slammed the phone down. Finally, he noticed Cori was there, and he looked at her with unfocused eyes. "What are you doing here?"

"Helping Ella bring the extra linens over." She ignored his rude question as she set them down on the table. "Let me help."

"No." He piled medication bottles, bandages, gauze pads and syringes in the box.

"I might not know about medical things, but there're other things I can do," she insisted. "Even if it's bandaging people. If it's my stomach you're worried about, don't.

I watched a *Friday the Thirteenth* marathon last night on TV and didn't feel sick once." She hoped to defuse the tension, but it didn't work.

Ben took a deep breath. He closed the box and secured the latch.

"This isn't a game, Cori," he said quietly. "The estimate is at least fifty people injured. Some of them could be dying and I'm the only doctor these people have to count on. We have two people with nursing skills and two emergency medical technicians who are out there supervising the transportation of the victims. Time is going to be of the essence tonight and I don't have time to baby-sit you to make sure you don't screw up."

She blamed her hormones for the tears springing to her eyes.

"That's not fair, Ben. Let me help."

The expression in his eyes was chilling. "If you feel sick, you get out." He picked up the box and carried it out of the room.

Cori didn't waste any time in picking up the linens and running after him. She tossed them in the back of the truck and jumped in the passenger seat. She rightly feared if she hesitated Ben would drive off without her. Ella climbed in next to her.

When they reached the school, she saw trucks and vans parked near the gym doors, which were propped open. Men, carrying stretchers, hurried inside.

Cori's first impression was noise—a lot of it—crying, voices echoing in the tall building and organized chaos.

"Doc! Over here!" A man wearing a dark blue shirt with a fireman's patch on one sleeve gestured to one end.

Ben turned to Ella. "Set up a triage," he ordered. He barely spared a glance at Cori. "And find something for her to do." He moved off quickly.

Ella looked around. "Gather up the children," she suggested. "They're going to be frightened. If I know Lorraine, she brought a pile of books. Use one of the classrooms to keep them occupied."

"There're so many people hurt," Cori murmured. Her shocked system couldn't take it all in as she looked over the large room. Nothing she had seen on television had prepared her for this.

"And more to come, I'm afraid." Ella patted her shoulder as she moved off.

As Cori circled the area, she found children afraid and crying. She picked them up, dried tears and tried to allay their fears. She found the stack of books the bookstore owner had brought and, later on, a large urn filled with hot chocolate.

"All because of a drunk driver," she overheard one of the men say with disgust to a friend as they walked past her.

She heard the steady *whop-whop* of the helicopter blades as it landed and later took off, along with high-pitched wails of ambulance sirens that arrived to pick up the injured. Time had no meaning as she read stories, comforted the children and even braided a little girl's hair in a fancy French braid to get her mind off her fears. Several more begged for fancy braids, too, and she accommodated each of them. She did anything to make the hours as normal as possible for them. And all the while, she heard faint voices crying out and sometimes she could hear the low pitch of Ben's voice as he treated a patient or gave out orders.

"I want my mommy," one little girl whimpered, climbing into Cori's lap. Tears streamed down her cheeks as she clung to Cori.

"I know, sweetie, but the doctor is helping your mommy feel better," she soothed.

She had no idea what time it was when an unfamiliar woman stepped in, claiming that she was now going to look after the children and that Cori was relieved.

"I'm going to help them work through the shock," she explained.

Cori looked at the kids, most of them now asleep. "I'd say they're doing pretty good if they can sleep."

"Why don't you go on home now," the woman dismissed her.

When Cori stepped inside the gym, she found it not as crowded. Ben was hunched over a cot at the other end of the building. She started toward him, but Lucia intercepted her.

"This is not a good time, my dear," she told Cori. "It's been a very long night for all of us and this is something you're not used to, especially in your condition. Why don't you go on home and rest? We've been able to transport the more seriously hurt and release the lucky ones."

Cori started to protest, but something in Lucia's face stopped her. She managed a brief smile and headed for the door.

"I guess no one remembers home for me is L.A.," she murmured, walking with leaden steps away from the school.

She didn't have to worry about her safety being out alone. Not here. But as Cori got closer to the cottage, the more she felt as if she were unraveling inside. She picked up her pace and was soon almost running toward the clinic and around to the small house in the back.

By the time she stepped inside the living room, she was shaking like a leaf in a strong windstorm.

"IF WE HAD a hospital closer, we wouldn't have had to worry about losing some of those people," Ben said through gritted teeth. He dropped onto a bench and ran his hand over his face as weariness set in. "I haven't felt this tired since I was interning. If it hadn't been for Dr. Willoughby coming out to help, I don't know what we would have done." Lucia had contacted the retired doctor who'd been only too willing to help. Ben had welcomed him with open arms.

"We would have coped as we had before," Lucia told him. She pressed a coffee cup in his hand.

He gulped down the liquid. "What's left?"

"Nothing. The Stanleys took that last family to their place." Ella dropped onto the bench next to Ben and closed her eyes. "I do hope this counted as overtime."

He smiled at her wry tone. "In your dreams."

"Bennie, everyone is gone and you must go home and rest." Lucia got to her feet and patted his shoulder. She stooped down and kissed him on the cheek.

"Yeah." He shook his shoulders to rouse himself and looked around, but didn't see what he was looking for. "Does anyone know where Cori is?"

"I sent her home hours ago. Someone came in to be with the children and I told her she would be better off home," Lucia told him.

Ben felt a faint tingle of fear crawl up his spine. "Was she all right?"

"Tired, but that is natural. I'm sure she went home to bed."

Why didn't he feel consoled by her words?

He pushed himself to his feet. "I think I'll check on her before I turn in."

"After the night you've had, you'd be better off getting sleep. I'm sure Cori's fine." Ella smothered a yawn.

Ben held out his hands and helped her up. "I hope so. Don't worry about coming in tomorrow, Ella. I can handle the office."

"Oh, I'll be in," she informed him. "Do you think I want you to mess up my files?"

Ben drove Ella back to the clinic and watched her drive off. He looked down the street that was known as Farrington's business district. Now, store and office lights were extinguished and all was quiet. After the absolute chaos of the emergency Ben couldn't comprehend the silence. He felt jumpy, as adrenaline still pumped wildly through his veins.

He thought about going for a long run. That was what he used to do to settle himself down. But first, he wanted to make sure Cori was all right.

When he approached the cottage he could see a light on in the kitchen and stepped around to the rear door.

"Cori?" he called out as he stuck his head in. "Cori?" Uneasy by the silence greeting him, he stepped inside. He noticed a pan covered with what looked like scorched milk was in the sink and heard the sound of water running in another part of the house. He headed for the bathroom and found the door ajar. Over the sound of the running shower he easily heard heartrending sobs.

He muttered an expletive and hurried inside. In the steam, he could see a shadowy figure behind the frosted glass. He pulled open the door and saw what he knew he'd feared seeing after hearing she had been dismissed. Not cruelly; he knew his mother better. But he should have known Cori would have gone through her own trauma out there and had no idea how to handle it. She huddled in a tight ball under the steaming water, crying as if her world had ended.

"Oh, baby," he murmured, grabbing a towel and reaching for her. He quickly wrapped the towel around her and turned off the water before gently pulling her out of the shower cubicle.

"I can't stop crying!" she sobbed, burying her face against the curve of his neck. She curled her arms around him and nestled in his arms as naturally as if she had done it for years. "I tried. I really did. I even tried to make myself hot chocolate in hopes that would help, but I cried so much while I warmed the milk, I burned it."

"Ssh, it's okay," he soothed, carrying her into the bedroom. He dried her off as best he could, then grabbed the quilt and wrapped it around her.

"All those children were so afraid because I couldn't tell them their parents were all right. All their crying and the pain as they feared the worst," she babbled, starting to shake uncontrollably. "It's still in my head. I can't get rid of the sounds!"

Recognizing her shocked emotions for what they were, he settled for rocking her and murmuring soft words in her ear until she started to calm down. He forgot he was tired. Forgot overworked muscles and eyes burning from weariness. All he knew was the woman in his arms had experienced something she hadn't been accustomed to.

Cori looked up at him with tear-drenched eyes. "I didn't let the children know I was scared," she told him with a note of desperation in her voice as if afraid he might not believe her. "I read to them and played games and let them talk. But I can't get all those sounds out of my head! They keep coming and coming."

"It's normal, Cori," he assured her. "I should have made you stay here."

"No!" she clutched his shirtfront. "I'm glad I went because I saw what you did. Saw why you need a hospital here."

Ben circled his fingers around her wrist to check her pulse and found it racing.

"How about I fix you some warm milk?" He started to get up, but her tight grip on his shirt refused to release him.

Panic flared in her eyes. "Don't leave me, Ben!"

"Okay, I won't leave you." He adjusted his hold on her as he sat back against the headboard, still cradling her in his lap. He picked up the towel and began drying her hair, rubbing the strands gently between the nubby fabric.

Then the quilt slipped just enough to reveal the tops of her breasts. The golden color turned to pale ivory as he looked farther down, noting the delicate curves and lines. He wanted to trace them all. He felt his body tighten with desire as he felt her lips pressed against his throat.

"Make me forget, Ben," she whispered, shifting her body until she faced him. She tossed the quilt off her shoulders and half sat up in his lap.

"No matter what happens between us tonight, you won't ever forget," he told her. "It will always haunt you."

"Then let me forget for tonight." She pulled his shirt free and took it off him with a sense of desperation in her movements. She straddled his hips, her fingers feverishly working on unfastening the metal button at his waistband. When she looked up at him, her eyes were large and dark. The shock had now been replaced by arousal.

He grasped her arms, keeping her from touching him again.

"We're not going to forget anything that happened tonight," he said in a harsh voice. "If anything, tonight we're going to create something new. Tonight, we're going to create a lot of memories that will be all ours."

Chapter Ten

Cori's Bedroom

The first thing Ben did was reach out to turn off the over-head light. The room was left bathed in a warm golden glow of one muted lamp.

Not taking his eyes off Cori, he easily unfastened his jeans and pushed them down his hips, kicking them off the bed. When he started to sit up to remove his shirt, she stopped him by placing her palm against his chest. He lay back and allowed her to roll the soft fabric up his chest. He expected her to pull it over his head and was surprised when she paused for a moment just as the fabric covered his neck and left his arms imprisoned by the sleeves. She pulled upward a little more until the shirt covered his face.

Cori did what seemed to come natural where this man was concerned. All she knew was that she had to touch him, assure herself that they were both still alive. She dipped her head and began nuzzling his nipple. It hardened immediately, but she only turned her attention to the other nipple, curling her tongue around the tip.

Ben groaned. He tried to pull at his makeshift mask, but had no way of getting it off since his arms were still confined.

"Cori," he muttered. "Take it the rest of the way off."

"Not yet."

He felt her movements, but quickly realized it only meant she had tossed the bath towel to one side. She moved to straddle his hips, her feminine warmth cradling his arousal with only the soft cotton of his briefs between them. He ached to have that remaining piece of clothing gone. He realized that the evening's events had left her feeling out of control and this was her way of regaining it.

"I need you," she murmured, scraping her nails lightly over his midriff.

Ben hissed a sharp curse when her nails danced around his erection. Since he couldn't see, he could only feel Cori's fingers trail lightly across his upper thighs and her body shift against his. He felt as if flames of fire traveled up his body with every stroke of her fingertips.

Her leisurely movements felt as if she thought she had all the time in the world. And it was killing him. But he wouldn't have begged her to stop if his life depended on it. He wanted her to keep that control she so desperately needed.

"I want to feel alive again." A sob sounded trapped in her throat.

"You are alive," he told her, then gasped when he felt her teeth gently pull on his nipple.

Even more of a shock to his system was the sensation of hot tears splashing against his skin. "Cori?"

"I want to know there is more to it," she whispered in his ear as her fingers danced lightly along his rib cage and lower.

Her breath feathered across the path her hands had begun.

Until that moment, Ben hadn't known a person's breath could literally shut down. But Cori's comment and caresses had knocked his breath out of his body. He could tell by the faint uncertainty in her gestures that she wasn't used to being the aggressor. Which made what was happening between them all the more sweeter.

Except as Cori's caresses grew even more daring, so did Ben's desire to plunge deeply into her and never stop. He wanted to show her what they could share together. Show her there was much more than she ever had with that other idiot. Once he started, he knew he wouldn't ever be able to let her out of his bed.

Unable to take any more, he struggled to release himself from his shirt. He was ready to tear the fabric into pieces by the time he was free. Within seconds, the shirt sailed across the room and he was able to look at Cori. She took his breath away.

Faint tan lines left her breasts and belly a warm ivory shade while the rest of her was a deep gold, thanks to her afternoon sunbathing sessions. Her nipples had begun to darken and there was a roundness to her tummy. There was no doubt she would only grow more beautiful during her pregnancy. The only thing that bothered him were the tear tracks across her cheeks. He vowed to make sure she never had reason to cry again. He reached out for her, and when she melted in his arms he twisted so that she lay back against the covers.

Ben angled his body over hers and captured her mouth, kissing her with a hunger that had been building up since that first day. Their mouths fused with an urgency that electrified the air. He framed her face with his hands and studied her features—not as her doctor but as the man who was falling for her. Falling hard. For a man who had long fought commitment, he discovered he had no desire to start running. Not if it meant having this delectable woman for all time.

He caressed her breasts, finding them silky and full against his palms, the nipples peaking as he rubbed them gently with his thumbs. But it was her moist and inviting mouth that tempted him the most. He couldn't stop tasting her. Her mouth opened under his, her tongue curling around his in silent invitation as their bodies strained to get even closer.

With her help, he slid off his briefs and pushed them off the bed along with the quilt. Pillows were shoved to one side as they stroked and touched each other with increasing intensity.

Cori moaned as Ben's mouth covered her nipple, coaxing it to life. He drew it deep into his mouth, wrapping his tongue around the nub. At the same time, his fingers delved deep within her. He muttered with satisfaction at finding her moist and pulsing around him.

"So hot," he murmured, finding the tiny nub with his thumb and rubbing it gently. "We're going to be very good together, Cori. We are going to have the ultimate experience here because we're going to be together all the way. You'll never feel alone again."

The skepticism she tried to hide from him told him she wasn't used to a man wanting her to have an equal amount of pleasure. How could a man not see how naturally responsive she was? He couldn't wait to watch her explode in his arms.

He made love to her mouth as his fingers also made love to her, and when she started to quiver under his touch, he moved over her and thrust deeply. The moment he buried himself inside, he felt the tiny explosions around him, her tight grip on his shoulders and the beautiful sound of her moans against his mouth.

Ben wanted to rear back and shout his feelings for Cori. He wanted the world to know she was absolutely perfect, that she was meant solely for him. They moved together as one, Cori's face buried against his shoulder as he strained to bring her to that peak again. To return to that heaven.

Cori had no time to think. All she could do was feel as one sensation after another built up inside her until she thought she couldn't handle any more. She tried to close her eyes as if she could block some of it out that way, but it only magnified the heat racing through her veins. She opened them again and found him looking down at her with an energy that should have frightened her if she hadn't felt that same intensity.

"Ben," she whispered just as bright lights exploded around her.

Cori felt as if all her bones had turned to liquid. She lay in Ben's arms, her head resting on his chest as the dim light bathed them both. She was so relaxed she seriously thought about going to sleep for the next week. She felt Ben reach under them, pull the sheet out and then cover them up. Her eyes were just closing as she watched his hand reach out and snap off the lamp. By the time the room darkened, she was sound asleep.

CORI FOUND HERSELF ALONE in bed when she woke up. Before she had a chance to feel lonely she saw a glass of orange juice on the nightstand and a note propped up against the glass.

Went out for a run to regain my energy level. Drink your juice. I'll be back soon to check your pulse.

                                        Dr. Ben

She laughed softly and immediately reached for the glass. Once up, she noticed Ben's T-shirt still lying on the floor. She pulled a pair of panties out of the dresser and tugged his shirt on, relishing the security it afforded her.

As she went through her routine in the bathroom, she couldn't help but think of last night. The sights and sounds of the accident—and how Ben's tender lovemaking somehow made them all bearable, made her feel so safe. Just the memory brought a warm smile to her lips.

When she made her way into the kitchen, Ben stood just inside the doorway. His T-shirt and shorts were soaked with sweat and tiny rivulets trailed down his face.

"I'd ask if you had a good run, but it looks as if I don't have to." She suddenly felt an attack of shyness as she realized she wasn't all that conversant in morning-after etiquette.

Luckily, that didn't deter Ben. He walked over until his chest touched hers. He kept walking, forcing her to back up until her hips bumped against the small table.

"Good morning," he said with a faint smile on his lips. "How do you feel?"

"Hi." She managed a faint answering smile. "I'm fine. Thanks to you."

Ben grasped her by the waist and hoisted her onto the table. He nudged his way between her knees, forcing them apart.

"Would you like to try that again?"

Cori's eyes widened. "But we—"

"But we what?" He nuzzled the soft area on her throat where her pulse pounded madly.

She giggled as his morning beard rasped against her skin. "Ben, we're in the kitchen!"

He looked up and around. "Yeah, we are. So?"

"And I'm on the table!"

"Are you uncomfortable?" he asked, now nibbling on her ear.

She wrapped her arms around him and resisted the urge to wrap her legs around his. "No."

"Then what's the problem?" he teased, running his hands up under her shirt. "Hm, isn't that my shirt?"

Cori found it difficult to speak. "Yes."

"Maybe I'll want it back." He pulled it upward and let out a wolf whistle when he bared her breasts.

"Ben!" she shrieked, pulling the shirt back down and trapping his hands at the same time. "What if someone comes by?"

"Then they'd definitely believe we've been getting it on since you came to town, wouldn't they?" He settled for running his hands across her midriff and down over the slight rounding of her tummy. He kept his hands cupped over it.

Cori couldn't help it. She found a playful Ben irresistible. "You are so bad."

His wolfish grin sent shivers along her spine. "And you love it."

That grin was her undoing. She pulled off his shirt, grimacing at the damp feel. "You're not exactly morning fresh, you know."

"I thought sweaty guys were a turn on."

"Not for everyone."

Ben pulled back slightly. "Maybe I should consider a shower." He stopped when he saw that siren's look in her eyes.

"Maybe I should make sure that you get the job done right. After all, it must be difficult to reach your back."

The water was soon running and the click of the shower door sounded just as Ben, not so innocently, commented, "Cori, speaking as a doctor, I can tell you that what you're washing isn't my back."

BEN WAS WHISTLING as he let himself in the clinic. He almost ran upstairs to change his clothing before Ella arrived. The last thing he needed was an interrogation from his eagle-eyed nurse about the previous night's activities. He was grateful his beeper hadn't gone off. Luckily, the only patients who'd remained in town were those who only suffered minor injuries. Everyone else had been considerate enough to remain healthy overnight.

"Benjamin, are you up there?" Ella's voice traveled up the stairs.

He quickly shrugged on a shirt and began buttoning it up as he trotted down the stairs.

"Where else would I be?" He tucked his shirt in his jeans and fastened his belt. "I thought I told you not to worry about coming in this morning."

"And I told you I wouldn't have you fouling up my filing system." She crossed her arms in front of her and stared at him.

Ben stared back. "What's wrong?"

"You didn't get any rest last night, did you?" She shook her head, clucking her tongue. "Charlotte said she saw you out running this morning. After the night you put in, you would have been better off sleeping than getting all that exercise."

"Surprisingly enough, exercise can be very restful." He walked on ahead of her to his office.

"All that running can't be good for a body," she said more to herself than to him as she followed.

"Actually, it's very good for a body."

"Are you sure we're talking about the same thing?"

Ben grinned since he knew she couldn't see his face. "I'm sure we are."

He shrugged on a lab coat while Ella brought in the appointment log. As part of their routine since that first day, they went over the day's appointments first thing in the morning while Ella fixed coffee and brought out pastries.

"My daily run also lets me eat one of these without guilt," Ben told her as he chose a raspberry danish.

"And I suppose you checked on Cori last night, too." She set a filled coffee cup in front of him.

"I wanted to make sure she was all right," he said carefully. He remembered Ella's three grown sons used to call her the "all-knowing one." He knew he'd better tread lightly before she ferreted out the truth.

"And was she?" Ella took the chair across from him. She sat back with her mug in one hand and a lemon danish in the other.

"The night's events had naturally unnerved her." He ate with more diligence than usual. "Cori had never seen anything like that. Unfortunately, most of the people in this town have. Otherwise, she was just fine."

Ella sighed and shook her head as she recalled another bad highway accident that had happened the previous winter.

"If there's one thing you can say about this town, it's that we've always come together in times of need," she said softly.

"True." He sipped his coffee. He leaned back in his chair and propped his feet on top of his desk. "Anything major today?"

"Just the usual." Ella read from the appointment log and made comments on each name punctuated by Ben's observations.

"There will also be a few from last night in today," she said. Then the phone rang and she picked it up. "Good morning, Dr. Cooper's office." Exasperation crossed her face. "Marge, you know we're not open yet. Yes, I answered. Fool me. Just a minute." She put the call on hold and turned to Ben. "I'll take it out front." As she opened the door, she turned back. "By the way, you might want to make sure that collar stays straight. Otherwise, people are going to see that hickey on your neck."

Ben guiltily slapped his hand against his neck.

"Dammit, Ella!" he growled as the chuckling nurse closed the door after her.

Ben had to laugh in spite of himself. "No wonder her boys walked the straight and narrow. They wanted to live."

"I HAVE TO GIVE YOU CREDIT. You never stop," Cori commented from her perch on top of the examination table where she sat kicking her heels against the side. "And you're much cuter than Marcus Welby."

"Thanks, I guess. Now stop with the compliments and read off those numbers so we can get this over with." He was taking inventory of each supply cabinet and Cori had volunteered to help.

She looked down at the sheet of paper in her lap. "Gauze bandages, one inch wide," she began.

For the first time, Ben had difficulty in concentrating. He knew it had to do with Cori looking so delectable in her short denim skirt.

Once they finished he walked over to her with the intention of helping her off the table. She had already put the inventory sheets to one side and gazed at him with devils sparkling in her eyes. That should have been his first warning.

"Now," she purred, grabbing hold of his lab coat lapels and pulling the coat back. "Let's talk about giving you that much needed physical."

Ben's grin threatened to split his face. "Doctor, I'm in your capable hands."

Chapter Eleven

The Williams Farm

"Has it been any easier working with Mrs. Timmerman?" Denise asked as she and Cori puttered in the kitchen. Denise had put Cori to work making a green salad while she hand-cut French fries. Ben and Stan were out back, each holding a can of beer as they discoursed on the best way to fire up the barbecue.

"I think she's finally believing that I just might have a brain. She actually complimented me. Said with a lot of hard work I might actually make something of myself," she said wryly. "Then I found out she recommended I be hired on for the fall semester as a paid aide. I was floored. They even said there was no problem about the baby coming in November."

"That's wonderful!" Denise gave her a one-armed hug. "Believe me, from her that's high praise. Nobody can fault her. She's a wonderful teacher and the kids really do love her."

"I never thought of myself working with children, but considering everything, it might be a good idea."

Denise glanced out the window. "We're in luck. It looks as if the men were able to get the fire going without blowing up anything."

Cori's gaze fluttered toward the window with a trace of alarm written across her face. "I didn't think barbecues were dangerous."

"It is if Stan's starting it up." She chuckled. "The last time he started up the barbecue, he used too much starter. The flames flared high enough to singe his eyebrows and burn the front of his hair. Ben told him he better have medical help standing by from then on."

"At least I only burn food." Cori observed her efforts with a critical eye. "How does that look?"

"That's fine. A lot prettier than when I make a salad." Denise looked at Cori with puzzlement. "You've never really cooked before, have you?"

"Not at all," she cheerfully admitted. "My father has a cook who looks and acts like a prison warden, but cooks like a dream. I once went down to fix myself some peanut butter and crackers and she acted as if I was going to turn the entire kitchen upside down and even threatened to quit. I never went down there again."

"I'd call you a poor thing, but it just doesn't fit," Denise said without malice.

Cori dried her hands on a dish towel and carefully folded it over the towel rack. "Poor little rich girl, that's me. A father who was always too busy making money to think about me. There were never vacations. Only business trips. Then I suddenly turned into an adult and he realized he couldn't pack me off with a nanny and tutor anymore.

"Now I realize there was no way I could have renovated that house and turned it into a bed and breakfast with any success because I didn't have any experience in that area, so I would have been a failure once more. I'm only hoping I won't blow it with junior here." She patted her round tummy, which was skillfully hidden by the empire waistline of her white eyelet dress.

"People see the expensive clothes and the self-assured way you handle yourself and forget that you've been thrown into entirely new territory. And not just the baby," Denise said. "Have you ever thought about calling your father?"

"Every day," she said honestly. "But there're things I need to work out in my mind first. Luckily, the school has decided to pay me a small wage and I have a place to stay."

"Could the one thing you need to work out have something to do with Ben?"

Cori wrinkled her nose. "You could tell, huh?"

Denise burst into laughter. "Of course I could! The man looks at you as if he wants to drag you off somewhere."

"I'm falling for him," she admitted, feeling the need to confide in someone. "And this isn't like any other time for me. This time I feel great—but I also feel horrible."

"Yeah, I always thought falling in love was like having the flu." Denise walked over and hugged her. "I wouldn't worry. I'm sure everything will come out fine. Ben wouldn't have it any other way."

"Hey, ladies, aren't you gonna join us out here?"

"We're on our way," Denise called out. From the refrigerator she pulled out two bottles of flavored seltzer and handed one to Cori. "I guess we better get out there and make sure they keep the fire in the barbecue pit."

Cori followed Denise outside. With the hot sun beating down, she was glad for the visor shadowing her face. As they reached the men, she found herself unable to keep her eyes off Ben.

Even dressed in cutoffs, T-shirt and battered running shoes, he looked good. He watched her every step of the way with a look that she recalled seeing the night before. She began to wish they were alone again. Ben had been called out in the middle of the night because Mr. Bowman overindulged in his favorite meal of corn beef and cabbage and was suffering from a massive case of heartburn. He crawled back under the covers around dawn and proceeded to show her the best way to wake up. Just thinking about it made her flesh tingle. Her secret smile brought a sly look to his face.

"Do you see that expression on his face?" Denise whispered to her. "I'd say you have the man completely under your spell."

She looked surprised. "Really?"

"Don't you realize the extent of your power?" She shook her head. "Honey, I wish I had half your looks and appeal. When I'm pregnant I'm miserable to live with and have puffy ankles the whole time. While you stand there looking as if you stepped off a magazine cover." She glanced down at Cori's ankles. "I bet they won't even have the nerve to swell. How far along are you now?"

"Five months. I look down and feel as if I swallowed a watermelon."

Denise shook her head. "Wait a few months. Then you'll see that watermelon."

"What lies about me did Denise tell you in there?" Ben asked, draping an arm around Cori's shoulders as she came up to stand at his side.

She tipped her head back so she could see his face without her visor obstructing her vision. "Holly Miller?"

He tossed his head back, groaning loudly among his friends' laughter. "What kind of friends are you?" he accused.

"Hey, leave me out of this." Stan held his hands up in mock surrender. "You should have known Denise would bring up that story."

Cori studied Ben out of narrowed eyes. "I imagine Lucia was very happy to have the sheriff bring you home after finding you and your girlfriend skinny-dipping out at that lake."

"I was grounded for a month and Holly's parents told her if she even talked to me she'd be sent away to a boarding school," he replied.

"But she found her way down to the Diner," Denise teased.

"You mean Myrna's?" Cori asked.

"No, we used to have this great diner that looked like a railroad car," Denise answered. "It first opened in the forties and for lack of a better name was called the Diner. Great jukebox and great food."

"The owner died about fifteen years ago," Ben took up the story. "His remaining family lived out of the state and didn't want anything to do with it. Unfortunately, no one had the money to keep it up, so the diner was eventually hauled off and the land sold."

"The car's over in Dawson's northeast field now," Stan continued. "He can't use the land for anything, so it's been sitting there, turning into another weed."

"That's sad! Fifties and sixties clubs have gotten popular again and it would have been a great drawing place just for the neighboring towns," Cori said, sipping her seltzer. "It's a shame no one can revive it."

"Probably too late now." Stan's expression was somber. "But we had some great times there."

"Hey, I do not intend to stand here and get depressed," Denise finally spoke up. "Come on, Cori, it looks like those steaks are almost done. We'll bring out the rest of the food.''

''Tell the monsters—I mean the kids—it's time to eat,'' Stan called after her.

Denise pulled bowls out of the refrigerator and unplugged the Crockpot, which held the baked beans. ''Why don't you take the beans out?'' She walked to the hall and yelled, ''Kids, wash up for dinner! And I do mean with soap.'' She shook her head as she walked back in. ''Amazing how dirty kids can get just playing video games.''

Cori laughed as she heard the stomp of feet in the distance.

''They sound like a herd of elephants.''

''Yes, I've noticed that, too,'' Denise said wryly.

''Food!'' was shouted in unison as three boys raced for the back door.

''Hold it!'' Denise called in the manner of a drill sergeant. ''Take a platter out with you.''

The boys lined up, each taking the bowl or platter their mother held out.

''Walk, *do not run,* to the table,'' she reminded their retreating figures. ''And do not even think of a food fight!''

''Okay'' came back in unison.

''Why do I bother when I know they don't listen,'' Denise said with the beleaguered sigh of a mother.

Cori laughed again as she watched the boys jockey for what they felt were the best positions for eating, then proceeded to fight among themselves until Stan put a stop to their horseplay.

''I just bet your baby will grow up to be the perfect child the rest of us mothers will hate because our children aren't like that," Denise said sagely as they carried bowls outside.

"But then again, my darling might end up as a star on 'America's Most Wanted,'" Cori said, tongue in cheek.

Denise halted for a moment and lightly touched Cori's arm. "Honey, you do realize we're all here for you," she said, sincerity warming her gaze. "You'll never have to feel alone through this."

Cori was touched by the woman's assurance. "I know that and I'm grateful."

All through the meal, Cori felt the warmth surrounding her like a favorite old quilt. Ben had done more than make sure she was healthy and ate correctly. He was wonderful moral support and she had learned that she could offer the same when he mourned the passing of a patient. Her four-man entourage accompanied her on her walks, even though she now took them early in the morning before it got too warm. And people who used to look at her curiously now greeted her with warm familiarity. She knew names of the children and their pets. She was slowly but surely feeling a part of the town.

Denise turned to Cori. "Since you worked on fundraisers before, how would you like to help the church fundraiser we're putting on next month?"

"Hey, Cori, say a quick no," Stan advised as he forked steaks onto the plates. "Denise does this every year, and every year we go through hell while she does all the organizing."

"Stan!" Denise cut a quick look at the boys.

"Trust me, they've heard worse on TV." He turned back to Cori. "Denise has already spent the past two weeks running around, picking up donations from everyone. Our living room is filled with just about anything you can think of—including Mrs. Peabody's ugly ceramic cats."

"A lot of people around here enjoy making things," Denise explained. "And they're always popular at the social we put on."

"Especially all the afghans Denise knits," Ben put in.

"My way of coping with nights of bad TV," she joked. "I'll show you after dinner."

"Tell me more about the Diner," Cori suggested as they ate. She and Ben sat on one side of the table, Ben's thigh rubbing companionably against hers.

"It was great," Stan spoke first. "All these wild neon signs, the jukebox going at all times."

"We got together there after every game. After all the dances. We celebrated going steady, even engagements," Denise added.

"It was understood by all the parents that we wouldn't get into trouble while we were in there," Ben went on. "We were there for burgers and Cokes—"

"And to pick up women," Stan expanded, then ducked when Denise playfully swiped at him. "Not me, honey. You were always the only one for me."

"You remember that."

After they ate, Denise put the three boys to work rinsing off dishes and putting them in the dishwasher while she took Cori into the living room.

Cori took her time, looking over the variety of handmade items. "People in town did all of this?" she asked, fingering a patchwork quilt.

Denise nodded. "In town and along the outlying areas."

"With all this talent, I'm surprised you don't have a craft boutique."

"Is that popular?"

Cori nodded. "My dad's secretary's daughter makes jewelry and sells it. She took me down to one and I was hooked right away. I think a boutique would be great for around here. And, you know, there's that empty store in town."

Denise didn't look convinced. "Cori, no one's got that kind of money."

Cori's mind was already whirling. "A few cans of paint, the crafters talk their husbands into building the booths and you find someone who will give you a break on the rent for the first year. It's done all the time."

"Not in Farrington."

"It's something to think about," Cori insisted. "If you all worked together you could have something. It's too bad that other restaurant closed. People would have loved the atmosphere. I'm not saying Myrna's isn't good, because it is, but the competition wouldn't have hurt." She picked up a fluffy baby blanket knitted in soft pastel shades. She pressed it against her cheek.

"Still, I know we need you helping on the fund-raiser."

Cori thought of the others she had helped with. Ones that dealt with millions of dollars. She knew this one would be a bare fraction of that amount, but she had an idea she would probably have a lot more fun.

"DID YOU HAVE A GOOD TIME?" Ben asked as they later drove back to town.

Cori suppressed a yawn. "It was great."

"Even with Denise talking you into helping her with the fund-raiser?"

"I was hooked once she explained the proceeds were put into a hospital building fund," she replied. "I heard one of the accident victims you treated made a nice contribution."

"He did and it was greatly appreciated."

Cori looked out the window. "Are we far from the field that has that diner you all were talking about?" she asked suddenly.

"A few miles." Ben was whistling under his breath.

She turned toward him. "Could I see it?"

"There's not all that much to see, Cori. It's nothing more than a rusted old relic in the middle of a field."

"An old relic that holds a lot of memories. Don't worry, I have a great imagination. Please?" she asked in a husky voice as she ran her fingers up and down his thigh.

He could feel himself weakening. But he already knew it never took much where Cori was concerned.

"All right, but ten to one the minute we get there I'll get a call and we'll have to leave."

"And maybe you won't." She playfully punched his arm. "Be optimistic, Ben! There are times when the people are polite enough not to get sick."

Ben pulled off the road, took several side roads and slowed to a stop. He jumped out of the truck and walked around to help her out.

"Careful, it's pretty rough going here." He threaded his fingers through hers as he led her across a field covered with dry grass. "Watch the rocks."

Cori grimaced as she felt an itchy feeling travel from her ankles to her calves—she guessed from the grass. The sound of insects echoed in her ears and she only hoped they wouldn't hop from the ground up her legs. Ben kept a steadying hand on her so she wouldn't stumble over the uneven ground. She looked up just as they rounded a clump of bushes and he gestured to a space ahead of them.

The silver railroad car set up on blocks looked tarnished under the still-blazing late-afternoon sun. Windows were smudged but unbroken and one door hung crazily open. With grass growing up around the building it looked as if aliens had abruptly dropped it into the field.

Cori recalled pictures of diners from the forties and fifties fashioned from railroad cars and streetcars. But this looked like a space-age automobile. She closed her eyes briefly and tried to visualize it the way it must have looked years ago. Luckily, it wasn't difficult.

"I spent a lot of evenings in this place," Ben said reminiscently. "Had a lot of good times."

"It's a shame someone didn't take it over." Cori started to step inside, but Ben held her back.

"We don't know what might have taken up residence in there."

"Please? I'll be careful. It's not as if bears live around here."

His shoulders rose and fell with a deep sigh. "If I say no, you'll go, anyway, so I guess I better go first." He took a tentative step inside and reached back to take hold of Cori's hand, pulling her up.

The counter was covered with bits of grass—obviously previous nests for field mice—as were the red leather seats and booths, now split open, their stuffing providing more nests.

"Oh, Ben, it's not fair," she murmured. "You can't let it stagnate out here."

"No one has the money necessary to revive it, and besides, what good would it do?" Ben took her hand and pulled gently, leading her out of the building.

Cori looked back once as they walked away.

"It still isn't fair," she said as Ben helped her into the truck.

"Cori, in the space of one day you're trying to save everything. I'm afraid it doesn't work that way."

Ben realized that taking her out there was a mistake. Because no matter what he said, she wasn't about to listen.

He opened his mouth to say something, but she spun toward him, a look of wonder on her face.

"Ben, I felt the baby move!" she whispered. She grabbed his hand and placed it against her abdomen. She seemed to be holding her breath. "Feel it? It's as if butterflies are flying around inside."

The tiniest of flutters seemed to tickle his palm. At that moment, Ben knew he could never think of the baby as anyone's but his.

Chapter Twelve

Dr. Cooper's Clinic

Ben was worried and he hated to admit it.

It was Cori.

Each day, he worried would be their last together. Even the mornings he woke up, with Cori warmly ensconced in his arms he feared she would decide she'd had it with rural life and call her father to come rescue her. And that fear twisted a vicious knot in his gut. Lately, he'd even taken to going past Cal's to check that her car was still under the tarp.

He might as well face it. He was in love with her.

Though he'd suspected it for a while now, he finally admitted it. Even though it was only to himself. Was he ready to tell Cori? He groaned at the thought, and turned over on the couch.

And what about the baby? Ever since he'd felt it move, he'd been hooked. He couldn't stop the fantasies from coming: him out playing ball with his son, teaching him to fish, maybe even one day passing on the clinic to him, as his father had done.

Somehow, he'd just come to think of the baby as his. But he had no idea how Cori would react to that. It was one thing for the town to gossip that he was the father, but quite a different thing for him to claim he wanted to be.

He shook his head, hoping to clear his muddled thoughts. But it did little good.

His tiny living room looked dull and drab after all the time he spent at the cottage with Cori. But right now, he couldn't handle going over there. He knew she was still at the school, and while she had put her stamp in every room it just wasn't the same when she wasn't there.

Cori had added her love for color everywhere by putting out bunches of dried flowers in small pitchers, throwing an afghan Denise had given her over the back of the couch and scattering her array of cosmetics throughout the bathroom. He knew he could never look at the cottage through the same eyes again.

Cori had already thrown herself wholeheartedly into fund-raising for Denise, who'd privately told him that Cori was the best organizer she'd ever seen. Vivian told him that Cori stopped by every few days and offered suggestions to jazz up her display window. Even Elliott had finally come around and added several shelves of vitamin therapy to his store.

All the while, Cori had brought up the idea of a craft boutique to everyone she talked to. Some were excited by the ideas, but more were skeptical. But that hadn't stopped her.

"Hey! Where are you?"

He jumped at the sound of the familiar voice.

"I'm upstairs," he called out and sat up on the couch.

Cori walked into the room with a bouncy step.

"I'm actually getting used to all that running," she told him, nestling herself in his lap. She finger-combed his hair. "And I carried on a conversation about Bugs Bunny and knew what I was talking about. I am making a lot of headway there."

Ben smiled. "Mrs. Timmerman better watch out."

She shook her head. "I'm not even close to her abilities, but I'm slowly climbing up the rungs. Is your stomach up to my cooking or do we go to Myrna's?"

"Actually, I had another idea in mind." He curved his hand around her nape and brought her face to his for a kiss. "Dr. Willoughby offered to cover for me tonight, thanks to Mama offering to cook him one of her famous dinners. So how would you like to go out for dinner and a movie tonight?"

Her delight turned to confusion. "It sounds great, but last I looked Farrington didn't have a movie theater."

"I was thinking more about going to the drive-in theater that's about twenty miles from here."

"A drive-in," she murmured. "A real drive-in theater?"

He nodded. "One of the last ones around. Right after we have the kind of dinner I wouldn't recommend to most of my patients. But since I'm always telling you you need to gain a little more weight I figure the extra calories won't hurt you."

Cori's eyes lit up. "Are we talking greasy hamburgers and fries?"

"Exactly."

"Sounds great!" She almost bounced in her eagerness.

"Really?" He was surprised by her reaction. "I thought I'd have to hog-tie you to go."

"No, lately, I have been craving a hamburger with everything on it and a ton of fries." She shook her head. "Seems junk food is all I want lately."

"Yeah, I've noticed the candy bar wrappers in the trash. Not to mention an empty Ding Dongs box."

"They taste good," she defended herself. "When can we leave?"

"An hour?"

"I'll be ready." She leaned in to him for a deep kiss that had both of them thinking about forgetting dinner and the movie and just staying where they were.

"Hm, I'll say you are," he mumbled when she drew back. With a deep sigh of regret, he levered himself upward. "I really need a shower, so I'll be by in about an hour to pick you up." He held out his hands and pulled her to her feet.

In deference to the late-summer heat, Ben wore khaki shorts and a T-shirt and kept his feet bare in running shoes.

He had barely approached Cori's door when it opened and she stepped out.

"Wow." He let out a low whistle of appreciation. "You look great."

"Really?" she asked with a hopeful air. She turned around in a tight circle. In bright pink bike shorts and a multicolored maternity top, she was the closest thing to heaven he'd ever seen. Her hair had grown quite a bit over the months and she wore it tied in a short bouncy ponytail to keep it off her nape.

It was on the tip of his tongue to tell her he was in love with her, but he couldn't. Not here. Not with the sun still shining overhead. No, he'd wait until later when it was dark and the moon was out. Yeah, that was it. He wanted his declaration to sound as romantic as hell. And confessing it in a doorway wasn't all that romantic.

"Then let's get out of here before someone decides they need me," he teased, grabbing her hand and pulling her toward the truck.

The drive went by fast as Cori sang along with the radio and treated him to some of the knock-knock jokes she had learned from the kids that day.

"You know, having these prekindergarten classes is great. They're already primed for school and they'll do much better," she chattered. "And did you know Mrs. Timmerman tats? Makes lace, that is. She learned from her mother. She brought in doilies she had made and they were beautiful. I told her I once read somewhere tatting was a lost art. She's donating them for the fund-raiser. We had the kids decorate posters today that the high school kids are going to take around to the other towns and put up. They're really cute."

"Posters in the other towns? I don't think they've done that before. Oh." He nodded his head in understanding. "Your idea."

"Denise thought it was great. After all, a local hospital would help those towns, too," she suggested. "They'd come to see you instead of traveling to the next doctor."

"What next?"

"The Diner."

Ben couldn't help laughing. "It was a rhetorical question."

"I know it, but I answered, anyway. Denise thinks it would be great if it could be revived."

"Cori, I hate to bring this up again, but your ideas need money. Something, you may have noticed, Farrington doesn't have a lot of."

"But if everyone worked together, there's no reason why costs couldn't be cut in half," she argued. "If anyone with construction skills donated labor and the hardware store donated lumber and materials."

"Homer donate something? That would be a miracle in itself. Look, I just don't want you to feel disappointed."

"I only will if you don't support me on this."

Ben took a deep breath. "Do you think we could put this on hold for the evening? This is the first time we've actually gotten away and I want you to enjoy it."

"Truce for the evening. That's fair," she agreed, snuggling up to his side.

Cori's eyes widened with delight when Ben drove up to a drive-in restaurant with the neon sign declaring it to be Beanie's.

"This is great!" She watched the car hops, dressed in denim shorts and red T-shirts, running around to serve the many cars parked around the circular restaurant.

"Yeah, it's real popular over here." He drove up and accepted a menu from a teen waitress who affixed a tray to his car-window opening. He handed it over to Cori. "What looks good to you?"

She visually devoured it. "Everything. Oh, I'll have a chili cheese dog, large order of fries and a large Diet Coke. No, make that chocolate shake." She handed him back the menu.

"Heartburn city," he murmured before turning to the waitress and giving her their order. "Good thing I brought along antacid for you."

Cori rolled her eyes. "That one time."

"That one time lasted half the night. No more onion dip for you after that." He tapped the section of the seat next to his thigh and she obligingly slid over until her bare thigh brushed against his. "So have you ever necked at the drive-in movies?" he whispered, nibbling on her ear.

"I've never even been to one," she confessed. "Unfortunately, they went the way of the dodo bird out there."

He noticed she didn't call California home. And took heart.

"Then you're in for an experience."

"Terrific. More than six months pregnant and you're talking necking at the show."

"Why not? Pregnant or not, you're still a sexy lady."

Cori made a face. "You get up in those stirrups and tell me how sexy you feel."

He laughed. Seemed he was always laughing when Cori was around, he thought.

Dinner continued in the same vein as they bantered back and forth. Cori literally glowed under Ben's attention. He wondered what kind of dates she'd had in high school because if anyone looked at her right now they'd think she was still back there.

"I'd love another shake," she decided.

Ben leaned over and whispered in her ear, "I hate to say this, hon, but you're starting to get a little pudgy. Are you sure you want to take a chance?"

"Aw, c'mon, let her live it up," the waitress said cheekily, obviously overhearing him. "After all, it's your fault she's eating for two." She laughed merrily as she bounced off with empty containers and to fill Cori's order.

Ben felt the silence the moment they were alone.

"I guess it's natural anyone would think that," Cori said quietly. "I'm sorry if she embarrassed you."

This was the opening he'd been waiting for. He plunged right in.

"Wrong. If anything, I wish what she said were true." He leaned over and placed his palm against her bulging tummy. "I'll be honest, Cori. I wish I was the man who had placed that baby inside you."

Cori blinked rapidly, holding her tears back. "Oh, Ben, don't make me cry," she murmured with trembling lips. "You know my overactive hormones get in the way at the worst times."

Ben smiled as what felt like a tiny foot pushed against his palm. "Soccer?" he guessed.

She smiled through her tears. "Ballet."

"Maybe hockey."

"Maybe we'll let her decide."

"Maybe he doesn't want ballet lessons," he teased, gratified to see her tears were quickly disappearing. "You know, if you want to find out, we could do an ultrasound. I haven't suggested one before since you're not at any risk."

She shook her head. "No thanks, I'll do it the old-fashioned way and be surprised."

"Here's your shake," the waitress interrupted them. She flashed Ben a saucy grin as she passed over the shake and the bill. "Have a good evening, you two."

"What movies are we seeing?"

"I forgot to check the paper today," he admitted. "When I looked last night, it was two comedies."

She nodded. Her cheeks hollowed out as she sucked on her straw.

When they reached the drive-in theater, the lot was about half-full. Mindful of Cori, Ben parked in the rear near the concession stand and the rest rooms. Except he parked the truck backward with the truck bed facing the screen.

"Is this a new way to watch the movie?" Cori asked. "I thought going to the drive-in meant you sat in the car and watched the movie."

"Call it an alternative to the back seat. I put an air mattress, a couple of large pillows and blankets in the back so we could be more comfortable," he explained, helping her out of the truck. He uttered a low grunt when he lifted her onto the truck bed. "From now on, you lay off the chocolate shakes.'' He picked up the speaker and looped the cord over the side of the truck.

But Cori was busy watching animated popcorn containers, soda cups and candy packages dance across the screen.

''Red licorice,'' she said suddenly. ''That sounds great.''

Groaning, Ben pulled himself up onto the truck bed. ''You have got to be kidding!''

''No.'' She turned eyes, now a limpid navy blue, on him. ''Please, Ben?''

He was ready to say no. Ready to remind her that while she might be eating for two, she still needed to watch what she ate. He opened his mouth to do just that—except a pair of blue eyes and a delectable mouth stopped him.

''Oh, hell,'' he muttered, pushing himself off. ''I suppose you want a Coke, too?''

She quickly nodded. ''And popcorn, with butter.''

''Popcorn, *no* butter.'' He pointed his forefinger at her. ''Fine, I'll be back.''

Cori sat on top of the blankets with her knees drawn up. At least as far up as the baby would allow. She rested her arms on her knees and watched Ben walk toward the concession stand.

He was tall, dark-haired and sexy, had a wonderful personality and was the owner of an incredible body she lusted after. Not to mention, explored every chance she got. Ben was the kind of man any red-blooded woman would appreciate. She knew she did.

And then it hit her—hard.

''I love him,'' she said, almost in wonder. ''Oh, my God, I love him.''

For a moment, she was positive she couldn't breathe.

She thought about the way she kept adding little touches to the cottage to make it more her own. And her lack of desire to return to California. She remembered Denise warning her pregnancy would bring out a strong nesting instinct. Were her feelings due to pregnancy or were they all thanks to Ben?

The more she thought about it, the more the truth loomed at her. It was Ben who instilled these feelings.

Now all she had to do was figure out how to break the news to him and hope he wouldn't take off running the moment he heard.

Not to worry, Courtney Peyton, a part of her heart whispered, *if anything, he'd run right into your arms.*

Her thoughts instantly brightened when the object of her contemplations appeared bearing snacks.

As he handed them to her, he ticked off each item she had requested.

"Milk Duds!" Her eyes lit up at the remaining box in his hand.

He held it out of her reach. "Hands off. They're mine."

"But, Ben." She got up on her knees and looped her arms around his neck. "Didn't you ever learn to share?"

"Don't worry, you have something else to look forward to." He held up a plastic bottle he had hidden under the blankets. "Riopan for when you're finished."

Making a face, she sat back on her knees. "You think you're so funny."

"I try." He pulled her back onto the blankets. "Come on, let's get comfortable."

"Do you realize we're the only people here who are over the age of twenty-one?" Cori commented after glancing at the variety of cars and trucks before them. "In fact, we might be the only ones here over the age of eighteen."

"Can't imagine why. The comedies listed didn't look like something that would appeal to teens."

"Unless—" she snuggled up against his side and slipped her hand under his shirt "—they're not here for the movies."

He arched an eyebrow. "And you thought we were?"

"Not after I saw all the blankets." She slid her hand up higher, pushing her fingers through the mat of hair. She halted and looked around. "Andy won't suddenly show up here, will he?"

He traced a pattern across her bare knee. "Not his jurisdiction."

"Good." She exhaled a warm puff of air in his ear.

"Yeah, I think we've shocked him enough."

Cori turned her head just enough to glance at the cartoon characters racing across the screen. "Bugs Bunny wins again." She turned her attention back to Ben.

By then, darkness shrouded them with secrecy as they indulged themselves in salty popcorn kisses.

"The movies were never this fun in high school," she whispered.

"It does seem to improve with age." He slid his fingers under her bra and gently caressed her breast. He smiled at her soft moan as his mouth covered hers in another soul-thrilling kiss. His tongue delved inside, curling around hers.

When Cori first heard the scream, she worried it came from her. Except she then realized there wasn't any way, at that moment, she could have screamed.

She turned her head in the direction of the sound. Her eyes widened with shock as she watched the grisly scene being played out on the screen.

"*Texas Chainsaw Massacre?* You brought me to see *Texas Chainsaw Massacre?*" She stuck her finger down her throat and made gagging noises.

"Considering the state of your stomach at times I wouldn't advise you do that."

"This is a horror film. You brought me to a horror film!"

"You love horror movies, so why should this one bother you?"

"Yes, I love them. At home, with a blanket wrapped around me and the lights on. Not out here where a homicidal maniac could appear at any time and chop us to pieces!" She reached past him and grabbed a handful of popcorn. "So be prepared to protect me."

"No problem there." He pulled her back against him. "Just remember that popcorn is for both of us."

Cori took a kernel and rubbed it against his mouth until he parted his lips. She nudged it inside, following it with a kiss.

"Popcorn never tasted so good," Ben murmured, inching his fingers under her blouse again. "More."

Pretty soon, kisses weren't enough as they lay on their sides facing each other.

"Too bad drive-ins aren't popular anymore," Cori whispered, unsnapping Ben's jeans. "They offer so many wonderful opportunities."

"That they do." He walked his fingers up her spine.

"And the blood and gore on the screen along with those blood-curdling screams add so much to the atmosphere." She feathered kisses along his jaw.

"True." He reached down and dragged one of the lightweight blankets over them.

She smiled as she felt her shorts being pulled down slightly. "You must have been a wild teenager."

"Nope, you weren't around to be wild with."

It could have been that point of no return for them if a familiar voice hadn't intruded. They immediately froze.

"Hey, Doc, Cori, how ya doin'?" Andy drawled as he walked past the truck with a popcorn container in his hands.

Chapter Thirteen

Farrington Craft Show

He watched her fondle tacky little knickknacks, caress colorful afghans and outrageous patchwork quilts—even look longingly at Mrs. Peabody's infamous ceramic cats. And all the time Ben wished it was him that was the object of Cori's rapt attention.

It had been that way all week. She was so wrapped up in the craft fair that she seemed to spend every moment conferring with Denise or courting the women in town to encourage handmade donations. He looked around the church basement: the tables were laden with items for sale, and what seemed like half of Farrington and the surrounding towns oohed and aahed over them. He had to admit, Cori had found her calling.

Last night, he'd come close to speaking what was on his mind all week. Over a pot-roast dinner at Myrna's, in the back booth, he'd almost told her that he was in love with her. But by the time the words came to his lips, Charlotte was back with a refill on Cori's milk and the moment was lost.

Myrna's might not have been the most romantic of places, but Ben was tired of trying to manipulate her into the moonlight. No, he decided, he just had to take her aside and tell her.

Gathering his courage once more, he pushed off from the wall and strode determinedly across the church hall. Cori was busily arranging more crafts on a far table when Mrs. Peabody beat him to her.

"Courtney, my dear." One of the first things Mrs. Peabody had ever told Cori was that she didn't believe in nicknames. She was the only one in town who insisted on using Cori's full name. "Looks like we'll make some money today to help build Dr. Cooper's hospital," she said, patting her hand.

"We sure will. Thanks to your kitties." Cori had personally sold several of them. With Mrs. Peabody's attention, this seemed like the perfect opportunity to talk to her about opening the craft boutique. She'd spent most of the morning doing just that with the talented women of town. As she launched into her spiel once again, she spied Ben walking over.

He had a strange look on his face and a purpose to his stride. He was probably upset with her for overdoing it again. All week he'd been lecturing her about the importance of rest and diet, and constantly trying to get her to stop for a picnic or take a drive out to the lake. But there was never any time.

Cori looked at Ben and just the sight of him distracted her from her sales job on Mrs. Peabody. All week she'd been just as determined. With all the planning for the craft sale, she'd never found the time to tell Ben what she finally realized at the drive-in. That she loved him. There had always been one more detail to cover, one more person to contact. It had gotten so bad that she even invited him over for a home-cooked meal one night, just to be sure they'd have some time alone. But then he got called out on an emergency. Probably just as well; she laughed to herself. After eating her cooking, the last thing Ben would want to hear was that she loved him and wanted to stay in Kansas with him.

But after today, the fund-raising was over. She'd find the time to sit quietly and bare her soul to Ben.

But first Denise had one more job for her.

"Here." She plopped a stack of paper in Cori's hands. "We voted you to be the person who stands at the door and hands these out."

"Why me?"

She chuckled. "Because when you smile, the men tend to lose their minds and will do anything we wives tell them to. So smile a lot."

Cori did just that. She handed out flyers to the incoming and reminded each and every visitor that the proceeds would go to the Farrington hospital building fund.

"Hey." Dan sidled up and spoke out of the side of his mouth. "Meet me by the snack bar in five minutes."

Cori looked curious. "Why?"

"It's important." He held his finger against his lips to indicate silence and walked off.

Five minutes later, Cori was able to pass the job on to someone else and quickly made her way to the snack bar where Dan, Zeke and the others were huddled together.

"You really think you could do something with the Diner if it was hauled out of Dawson's field?" Dan asked.

It took Cori a moment to realize the significance of his question. She didn't hesitate in answering. "Yes, I do."

"With the right equipment, there would be no problem in towing it," Zeke chipped in. "All we'd need to do is find some land to sit it on. We think we have a way to get that."

Cori leaned forward so she wouldn't be overheard. "Really?" Excitement colored her voice. "How?"

He nodded. "We're working on it. You know, a lot of people miss that old place. Oh, Myrna's is fine for us old folk, but the younger ones need something that's all their own. And the Diner holds memories for a lot of us. I proposed to my wife there." His faded eyes warmed with memory.

"We think if we got the Diner up and running again, there'd be no reason for the people to argue against the idea of that craft store you're tryin' so hard to get people interested in," Dan explained.

Cori unconsciously placed her hand against her bulging abdomen. She wasn't sure if it was a foot or a hand pushing against her palm. The baby had gotten so active she couldn't remember the last time she had had a full night's sleep.

"Time is starting to work against me," she murmured. "Why don't we talk about this during our next walk?"

All four nodded and walked off.

"What are you five cooking up now?" Ben came up from behind and draped an arm around her shoulders, drawing her against his side.

Cori noticed the number of approving smiles sent their way.

"You know, it has taken me a long time with innocent comments and not-too-subtle statements to persuade these people that the baby isn't yours," she muttered. "And now you're getting all cozy in public."

"I told you before. I don't mind if they think the baby is mine." He smiled and nodded at those looking at them.

"You two just can't keep your hands off each other, can you?" Andy shook his head in wonder as he walked past them.

Cori could feel her face burning a bright red. Since the fiasco at the movies, she couldn't face the sheriff without embarrassment coloring her features. Ben had later learned Andy had been there with his son. The fact that the sheriff recognized his truck was pure coincidence. She was positive Andy was enjoying finding them at inopportune times, though. Ben tried to tell her she was imagining it, but she didn't miss that amused glint in Andy's eye every time he saw them together.

"Are you getting tired?" Ben asked, wincing as one little girl ran by screaming happily as another girl chased her. "Man, those kids are loud."

She smiled and shook her head. "Not at all. I've been having so much fun this afternoon. People are even buying Mrs. Peabody's cats," she whispered, although the noise around them wouldn't have allowed anyone to eavesdrop on them. "One woman said she read somewhere that cats are now eclectic art. Especially if they're painted purple."

Ben stood behind her with his arms wrapped around her middle, his hands splayed possessively on her tummy and his chin resting on top of her head. "Wait until the town Halloween party. We dress up and get pretty wild then."

"I can't wait," she said softly, but he could still hear her.

He was afraid to ask. "You'll be here then?"

She turned her head and looked up. "Do you want me to be?" The intensity in her gaze told him there was more to her question than what she said aloud.

He tightened his hold. "Yes, I do. Very much."

She smiled. "Then I better start looking around for a pumpkin costume. I can't think of anything more appropriate, can you?"

"I think you'll make the cutest pumpkin in town."

"Cori, my darling, Denise told me all you have done to help her set this up." Lucia swooped down on them, giving each one a hug and kiss. She looked fondly at Cori.

"Do you realize we have already brought in more money than we did last year? You will come out to dinner next week." She turned to her son. "Bennie, do not let her get away." She leaned over and said in a not-so-subtle whisper, "The best part is we already know she's fertile." She patted his cheek and walked on, calling out to someone.

"She can embarrass a son like no other," Ben revealed with a deep groan.

"I've heard it's a mother's lot."

He looked around, suddenly uneasy with everyone's eyes on them. He was beginning to hate this lack of privacy. "How much longer do you have to hang around here?"

"At least another hour." She eyed the snack bar. "I'd love one of those big soft pretzels Ralph has."

"Did Ella weigh you today?"

"Yes, and she said I'm doing fine." She looked smug. "Pretzel, please." She arched an eyebrow. "You might get lucky later on."

"You're on." He dug into his jeans pocket.

"Hi, Doc. Cori." A glowing Thalia walked up to them. A small diamond sparkled on her left ring finger. The man standing behind her looked more like a bean pole than a human being and he continually pulled at his collar as if it was choking him. But the look he gave Thalia was filled with love and wonder.

Regina had artfully colored Thalia's previously orange hair a pale golden blond that did more for her face than the previous ash-blond shade. She even wore brighter cosmetics now.

"You look great," Cori said sincerely. "That dress does a lot for you."

She blushed. "Vivian helped me pick it out." She looked up at her fiancé who nodded. "We set the date. December tenth."

"A Christmas wedding!" Cori smiled.

"We're hoping you both will be there," Rawley mumbled.

"Wouldn't miss it," Ben assured them.

"We told Mrs. Raymond we want to buy her wedding ring quilt." Thalia blushed again. "We better go over and pick it up."

"That's a romance helped along by you," Ben said after they were left alone. He had gotten Cori her pretzel and they stayed in a corner while she nibbled on it and shared bites with Ben.

"And all because I accidentally turned her hair orange." She shook her head in wonder. "It must be a gift."

He chuckled. "I'm not sure the others would call it that."

"Cori, it's time for you to spell Ella," Denise called out.

"And, Ben, you promised to help me get away from my wife before she corrals me to do something else!" Stan called out, earning a warning look from Denise. "She's killing me!"

"Set your watch. I'll be back to rescue you in an hour." Ben knew kissing Cori in public was going to feed the gossip mill for a week. So he did more than kiss her. He pulled her in his arms and kissed her twice. By the time he allowed her to come up for air they both looked dazed.

"Way to go, Doc!" someone shouted with a loud whoop and applause.

"Hey, Doc! You keep on doing stuff like that and our wives will expect the same!" another man called out.

"Only if it's with the doc and not you," one woman teased amid ribald laughter.

Cori burst out laughing. "I guess we did it again."

"WHEN ARE YOU GOING to do something about Cori?" Ella demanded, slapping the top of Ben's desk with the palm of her hand.

Ben smothered a jaw-cracking yawn. He'd been up half the night delivering a baby who wasn't too eager to enter the world. The last thing he wanted was a battle with Ella, but he knew Ella always believed in striking when she thought her prey was most vulnerable. Right now, he was about as weak as that baby he delivered. Correction, the baby probably had a hell of a lot more energy.

"Last I checked, she was doing fine, even if she did get mad when I told her she had to lay off the Ding Dongs. She tried to tell me it was part of her dairy allotment, but I told her it wouldn't work." He poured himself another cup of coffee in hopes the caffeine would kick in soon. "Are you sure you didn't make decaf this morning?"

"Positive." She fixed him with a stern look. "I hope you realize the town consider the two of you a couple."

"I'd say so." He picked up a file folder and opened it, making the necessary notes. "You know, it was amazing. Marge was fully dilated, the contractions were coming hot and heavy, she was ready to push with all her might and that kid still refused to come out."

"If you were the newest member of that clan, would you want to come out?"

Ben thought of a family where the smallest measured six feet, six inches. "A couple more kids and they'll have their own basketball team. Just wish I'd had a chance to get back to bed before coming in here."

Ella made a harrumphing sound. "As if you would have slept."

He groaned. "What do you do? Talk to my mother?"

"Don't have to. I have boys of my own. I know how you men think. So what are you going to do about Cori?" she demanded.

Ben ran his hand over his face. With the lack of sleep the night before, he wasn't prepared to handle Ella when she was on the rampage.

"Are you saying what I think you're saying?" he asked wearily.

She crossed her arms in front of her chest. "Yes, I am. I'm talking marriage. The girl will have a baby soon and there's no father."

He leaned back in his chair and propped his booted feet on top of his desk. "And how do you know she's not just staying here long enough for her father to calm down before heading back to L.A?" He knew she'd at least be there until Halloween, but he didn't dare tell Ella.

"I've seen the way she looks at you and the way you look at her. Considering how she feels about you, I don't think she's all that eager to go back to her old life. Before you know it, it will be November and she'll have her baby. So why don't you do the right thing and ask her to marry you?"

"Why don't you let me work this out my way?" He knew the minute he said it he'd made a mistake. Just as with his mother, there was no winning with Ella.

Her glare could have turned him into a ten-year-old boy.

"You're sleeping over there every night. If you think no one knows that, you're even dumber than I thought you were. You should be married. She should be married. The two of you obviously must have strong feelings for each other. Give that baby a family."

"Ella, let me handle this, okay?" He closed the file folder and put it to one side. "Cori and I are progressing at a rate we're both comfortable with. Why don't you leave it at that?"

The woman's entire body seemed to rise and fall with her deep sigh. "You always were slow in some things, Ben. Just don't keep things at your rate for so long that she decides there's nothing here for her and she leaves."

Ben's body tightened at the idea of losing Cori. She had already become a large part of his life.

"Considering her car is still under a tarp at Cal's, I don't think that will happen all that soon."

"All it would take is a call to her father and that car would probably be hauled out of here. And so would she." She shook her head at his stubborn bent. "Just tell me one thing. Are you in love with Cori?"

He jumped to his feet, feeling the electric charge from her question hit him. "Dammit, Ella! I haven't even told her yet!"

"Then I suggest you do just that." She cocked her head to one side as she heard a bell from the front of the office. "The Petersons are here with their kids. Since they were on vacation they weren't able to get in before for the school vaccinations. At least that's something I know you can do without any trouble." With one last look at him, she stalked out of the office.

Ben dropped into his chair and buried his face in his hands. "I can't believe this," he muttered.

Trouble was, he could. Because Ella only voiced concerns he had been having. Why the hell hadn't he told Cori sooner? Because he was a coward and feared she didn't have the same feelings he did. Except every time he recalled their time together, he knew that couldn't be true.

Maybe it was time to start saying a few things out loud.

"IT WOULD WORK," Dan told Cori.

The young woman and four elderly men had started out for their walk, but this time they led Cori to a spot not far from the gas station and announced their idea.

Zeke explained he knew the owner of the land and could arrange for the lease.

Dan, who used to work for the county, could arrange for a truck to tow the restaurant to the spot. Alex checked the records and found out the town owned the restaurant, and spoke with Mayor Holloway at their last poker game. And Carl thought he could get Ralph to help outfit the interior, in return for not telling his wife about the weekly poker game.

Hope bubbled up inside Cori. She bounced up on her toes and bestowed a kiss on each grizzled cheek. "You are all wonderful! Talk about a great chance to bring it back to life."

"Hell." Dan looked sheepish at such a display. "Retirement has been a bitch, so this should keep the ole ticker goin' for a while. But we're still going to need money."

Cori looked at the weed-covered lot and visualized a parking lot, the diner all shiny and filled with customers.

"I can take care of that," she said finally.

For once, she had a plan that she knew she wasn't going to allow to fail.

BEN BARELY HAD CLOSED UP the clinic and sent Ella home before Cori was at his side.

"You have to see this." She pulled on his arm.

He looked at her, noting her shorts and tank top. "I already like what I see."

"No, this." Cori grabbed his hand and tried to pull him off the step. "Come on, it's just a short walk."

"To where?"

"You'll see," she said mysteriously.

Cori led Ben to an open piece of land not far from the gas station. They stood on the side of the road, staring at it. Cori, with satisfaction. Ben, with confusion.

"So?" he asked.

She took a deep breath. "You are looking at the new location for the Diner," she announced.

He shook his head as if to clear it. "What do you mean?"

"I mean, as I speak, arrangements are being made to move the Diner here," she told him. "Thanks to Zeke and the boys."

"But—" Ben was clearly flabbergasted.

"They said it was a landmark that didn't deserve to be shuttled off and forgotten," Cori continued. "You should see them! This is the best thing that's happened to them since retirement. We can do it, Ben. I know we can."

Ben ran his hand over his hair as he spun around in a tight circle. He didn't want to ruin her joy, but she had to face the facts.

"You really think you can get use of the land?"

She explained that Zeke had already taken care of that.

"What about the Diner? Who's talking to the owners?"

She told him about Alex's work.

"How would you get it here?"

She mentioned Dan's connection.

"Where do you plan to get the money?"

Cori didn't falter. "I have connections."

He didn't have to think long on that one. "Your father."

"He has the money and he knows people who are willing to invest without having a say in what's going on. He's done it before. And this time, I have a sound plan to give him."

Suddenly upset at the mention of Sean Peyton, Ben took her arm and started walking back toward town. He had a niggling fear this might be the first step in Cori's flight back west. He could only hope he was wrong. "You haven't talked to your father in more than four months. What makes you think he'll take your call now?"

"I'll hit him in the only soft spot he has. I'll tell him one of his fondest wishes is going to come true. That he's going to be a grandfather. And once he's recovered from that, I'll invite him to Thanksgiving dinner. Lucia suggested having him out."

Ben stopped so quickly Cori stumbled. He spun around and grasped her other arm, pulling her around to face him.

"And what if he wants you to come back to California instead?" he asked in a raw voice.

In his heart, he knew no other woman had the dazzling smile Cori had. The one she was giving him now. He made a silent wish that he'd be lucky enough to see that smile for the rest of his life.

She paused long enough to loop her arms around his neck, "Then I would just have to tell him I can't do that because during my time in Farrington I happened to fall in love with the town's doctor."

"Dammit woman," he growled, pulling her into his arms. "You picked the most incredible time to make up a statement like that."

Cori didn't stop smiling. "You're not running for the hills—if you could find any here to begin with—so I gather what I said doesn't scare you."

Ben's face changed from tense to elated. "Not when I love you so much that it almost hurts."

The trucks and cars passing by all honked their approval as Ben kissed her with every ounce of his being.

Within ten minutes, everyone in town was speculating on the wedding date of Cori and Doc Cooper.

Chapter Fourteen

Regina's Cut 'n' Curl

"Why do I have to go?" Cori tried digging in her heels, but Denise was having none of it.

"Because I want your input on this," Denise explained as she shepherded Cori toward the beauty shop. "I want a new hairstyle and I'm hoping you can help me find one that will look good."

"Trust me, I'm not one to ask when it comes to hair! Regina is the expert," Cori protested. "Besides, the shades are drawn at the shop. Maybe she's out to lunch or something."

"Oh, sometimes she has to do that to keep out the afternoon sun," she said in a loud voice, rattling the door as she opened it. "Come on, Cori."

"But the afternoon sun doesn't shine in this direction," she mused, then yelped in surprise as Denise literally pushed her inside.

Cori froze when lights came on and women jumped out yelling, "Surprise!"

Crepe garlands in pink and blue were hung from the ceiling and a cake sat on a card table set up by the shampoo sinks.

Cori looked around, stunned by the number of women present.

"I don't know what to say," she stammered.

"A speechless Cori!" Denise laughed. "Let's record this moment for Ben, otherwise he won't believe it!" She pushed her toward a chair. "This surprise shower wasn't all that easy to plan, so you better enjoy it."

"A shower?" she numbly repeated, still unable to believe what was before her eyes. "For me?"

"Of course, for you. Do you see anyone else around here who's pregnant?" Regina chuckled, coming up to hug her and guiding her over to the cake table. "Darlin', if anyone deserves a baby shower, it's you. So come over here and sit down. We have plans this morning. And one of them is consuming this cake!"

Cori stared at the large sheet cake decorated with frosting baby buggies, booties and rattles in each corner.

"This is so nice of all of you," she said in a barely audible voice. She sniffed.

"Hormones at work again," Denise said with an understanding smile. "Honey, we all cried at our showers, so go ahead and let it out." She handed her a handkerchief.

Cori buried her face in the soft cotton and soon blew her nose. "I just didn't expect this."

"Look at my girl!" Lucia shrieked, throwing her arms around Cori who still looked shell-shocked. "Is she not beautiful?" She looked at Cori as if she were her own daughter. "My darling, if anyone deserves this shower, it's you. You have given so much of yourself during the months you've lived here that we wanted to do something special for you." She enfolded her in her arms again.

"She's right," Vivian explained. "After all, you didn't even know about the baby until you showed up here. We feel as if this little one is as much ours as yours."

That was when Cori knew she had been accepted.

The afternoon passed quickly as Vivian set up the games, such as coming up with odd names for babies. Regina handed the gaily wrapped gifts to Cori who found herself the recipient of blankets, toys, a musical mobile, tiny clothing and a beautiful baby afghan from Denise.

"I left one corner blank so I can work in the baby's name, birth date, time of birth, weight and inches," Denise explained as Cori ran her hand over the soft blanket.

"It's so beautiful," she murmured, noting the intricate work and knew this had to have taken many hours of Denise's time and was obviously a labor of love. She raised tear-bright eyes. "I'll hate to use it."

"But that's exactly what it's for." Denise looked pleased by Cori's reaction. "To cover the baby up."

"The way he's been kicking lately I don't think he's going to want any kind of covering."

"Just wait another month!" several called out on a wave of laughter.

By the time the party was over, Cori felt overloaded with emotion and dazed by the gifts surrounding her, many of them made with obvious affection.

She raised her eyes to study Denise.

"I usually hate surprises," she confessed.

Denise laughed. "You handled this one well." She began gathering up boxes.

Cori waited a beat. "Then I guess you won't believe me if I tell you I hope your next one is another boy."

BEN WAS BARELY ABLE to walk inside the cottage before he was assaulted by a jubilant Cori.

"Hi!" She jumped up, throwing her arms around him. "Look at what I got!"

Ben stared at the pile of baby clothing, toys and even a bassinet in one corner.

"Denise said I could borrow it." Cori walked over to run her hand over the lace trim on the bassinet. "And she made a beautiful afghan." Wonder colored her voice. "Ben, they gave me a surprise baby shower."

"Hey, that's great." He wrapped his arms around her and drew her back to him. He looked down at her. "You're not going to turn on the waterworks, are you? 'Cause if so, I'll need to get a couple of bath towels for mopping up."

"No." She blinked rapidly and sniffed. "It's just that no one has ever done so much for me." She absently ran her hand over her rounded tummy.

"Maybe they like you," he whispered, kissing the curve of her ear. "That's understandable."

She turned in his arms and stood as close as her belly would allow.

"I know I'm terrible for saying this, but I look and feel like the Goodyear blimp. Do you think I might be farther along than we thought?"

"You're right on the target weight since you gave up the Ding Dongs," he assured her. "I wouldn't worry. It just means we've had to get more inventive," he teased her.

Cori butted the top of her head against his chest. "You love to embarrass me, don't you?"

"No. I just love you." There, he'd said it. And it felt good.

Cori just looked at him, stunned. Then she broke into a big smile. "You do?" she asked in a sweet voice.

Ben nodded. "Yeah, I do." He reached out and pulled her into his arms. "Know what else I love?"

She shook her head.

"I love watching you on top of me," he murmured, trailing his hands up and down her back in a slow caress. "Admit it, you do, too. It makes you feel in charge." He dropped a kiss on top of head, and before she could even reply he swooped her up into his arms and carried her into her bedroom.

As he lay her down, Cori looked up at Ben and in that instant realized how much she needed him. Not just physically, but emotionally, too. She needed Ben in her life—today and forever. With her body, she'd tell him that. She reached out to unbutton his shirt, and within seconds they'd both shucked their clothes.

As their mouths fused with hungry intent, Ben raised his hips, thrusting deep inside her. She was already moist and receptive for him, moving her hips in quick countermovements. Their breathing quickened with each thrust. Cori stared into Ben's eyes and saw the love shining from the deep brown depths. She tightened her inner self as she felt the ripples begin deep down and move outward.

As those ripples turned into a tidal wave that engulfed them both, she said, "I love you, too."

BEN WRAPPED HIS ARMS around Cori, holding her spoon-fashion.

"You know," he said once he caught his breath. "You should be given a baby shower more often."

Cori's shoulders shook with laughter. "You have such a romantic nature at times."

"I do when it counts. Who brought you flowers yesterday?"

"Zeke."

"Oh." He thought for a moment. "All right, who took you out to the lake again?"

"You did and Andy showed up ten minutes later." She reached over the side of the bed and retrieved his shirt, pulling it on. She fastened three buttons. "I am never leaving town with you again unless we are going to your mother's or the Williamses. No more dark corners. No going off to look at the moon over the lake."

"Is that why you refused to go swimming with me?"

"We didn't have any suits with us!"

"So?"

"So the last thing I want is for Andy to catch me naked in the lake. That might be the one time he'll talk!" Cori grimaced and covered her tummy with her hands. "Major kicking." She gave a sigh. "I can't sleep on my back anymore. And there's certainly no way I can sleep on my stomach. I just know this baby is getting even with me."

"Probably wants revenge for those chili fries you ate when we went out last night." He drew her back to him.

Cori snuggled even closer and rested her palm against his abdomen. She looked sadly at the flat plane, then looked at the bulge below her breasts that had increased to what she considered an alarming size. She wondered if she would ever be able to regain her previously flat tummy.

"I'm always going to look like this, aren't I?" she said sadly. "I just know the baby has taken up permanent residence in there and will refuse to leave."

"You keep up with the chili fries and the kid will be out of there tomorrow," he teased.

Cori widened her eyes to saucer shape. "What an incredible insight," she drawled. "I am so impressed. Did you learn that in medical school?"

"Bet your boots, I did." He started tickling her side.

"No!" she shrieked. "You know I hate you tickling me."

"You cast aspersions on my medical training and you pay the price."

Cori stilled his hand. "Stop it, Ben. I need to talk to you, seriously."

The gravity in her voice made Ben stop and look down at her. "What is it?"

"Today brought a few points home to me. Number one is I have to settle with my dad."

"Before or after you hit him up for financing the Diner?" he asked on a smile.

Cori looked sheepish. "Definitely before. I told you I wanted to invite him to Thanksgiving dinner."

"Why not Halloween since it's coming up?"

She knew he was teasing. "You don't invite someone to Halloween dinner, you fool. Besides, by Thanksgiving, the baby will be here. Maybe seeing the baby will soften him up."

"There's one thing seeing the baby will do," Ben countered.

"What's that?"

"Make him want to shoot Rufus." Ben ducked just in time to soften the blow of the pillow Cori threw at him.

"I CAN'T GO."

Ben looked up at the figure standing in the bedroom doorway. He swallowed and tightened his facial muscles so he wouldn't laugh. He sensed if he did he wouldn't have long to live.

"You look...cute," he said finally.

"I look like a round orange ball!" Cori wailed.

"Pumpkins are round and orange," Ben said carefully, picking his way through the mine field as best he could. "But I must say the legs are spectacular."

Cori adjusted her hat made up to resemble green leaves. Thanks to Denise's help, she wore a puffy orange costume and orange tights. To complete the look, she had drawn tiny green vines along her cheeks and wore a bright pumpkin orange lipstick.

"I didn't even need any stuffing." She carefully made her way to a chair and debated whether struggling to get down into it was worth all the trouble.

"I can understand that," Ben mumbled behind the cover of the evening newspaper. His body shook with restrained laughter.

Cori held up her legs to study her black flats. "I don't even see my feet anymore," she mourned. "Are you sure the baby isn't due real soon? Such as tomorrow?"

"Sorry. You've got a few more weeks."

"It's not fair. I can't even blame you for this." She gave a deep sigh. "Do we have to go to the party?"

"We could stay here for our own trick-or-treat party, but then everyone would figure out what's going on."

Cori glared at him. Ben, wearing jeans and a white T-shirt, black leather jacket and black boots was devastating.

"That is not a costume."

"Sure is."

"As what?"

He shot her his you-should-know-the-answer-to-that look. "I'm going as James Dean." He glanced at his watch. "Are you ready?"

She seriously thought about sulking. "Yes."

Ben got up and walked over, holding out his hands. With a soft grunt, he pulled Cori to her feet.

"If you hadn't let me eat all that junk food the past few months, I wouldn't have gained so much weight." She looked as if she was ready to stamp her foot.

"Cori, I hate to bust your balloon—" he paused as he looked at her rounded shape "—but some of that weight is the baby."

"If you try to tell me I'm going to give birth to a twenty-five-pound baby I will personally shoot you." Cori walked over to the small coat closet and pulled out her parka. Thanks to Dina, she was able to arrange to have some warmer clothing sent to her. Her friend had been filled with questions and anxious for answers that Cori promised to fulfill soon. She didn't want to tell Dina about the baby until she could talk to her father. Except in phoning her father's office, she learned it was closed for three weeks and calling him at home only netted her the answering service. She left her name and telephone number, asking that he call her.

Ben assisted her with her parka, then wrapped it around her middle, but it refused to meet. He shook his head.

"I have a sweater on under my costume," she explained.

"As long as you're warm."

The town hall was filled with the residents dressed in everything from the usual Halloween witches wearing black dresses and holding old-fashioned brooms to more elaborate costumes such as one man sporting long sideburns and wearing a sequined suit.

"You look good as a pumpkin," Dan teased. "Just hope no one decides to turn you into a pie next month."

"You should talk." She eyed his faded coveralls and plaid shirt with the sleeves rolled up to his elbows. He carried a pitchfork. "What are you?"

He looked insulted she didn't recognize his costume. "I'm that painting with that farmer and his wife. 'Cept my wife refused to go as the old crone in the picture, so she's dressed up as Mother Goose. At least she didn't bring any of the geese with her. They tend to snap at people." He turned and smiled at Ben. "Hey, Doc. James Dean, right?"

Ben nodded. "I'm glad to see some people recognize an icon." He turned to Cori and grabbed her hand. "C'mon, let's dance."

"This should prove interesting," she drawled, following behind him. "We'll be fine as long as we don't have to get any closer than five feet."

After that, Cori didn't think she sat more than ten minutes. She was positive she danced with everyone, and when a large green lizard walked up and held out his foot, she dug up a bit more energy and walked back out on the dance floor.

"So, Godzilla, eat any good cities lately?" she asked brightly as she vainly tried to twist and found it next to impossible.

"Just the usual." His voice was muffled but unmistakable.

Cori leaned forward to get a better look, but could only see a pair of eyes blinking behind the eyeholes.

"Andy?" she asked in a hushed voice.

He nodded.

"You really should try this costume when you're ousting the teenagers," she advised. "After one look at you, they'd never try anything again."

"It only works on Halloween."

She started laughing when he swung her to the side and around his green scaly body. The next time he spun her, she whirled right into Ben's arms. He nodded to Godzilla and danced her into the middle of the crowd.

"That's Andy," she told him.

"Yeah, he likes to show his humorous side during the holidays," he replied. "Having fun?"

"Yes!" She suddenly laughed when Ben bent her backward in a dip worthy of Fred Astaire.

"How many pumpkins can claim they can dance to Chubby Checker?" he asked after the music stopped.

When Cori later walked out of the ladies' room she noticed Dan and Zeke talking to Ben. Ben's face creased in a smile and he slapped both men on the back. She couldn't stop watching him and only hoped she didn't look lovestruck.

What would marriage to him be like? she wondered. Would he care for the baby she was carrying? It was easy enough for him to act that way now because he had no claim. But they spent all their time together, she reasoned. That had to mean something. He told her how much he loved her and she knew he didn't want her to leave Farrington. Which wasn't a problem since she didn't want to, either.

Was he waiting for the baby to be born first? She rested her hand on her tummy, feeling the rolls and kicks from the baby. Obviously, the baby had decided to dance right along with mom.

"Ready to go?" Ben walked up. He looked at her quizzically. "Are you all right?"

She mustered up a smile. "Just a little tired. I haven't danced so much in quite a while."

"I'll get your jacket."

Ben later settled her in the warmth of the truck cab and climbed in beside her.

It took a moment for her to realize he was taking a different direction home.

"Where are we going?" she roused herself to ask.

"Just a little side trip," he said mysteriously. "Just do me a favor and close your eyes until I tell you you can open them."

"This better not have anything to do with the lake." But she obediently covered her eyes with her hands.

"Far from it."

Cori felt the truck soon slow to a stop.

"Keep them closed." Ben instructed as he climbed out of the truck and helped her out. He guided her to a spot, then stopped. "Okay, now you can open them."

Cori took her hands away and stared at the sight before her. A long silver building glowed dully in the night while a hand-lettered sign off to the side could be read courtesy of a nearby streetlight.

"Oh, Ben," she whispered, staring at the sign, which read The Diner—Open This Spring. "They did it. They did it!" She hopped up and hugged him tightly.

"Dan said they didn't want you to know in case it didn't work out," he explained.

Cori hung on to Ben and chuckled when he handed her a handkerchief.

"You know, something tells me you'll still be putting out the tears twenty years from now," he teased gently.

Cori knew it wasn't a proposal, but for the moment it was good enough.

IT SEEMED THEY HAD barely returned to the cottage when the phone rang. Cori picked it up and was surprised to hear a familiar voice.

"So what exactly have you been doing all these months?" Sean Peyton roared over the phone.

Chapter Fifteen

Lucia Cooper's House

"I can't believe I'm still pregnant!" Cori grumbled, using the electric mixer to whip the heavy cream under Lucia's direction.

"My darling, all first babies are late," the older woman told her.

"Mine wasn't supposed to be." Cori looked down at her dress. She was positive she was all tummy. "When Daddy called me back and I invited him out here, I was positive I could greet him at the door with the baby and he'd forget about our past differences. Instead, he's going to see me like this!" She absently rubbed at her lower back. "I hurt all over, I almost live in the bathroom and I look as if I'm ready to burst at any second."

"You look lovely." Lucia stopped to hug her before she checked on the turkey. "The two of you spoke on the phone and patched up your differences and I think he will be so happy to see you it won't matter how you look."

"But this isn't right. Today was supposed to be dinner with all your family," Cori protested.

"And I told them we would be up later for dessert," she replied. "It is important you and your father have time to talk. I am only too happy to do this. And I will tell your father what wonderful things you have done for so many of us."

"That should prove interesting." She grimaced. "I'll be back." She walked out of the kitchen with that waddle all heavily pregnant women have. She stopped and looked out the window. "Does that look like snow?"

"We never have snow this time of year." Lucia looked over her shoulder. "But then, it appears we will this year. I hope Bennie and your father get back soon. The airport said your father's plane will be on time." She cast Cori a curious look. "Are you all right?"

Cori gave a deep sigh. "I will be as soon as the baby comes."

Cori was grateful Lucia kept her busy in the kitchen so she didn't have time to worry about seeing her father for the first time in almost seven months. Not to mention worry what his reaction would be when he discovered she was nine months' pregnant. She thought of breaking the news to him when he called Halloween night, but she didn't want to do it over the phone. Instead, she said she'd settled in a lovely town and wanted him to come out for Thanksgiving. She didn't say anything about Ben because she felt that would also be better for Sean to see for himself what a wonderful man Ben was. Sean had planned to arrive a few days earlier, but an emergency had forced him to fly to New York first and he had to change his reservation to Thanksgiving Day. Ben volunteered to pick him up at the airport. He insisted Cori stay behind due to her advanced condition. Considering the weak state of her bladder and nagging backache, she was glad to stay with Lucia and help her with the dinner preparations.

When she returned to the kitchen, she picked up a celery stalk and started munching on it.

"Have to start losing that weight one way or another," she explained.

"Everything will be fine," Lucia assured her in her musical, accented voice.

"Easy for you to say. You've never met my father."

"No, but I know you and you shouldn't have anything to worry about. Not once he realizes how much Ben cares for you."

"Then I wish he'd do something about it," Cori muttered.

Lucia clucked under her tongue. "I think he's afraid."

She couldn't believe what she was hearing. "Afraid? Why?"

"He's afraid you'll decide to go back to California."

"Why would I do that when everything I love is here?"

Lucia gave a happy exclamation and hugged Cori as best she could. "And that is what you will tell Bennie." She straightened up and ran to the window. "There they are now." She ran back over to Cori and started to pull off her apron, then settled for smoothing a loose strand of hair away from Cori's face. "We will show your father the new Cori." She smoothed the front of Cori's apron over her bulging tummy. "You go to the door, but don't get chilled." She shook her finger at her.

"I smell something good!" Ben called out as he swung open the front door.

Cori reached blindly for Lucia's hand and the older woman squeezed back and gave her a gentle push.

"Don't worry, I'll be right behind you."

Cori walked into the living room just in time to see Ben taking Sean's overcoat. Sean's back was to her. When the older man noticed Ben's gaze directed over his shoulder, he turned around.

At first, his face turned red. Then purple. Then white.

"What the hell!" He spun back around with fists clenched. "What have you done to my daughter?" he growled.

"Daddy, no!" Cori ran as best she could to her father and grabbed his arm. "Ben didn't get me pregnant!"

"Well, you didn't do it by yourself!"

She winced at his strident sound. "It was Rufus."

His face turned purple again. "*Rufus!* That insolent puppy got you pregnant? He'll pay for this!"

"No, he won't," Cori said firmly. "Daddy, it didn't take me long to realize he was a mistake in my life, but this baby isn't." She rubbed her tummy.

Sean turned from Cori to Ben and back to Cori.

"Bennie, introduce me to Cori's father." Lucia sought to break the tension.

Sean looked up and didn't stop staring.

"Sean Peyton, madam." He stepped forward with his hand outstretched.

"Lucia Cooper, Bennie's mother." She smiled warmly. "We are so glad you could make the time to visit."

"For my only daughter I'll do anything." He cast a wary gaze at Cori's condition. "Should you be walking around?"

"Cori's in perfect health, sir," Ben explained.

"Did Ben tell you he's the town doctor?" Cori added.

Sean looked at the younger man with suspicion etched on his face before turning back to his daughter. "But who takes care of you?"

"Ben does. But he drove me to the hospital to arrange everything there for when the time comes," she replied.

"Where's the hospital?"

"About a hundred miles."

"*What?*" He turned on Ben. "Are you saying she has no adequate medical care in case of emergency?"

Ben looked more than a little tense. "Cori has excellent medical care here," he said tersely. "And in case of emergency I can call in a medical helicopter. I don't intend to let anything happen to her."

"Come, Mr. Peyton." Lucia walked over and linked her arm through his. "You must be tired after that long flight. Would you care for some coffee before dinner? Please, let me assure you, Ben has matchless credentials from the hospital he was affiliated with before he moved out here. Cori couldn't be in better hands."

Sean shot Ben a suspicious look as if he already figured out just what Ben's hands had been doing for the past seven months.

"Now you must tell me about your business," Lucia invited. "Cori explained you deal in high finance."

"That's right." He was rapidly thawing under her warm smile.

"Your mother is a miracle worker," Cori murmured to Ben as she grabbed his hand and squeezed it.

"I know she just saved my life." He looked into her face. "Are you all right?"

"I would be if I didn't spend so much time in the bathroom. I think my bladder shrunk."

Ben helped Cori onto the love seat and sat next to her. This time, Sean didn't look as distrustful.

Cori shifted in her seat, trying to find a way to get comfortable. She wanted everything to be perfect today and here she was fidgeting like an erring teenager.

"When do you plan to come home?" Sean asked abruptly.

Cori straightened up. "I am home."

He looked around the house and saw a warm, lovely, homey room, but little compared to the luxury of his own estate. Except, down deep, he knew his home didn't exude the family warmth this one did. Nor could he deny he couldn't remember ever seeing Cori looking so happy and content. "Here?"

"I live in a guest cottage behind the clinic," she explained.

Sean scowled at Ben. "Sounds handy."

"I also have a job with the local school as an aide," Cori went on.

Sean snorted his opinion of that piece of news.

"Cori has become a very important part of our town," Lucia said with a warm smile.

"Your son drove me through town and there didn't seem to be all that much to it."

"There's more than enough!" Cori staunchly defended her new home.

"Compared to what you had?"

She met his gaze. "Yes."

He shook his head as he tried to take it all in.

Lucia stood. "Now we must go in and eat. And I only want happy conversation. I do not allow strong words at my table." She led the way.

Sean watched Ben help Cori to her feet. He couldn't miss the look that passed between the couple and, for a moment, he felt uneasy, as if he'd spied on something intimate. He made his way to the table and sat where Lucia indicated he should.

Ben carried out the platter bearing a large golden brown turkey while Lucia and Cori brought out serving dishes filled with fluffy white mashed potatoes, green beans, cranberry sauce and rolls.

During the meal, Lucia managed to keep the conversation going as she asked Sean about his work and questioned him on his opinion of various European cities. She became especially animated when he spoke of Italy.

Cori was glad for the distraction as she tried to eat. She picked at her turkey and only managed to crumble her roll on the plate. Ben noticed and shot her a look filled with concern.

"Are you all right?" he murmured.

She shifted in her chair. "I just can't get comfortable," she whispered. "Please, don't tell Lucia. I don't want to ruin her dinner."

His gaze sharpened. "Can't get comfortable, how?"

She shot a look at the parents and realized they were still conversing. "My back aches and I keep feeling a pulling across my abdomen."

Ben started to open his mouth to ask how long she had been feeling this way when a look of shocked horror crossed Cori's face and she jumped up.

Lucia and Sean looked up—Sean with confusion, Lucia, knowing.

"Everything's all wet!" Cori cried out.

Ben muttered a curse. "How long have you been in labor?" he demanded.

She turned on him. "What labor?"

"What you've been going through is damn labor!"

"Don't you shout at my daughter!" Sean roared.

"What Ella described to me as labor didn't feel anything like this!" she shouted back, then started to cry.

"All of you stop it," Lucia ordered, swiftly coming to Cori's side and putting her arms around her. "Come, dear, let's get you comfortable. Bennie, get your bag out of the truck and call the helicopter. I don't think you will be able to drive her to the hospital in time."

Sean sat there openmouthed as the activity flowed around him. Within seconds, Ben had been outside and came back carrying a black leather bag and a box. He stopped in the kitchen for a moment, used the phone, cursed and hung up.

"We never have snow this time of year," he muttered, then spoke louder. "The winds are too strong. The copter can't take off in this storm!"

It hit Sean like a ton of bricks. "Are you saying Cori is having the baby *now?*"

"Exactly." Ben brushed past him.

Sean was on his heels as Ben walked swiftly toward Lucia's bedroom.

He handed Lucia the box, which she opened and quickly took out the necessary items.

Lucia had changed Cori into a nightgown and settled her on the bed. Lucia moved her only enough to make up the bed.

Ben turned to Sean. "Out."

He tightened his jaw. "She's my daughter."

Ben stared him down. "And she's my patient."

"But if we can't get to the hospital and the helicopter can't pick me up, I can't have the baby now," Cori cried.

Ben flicked a look at his mother. She smiled and nodded and, while murmuring words of assurance, escorted Sean back out to the living room where she left him with a brand new bottle of Scotch.

Ben sat on the edge of the bed and took hold of her hands. "Honey, I need to examine you."

Cori took a deep breath and bent at the waist. "I'm in pain and you want to examine me? I don't think so!"

"I have to." He waited until Lucia returned. She sat at the head of the bed, holding on to Cori's shoulders while Ben donned gloves and quickly examined Cori.

"She's dilating fast," he told his mother. "Either she's been in active labor for longer than even she realized or this baby just wants out now."

"Ben, it really hurts! I need something for the pain!"

He grimaced. "Cori, you're too far along. I can't give you anything. Just relax and breathe the way Ella showed you to."

"Relax?" With a great show of strength, she reached forward and grabbed hold of his shirtfront. "You try pushing a bowling ball out your eyeball. Then we'll talk about *relaxing!*" She screamed in a voice shrill enough to break eardrums.

After that, it was all a blur for Cori. She was vaguely aware of holding tightly on to Lucia's hand and listening to Ben's chatter, but nothing came through.

"Concentrate on something," he ordered. "Think about our wedding."

"Wedding?" she almost sobbed. "Cooper, this is a hell of a time to propose."

"Better late than never. Now, push! Okay, I've got the head. Push again, darlin'."

She could feel the pain ripping her in two and he wanted her to do it again. Then, all too quickly, it seemed over. She lay back panting, barely hearing anything going on around here.

"You've got a beautiful little girl," Ben whispered.

She looked up at him and limply raised a hand to stroke his face.

"You're crying," she whispered.

"Yeah, well, this one's special." He kissed her on the cheek. "Now one more push for the afterbirth and we're all through."

Cori groaned but complied. By then, Lucia had cleaned the baby, all the while murmuring Italian to the little one. With a broad smile she carried the baby to Cori who cried and did what all mothers do—counted the fingers and toes.

"Shall I take her out to meet her grandfather?" Lucia asked.

Cori nodded. "Tell him her name's Elizabeth."

By the time Lucia appeared, Sean had consumed half the bottle of Scotch and looked wild-eyed.

"What happened?" he demanded, staggering to his feet.

She smiled as she approached him with her blanket-wrapped bundle. "Sean, meet your granddaughter." She held back the corner and shielded the tiny face.

Sean almost cried as he looked down. "She looks like her mother," he said softly, tentatively touching the downy cheek with his fingertip.

"Cori said to tell you her name is Elizabeth."

His chin wobbled even more. "That was her mother's name. God rest her soul." He took a moment to compose himself. "Are those two in there serious?"

"Very."

"Why would he marry a woman who had another man's baby? How do I know he'll treat her right?"

Lucia's smile disappeared. "Ben loves Cori more than life itself. He would never hurt her. As for Elizabeth, he might not have planted the seed that gave her life, but he has nurtured her these past months and he brought her into this world. As far as he is concerned she is his daughter."

Sean nodded jerkily. "Well, ma'am." He wiped his eyes. "I must admit you put on a hell of a Thanksgiving dinner."

BEN SAT ON THE EDGE of the bed, holding the baby in his arms. He was so taken with the sight of the wrinkly, pink newborn, he could barely take his eyes off her. Of all the babies he had delivered in his practice, she was the most special. Because, Ben knew, she would be his.

He looked up at Cori. "I love you," he said fiercely. "If I'd known this would happen, I would have had you in the hospital days ago."

She touched his cheek in reassurance. "But everything went all right because I had a wonderful doctor. Although I would have hoped for a more romantic proposal." She grinned cheekily. "Still, your mother was a witness so I know you can't back out."

"I don't intend to." He kissed her deeply.

Cori moaned softly, holding on to him with all her might. "So do you think Elizabeth Peyton is pretty?"

"Beautiful. Looks just like you," he told her. "But I thought we could give her the name Elizabeth Peyton Cooper."

She started crying. "And here I thought that would stop. Oh, Ben, I love you so much!"

"Enough to stay in Farrington and see if you can bring that diner to life?"

"Enough to stay in Farrington and have lots of babies and whatever else I can manage to do," she told him.

"I guess I'll have to come back for a wedding."

They looked up to find Sean and Lucia in the doorway.

"You may as well stay around, Sean, because I intend to marry your daughter as soon as possible," Ben informed him.

Sean walked forward and kissed his daughter's cheek.

"Ben and I stopped by the garage on the way here to talk to that mechanic," he mumbled. "He'll have your car ready in a week. At least you'll have your car. Now what about a wedding present?"

Cori looked at Ben with a question in her eyes. She smiled when he nodded. She looked up at her father.

"Daddy, I have this business proposition for you..."

Epilogue

The Diner

Ben couldn't remember ever feeling so tired. Or fulfilled.

Thanks to Sean, Farrington had a hospital. Small but filled with up-to-date equipment for any kind of emergency imaginable. The clinic was now housed in a corner of the hospital and the building renovated into a house for Dr. Cooper and family.

After finishing for the day, he'd driven out to Cori's pet project. Thank goodness, spring had finally come after a long cold winter and, with summer here, he felt as if his life had come full circle. Ironically, with Cori and Beth in the house, the past cold snowy nights hadn't mattered. Only the nights he'd had to go out on an emergency. Those times were fewer, though, thanks to another doctor looking for small-town living. There was hope for the town, after all.

He parked in the parking lot, already filled with cars. The front doors were open and the rock-and-roll sounds of Bill Haley and the Comets poured out of the building.

Stepping inside was like going back in time.

Walls were filled with photos from fifties and sixties teen movies, also a large poster of James Dean. Cori, after a lot of calls and cajoling, had managed to find a Wurlitzer jukebox, which presided over one corner. Red vinyl booths were filled with young people.

Luckily, Ralph and Charlotte hadn't taken offense when the Diner opened. They hadn't minded losing the younger crowd who now packed the place almost every night. And the older ones enjoyed having Myrna's all to themselves. Except for Dan and Zeke who always occupied a rear booth. They seemed to enjoy the chaos as much as the kids did.

Waitresses wore poodle skirts and saddle shoes and were known to dance with their customers when the right song played.

But it was the hostess that caught his eye.

A black poodle skirt flared around shapely calves and a turquoise angora short-sleeved sweater hugged even more curves. The black scarf tied around her neck and the matching scarf encircling a blond ponytail were perfect touches along with the black-and-white saddle shoes. The only jarring note was the baby backpack the hostess wore with a towheaded baby peacefully sleeping against her mother's back. The woman looked up and bounced over to him.

"Hey, handsome, looking for a good time?" she murmured, greeting him with a kiss that brought catcalls from the diners.

"Always." He kept his hands on her waist. "I can't believe she can sleep through all this."

"Are you kidding, she loves it." She took his hand. "How's Brad working out?" she asked about the new doctor.

"Just fine. With luck, I have the next thirty-six hours free."

Cori kept walking until they reached the rear door and outside. She spun Ben around until his back was to the building and leaned into his embrace.

"I am so glad to hear that," she said throatily. "Because your mother is desperate to have her newest grandchild to herself and I think that would be a nice idea, don't you? For her sake, of course."

His lips curved upward. "Of course."

Their mouths met hungrily as they took advantage of a rare moment alone. With a new baby, the building of the hospital and Cori's work on the diner, time wasn't always on their side, but they always seemed to manage.

Pretty soon, Ben's shirt was unbuttoned to reveal his bare chest with Cori nibbling on one of his nipples while his hands were busy under her sweater. They were breathing hard and had the awareness they would soon have to stop before they reached the point of no return.

"Home in five seconds?" he asked in a raw voice.

"You got it," she said huskily, fingering his belt buckle.

"I swear I'm going to have to throw a bucket of cold water on you two. Don't you ever stop?" Andy asked as he rounded the corner.

Ben and Cori smiled at each other, then simultaneously replied, "Never."

MILLION DOLLAR SWEEPSTAKES (III)

SWP-H1095

You're About to Become a *Privileged Woman*

Reap the rewards of fabulous free gifts and benefits with proofs-of-purchase from Harlequin and Silhouette books

Pages & Privileges™

It's our way of thanking you for buying our books at your favorite retail stores.

Pages & Privileges™

Harlequin and Silhouette— the most privileged readers in the world!

For more information about Harlequin and Silhouette's PAGES & PRIVILEGES program call the Pages & Privileges Benefits Desk: 1-503-794-2499

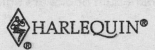

HARLEQUIN®

HAR-PP74